THE RUFFIANS

Rick Johnson

Editing: Alison Greene
Book & Page Formatting: TP peaCOCKing
Cover Art: TP peaCOCKing

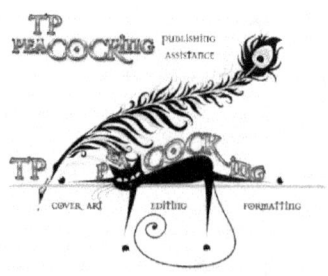

BLURB

The Ruffians are a legendary canine neighborhood watch group. They patrol the streets at night and keep the neighborhood safe from unsavory characters. There's something fishy going on by the duck pond in the park. The squirrels are eating all their nuts plus all the nuts stored up for the winter's supply. Mystified by this discovery The Ruffians realize that unless they can solve this unusual development by the time winter arrives, there won't be any squirrels left at the park with nuts.

The Ruffians investigation into the matter is stymied by the unexpected invasion of Russian terrorists in the neighborhood. Forced into an uneasy alliance with their arch-nemesis, The Godfather, and his career criminal counterparts, The Fang Mafia, Butch, Jim, Dandy, Empty, and Mixer are in for the battle of their lives.

Betrayal and deceit abound as a sinister force plots the complete and total destruction of the very existence of The Ruffians. The Ruffians are drawn into a final and epic confrontation that will forever shape the animal kingdom.

However, there's Butch. Don't ever forget about Butch. That would-be nuts!

DEDICATION

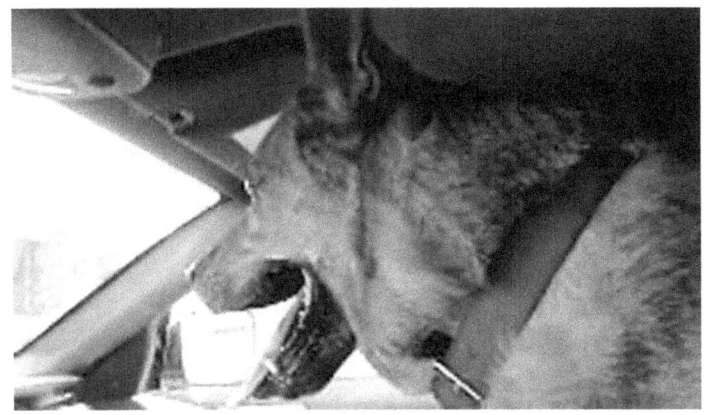

To My Dog

TRADEMARK ACKNOWLEDGEMENTS

The author acknowledges the trademarked status and trademark owners of the following wordmarks mentioned in this work of fiction.

Alpo ~ Purina
Apple Jacks ~ Kellogg's
Armour Vienna Sausage ~ Armour Star
Baby Ruth ~ Nestle
Blue Bell ~ Blue Bell Creameries
Butterfinger ~ Nestle
Cap'n Crunch ~ Quaker Oats Company
Capitol One
Chef Boyardee Mini Ravioli ~ Chef Boyardee
Chrysler ~ Fiat Chrysler Automobiles
Coke ~ Coca Cola
Del Monte Foods
Dolche & Gabbana
Donald Duck ` Walt Disney Productions
Duracell ~ Berkshire Hathaway
eHarmony
Essie
Facebook
Ford ~ Ford Motor Company
Frosty Mini Wheats ~ Kellogg's
Fruit of the Loom
Fruit Loops ~ Kellogg's
Grey Poupon Dijon Mustard ~ Kraft Foods
Here Kitty
Hibachi Grill
Holiday Day Express ~ Intercontinental Hotels Group
Honey Boy Pink Salmon

Huckleberry Hound ~ Hanna-Barbera
Jeep ~ FCA US LLC
Jeopardy ~ Sony Pictures Television
Kentucky Fried Chicken ~ Yum! Brands
Kibbles 'n Bits ~ Big Heart Pet Brands
Kip Nail Lacquer
Kodak ~ Eastman Kodak Company
Listerine ~ Johnson & Johnson
Little Debbie Oatmeal Crème Pies ~ Mckee Foods Corporation
Lucky Charms ~ General Mills
Macdonalds
Mattel
Milk Bone ~ Del Monte Foods
Milk Duds ~ The Hershey Company
Moon Pie ~ Chattanooga Bakery
Motel Six
Mr. Clean ~ Proctor & Gamble
Oakland Raiders
Oral B ~ Proctor & Gamble
Oscar Mayer Cheese Dogs ~ Kraft Heinz
Oscar Mayer Delifresh Smoked Turkey ~ Kraft Heinz
Ozarka ~ Nestle Waters
Pampered Chef ~ Pampered Chef, Ltd.
Pedigree Beef and Country Stew ~ Mars Incorporated
Pepperidge Farm Goldfish Crackers ~ Campbell Soup Company
Pepsi ~ PepsiCo.
Pine Sol ~ Clorox
Pizza Hut ~ Yum! Brands
Pringles ~ Pringles Manufacturing
Ramada Inn
Scooby Doo ~ Warner Brothers Animations
Skittles ~ Wrigley Company, a division of Mars, Incorporated
Snickers ~ Mars, Incorporated
Star Wars ~ Disney
Sony
Spiderman ~ Marvel Comics
Tabasco Sauce ~ Mcllhenny Company
The Animal Planet Channel ~ Discovery Communications
The Cooking Channel ~ Scripps Network Interactive

The Discovery Channel ~ Discovery Communications
The History Channel ~ A&E Television Networks
The Weather Channel ~ The Blackstone Group, Bain Capital, and NBCUniversal
The Western Channel ~ Starz Encore
Totino's Pizza Rolls ~ General Mills
Tupperware ~ Tupperware Brands
Walmart
Whirlpool
Wolf Brand Chili ~ ConAgra Foods
You Tube ~ Google

PROLOGUE

Dogs have owned humans for a long time. It's never been the other way around. I got lucky when I picked out my human. I wound up with a good buddy. Please notice that I didn't say master or daddy. Humans have never been the master of dogs, and if my buddy was my daddy, I would be making the rounds on the late-night network talk shows, and my buddy would be housed in an institution designed for some seriously disturbed people.

My buddy and I live at 3880 Furs Avenue. While my buddy is at work, I love to sit in the backyard and watch the activity in our neighborhood. I see Sally the Siamese cat prancing down the center of the street like she owns it. Sally and I had a summer fling a couple of years ago, but I broke it off before it got out of hand. I tried to explain to Sally that the other animals would really never accept our relationship, and it wouldn't be fair to the kids. Sally took the breakup hard. She hasn't spoken to me since. Sally refuses to look my way, but I know she's giving me the once-over out of the corner of her eye. Hey, who wouldn't?

I'm also checking out the one-hundred and twenty-five pound cement birdbath sitting by the rusted chain-link fence in our backyard. I watched my buddy drag and wrestle that heavy birdbath into the backyard all by himself. He was so happy that he finally had a chance to give the birds some water every day. He even went out and bought a brand new twenty-five-foot tan water hose just for the occasion. Every day my buddy comes home and fills the birdbath with fresh water, there's only one problem. The birds never came. The only visitor to the birdbath is one red wasp. Now my buddy comes home from work every day, and fills the birdbath with fresh water for one single red wasp. One afternoon I was watching the red wasp drink water, and two mockingbirds flew overhead. Neither bird looked down at the bird bath. I looked at the wasp, and the wasp looked back at me and shrugged its shoulders.

The only problem I have with my buddy is the name he decided to proudly bestow on me. Since I'm a shepherd mix, my buddy decided to call me Mixer. I've taken a lot of ribbing from the guys over the years about my name.

The house sitting to the east of my buddy's house is the home to Emperor Maximillian Plutarch Tiberius Young. We call him Empty. Empty is a full-blooded German shepherd dog. Empty loves to fight, well, when he's not staring at himself in a mirror. Empty's ego is about the size of The Grand Canyon. In the canine world, he's what we call a mirrorholic.

The house sitting to the west of my buddy's house is the home to two American beagles, Jim and Dandy. Jim and Dandy are television junkies. Jim loves watching The History Channel and The Discovery Channel while Dandy is addicted to The Cooking Channel. In addition, living with Jim and Dandy is Butch, an American pit bull terrier. Butch is gay. Butch watches over Jim and Dandy like a mother hen.

Don't let Butch being gay fool you about his dog hood. One time a burglar broke into Butch's buddy's house and what Butch did to that fellow ought to be illegal in all of Rhode Island and parts of Arkansas. Then I saw Butch break a toenail once and squeal like a girl. Go figure.

We gather every night in my buddy's backyard and discuss current events. We patrol the neighborhood every night and keep it safe from trouble. We're more than five pals. We aren't cosmic caped canine crusaders. We are The Ruffians.

CHAPTER 1

It's Monday night, and I don't have to worry about my buddy coming outside and interfering with our nightly meeting. The Oakland Raiders are playing a Monday night football game, so I know for the next several hours my buddy is going to be glued to his plaid cloth covered recliner in front of the television set. I'm glad the Oakland Raiders are playing in the Monday night football game. It'll give my buddy a break from The Weather Channel. My buddy's a Weather Channel freak. He sits for hours on end and stares at the weather girls. He's always screaming for me to come check out the high weather fronts and warm depressions. Okay, my buddy might need a life.

I don't worry about my buddy forgetting to eat during the football game. I see a can of Wolf Brand chili and a box of banana Moon Pies sitting on the white fake marble kitchen counter. Great. My buddy has his halftime snacks planned out. Good boy.

I decide to wander into the backyard and wait for The Ruffians meeting to start. I know that I'm going to be a few minutes early, but I'm hoping to catch a glimpse of some hot babes walking their buddies down the street. The September air is warm enough that the dogs should be out walking their buddies, and it's cool enough to make the strolls comfortable. I'm hoping to catch a glimpse of the golden retriever walking her buddy. She's new to the neighborhood, and I haven't had a chance to learn her name, but wow, does she put the bow in wow when she wriggles her hips.

I wander into the backyard, and I'm surprised to see Empty already waiting for everyone to show up at the meeting. Empty is never early. He prefers to call it fashionably late. We all know the truth. Empty has a hard time tearing himself away from the full-length mirror standing in his buddy's hallway.

"Hi, Mixer," he says. "What's up and don't even think about saying the ceiling. That line got old years ago."

So Empty wants to take away my intelligent little quip. That's no problem, I'll just think of a new bright quip to dazzle him with. I look over at him and say, "Not much."

Before Empty can reply we hear the sounds of happy baying as Jim and Dandy come tearing out of their buddy's backdoor and two white, black and brown bundles of joy streak to the chain-link fence. Butch comes ambling behind them and Jim and Dandy patiently wait as Butch takes his time strolling across the backyard. You would think that Butch is a model on a runway as he leisurely looks all around at his surroundings as he struts. What a diva.

Butch finally makes his way to the fence and Jim and Dandy use his back as a springboard to leap over the fence. Butch leaps and uses his two-front paws to grab the top of the fence and lazily climbs over. Okay, Empty is an egomaniac and Butch is a show off. Nobody said we were perfect.

Butch looks around and eagerly asks, "Does anybody want to sniff butts?"

Empty makes a gagging sound.

"You need to positively grow up," Butch says. "We're dogs. It's what we do."

Empty's gagging sound grows louder.

I ignore the question.

"Butch, you ought to be ashamed of yourself. There was no reason to use the word positively. You just absolutely, positively abused an adverb. Now you have me abusing adverbs. What am I going to do with you?" Jim fusses.

"I'm a gay man," Butch replies. "Gay men say positively."

"You're not a man. You're a dog," Dandy corrects.

"Whatever."

"I saw Rachael cooking on a television show," Dandy pipes in. "She looked delish." Empty and I smile at Dandy. Butch reaches over and pats Dandy on top of the head with his right paw.

Jim looks at me and says, "I saw Sally the other day. You need to talk to her. She's a scorned woman. She's throwing herself at every animal in the neighborhood. She's a scorned female on a one way catnip trip of no return."

"She won't talk to me," I say. "Besides, she knows it's over between the two of us. She's going to have to pick up the pieces of her broken heart and move on. The days of us catting around together are over. It's for the best."

Butch looks at me and declares, "You're a dog."

Empty butts in and asks, "Why doesn't she do like other cats and lie on top of the television set and stare at people? That would give her something to do."

"Cats don't do that anymore since the new flat screen televisions have come out," Jim responds. Jim is the intellectual of the group, and the only Ruffian that wears glasses.

"She could use the back of the couch," Empty replies.

"That would bring back too many memories of me," I brag.

Butch looks over at me and says, "Next you'll be trying to claim that you're an animal in bed."

I can see this line of conversation is headed straight for the litter box, so I try to think of a way to get the conversation steered away from mine and Sally's past relationship. "Has anyone ever wondered what would happen if you gave a mime the silent treatment?" I ask.

The guys are staring at me and not saying anything. I can see they're going to be a tough audience tonight.

"We can still sniff butts," Butch suggests.

This time Empty sticks a paw in and out his mouth as he starts once again making his gagging sounds.

"Let's quit the small talk and get down to the business at hand," I say. "Where are we going to patrol tonight? I know the neighborhood is usually quiet, but you never know when trouble might pop up at the most unexpected time."

"Speaking of trouble," Jim exclaims, "Dandy has something to say. I think that it might be an issue we need to address."

Dandy looks nervous about speaking, so Empty gives him a nod with his head indicating that's it's all right to speak up.

Dandy clears his throat, looks around at us, and says, "I saw a Russian wolfhound in the neighborhood. I actually saw two of them roaming the streets."

Jim lets the actually adverb slide as the impact of Dandy's statement hits home. We have Russians in the neighborhood. I feel a chill, and I know that it has nothing to do with the night air.

Butch reaches out with his front paws and pulls Jim and Dandy closer to him. I move closer to Empty.

Empty grins and says, "Great Lassie in Heaven, we have terrorists in the neighborhood."

"Let's do it," Jim yells.

We know what he's talking about.

We gather around, do a group high five, and yell, "We are The Ruffians!"

CHAPTER 2

The slamming of the front door wakes me up the next morning, and I know my buddy has gone to the place he calls work. I'm not sure what he does at that place, but I do know that his leaving gives me room to stretch out in the bed for a few more hours. I always look forward to my time alone in the bed. You ought to try sleeping with a guy who mumbles about The Weather Channel all night. After a while, you start going through your own tropical depression.

I sleep for a few more hours and then wake up to the sight of sunlight streaming through the rips in the aluminum foil my buddy has taped over his bedroom window. I've yet to figure that one out. Okay, so my buddy might be a bit of a nerd. I quit staring at the streams of sunlight and glance at my buddy's pillow lying upon his side of the bed. My buddy is also a germ freak. He hates laying his face on a pillow that has been lying upon the floor all day. He'll change the pillow case every time he finds his pillow lying on the olive-green shag carpet. He'll also spend a few minutes grumbling about how I should leave his stuff alone while he's at work. I stand on the bed, stretch, yawn, shake my rear end a couple of times, and then use my nose to flip his pillow off the bed onto the floor. I love watching my buddy freak out. I should be ashamed of myself, but I'm not.

I leap off the bed and wander into the kitchen. I glance up at the white plastic clock hanging above the kitchen sink. It's almost noon. The other Ruffians are probably still asleep. They aren't early risers like I am. I check out my silver metal food and water bowls sitting beside the refrigerator. I check out the water bowl first. The bowl is filled with clear, fresh water. Clear, fresh water is good. I check out the food bowl. It's filled with brown, dried, chicken flavored soybean nuggets, bleah. I use my nose to flip over the bowl of dry dog food and watch the little brown nuggets of soybean and chicken flavoring scatter across the kitchen floor. My buddy's going to freak twice when he gets home from work. All I can say is he had better be holding a bag of burgers when he walks through the door.

I decide to go into the backyard and check out the neighborhood. I leave through the doggy door my buddy installed for me. I scan the neighborhood. Nope, nothing is going on here. Wait a second. I spot Sally slowly walking down the center of the street. Whoa, judging by the bags beneath her eyes, she must have really had a rough night. I think she is giving new meaning to the word catnip.

I know I should wait for the other Ruffians to wake up, but I decide instead to stroll down to the park and check out the babes. I'll be back before the other Ruffians know I'm gone. It'll be nice to hit on some babes without Empty horning in on the action. When it comes to trying to score with the babes that Empty has no shame. He's a dog.

I walk over to the gate leading to the side yard and use my nose to flip up the metal latch. The latch stays up so I use my left paw to reach underneath the gate and pull it toward me. The gate swings open, and I smell the fresh air of freedom.

I take off walking along the street to the park. It's a beautiful day. The sun is shining. The sky is an awesome shade of blue, and I don't have a care in the world. And then it happens. I spot a dog standing beside the stop sign on the corner of Crabtree and Spruce Streets. The dog is one I've never seen before and the conversation from last night comes flooding back into my memory. I feel a cold knot form in the pit of my stomach. I recognize the breed of the dog. It's a Russian wolfhound. It's true. We have a terrorist in the neighborhood.

The terrorist starts walking slowly toward me, and I think about turning and fleeing back to my buddy's house. I immediately scoff at that idea. I'm a Ruffian. The terrorist has no way of knowing that I'm the fleamare his momma forgot to warn him about. I almost feel sorry for him.

We slowly advance toward each other down the center of the street until our noses are almost touching. It's time to let the Russian know that he has finally met his match. I search my brain trying to think of an intimidating line that will have the wolfhound shaking in his paws. I got it. I say, "What's up?"

The Russian wolfhound growls at me. Okay, he wants to play tough guy, uh?

I growl back.

The terrorist pulls his lips back over his fangs and starts snarling at me. I know he just didn't do that. I snarl back.

The Russian wolfhound is really putting some effort into his growls and snarls. He sounds like two dogs. Then I realize why. There are two dogs. His buddy has come to stand beside him. Where did he come from?

I try a different tack. I say, "What do you get when you cross a pig with a pawn shop?"

They quit snarling and look at me.

I scream, "A ham hock!"

The wolfhounds start snarling again. It looks like they're going to be a tough audience. I tried being the nice guy, but now it's time to show the furry invaders why I'm considered the Clint Eastwood of the canine world. I give the wolfhounds my biggest snarl. Let's see the punks deal with that.

They snarl back and advance a small step toward me. So they want to play the game this way. I think about that saying, 'When the going gets tough, the tough gets going'. It looks like it's going to apply here. I spin one-hundred eighty degrees, and I'm gone.

I'm flying down the center of the street. I must look like a canine airplane streaking down the runway. There's no way the wolfhounds can catch up to me. Somebody forgot to tell them that. I feel the panting of their hot breath on the back of my neck. I stick my tail between my hind legs and crank it up a notch. The Russians are growling and snarling and yapping right behind me. I can't understand a word they're saying. This is great. I'm being chased by a couple of dogs in my own neighborhood who can't speak English.

My devious mind comes up with a plan. I take a hard right on Cedar Court Drive. I'm going to cut through K.D. Mitchell's backyard and escape through the woods leading into the park. There's no way the wolfhounds can keep up with me in the woods. I know the back of those woods like the back of my own paw. I see K.D. Mitchell's house. I see something else. K.D. Mitchell is standing in her front yard holding a water hose. She's not watering anything. The hose isn't even hooked up to the faucet. She's just standing in the front yard holding her green water hose. Humans. Go figure. Everybody knows K.D. Mitchell is the sweetest person in the world until 11:00 a.m. At 11:01 K.D. Mitchell turns mean. No one can explain it, not even K.D. Mitchell. I'm not taking a chance. I don't want to wind up being the main ingredient in a doggy pot pie. I streak by K.D. Mitchell's house. I look over and give her a wink. She glares at me.

I decide on another course of action. I'll cut through Ms. Kolinsky's backyard. I'll climb through the hole at the back of her brown, wooden privacy fence. Maybe Ms. Kolinsky will be out lying on her beach towel and sunbathing in her backyard. Talk about something that will put the bow in your wow.

I run into Ms. Kolinsky's backyard and glance over at the spot where she usually lays her beach towel. Major league bummer. The white towel is there but there's no Ms. Kolinsky. I spot another problem that I wasn't counting on. Someone has taken a sheet of plywood and repaired the hole in the back of Ms. Kolinsky's wooden fence. I'm trapped.

I spin around and see the two wolfhounds have slowed down to a walk as they advance toward me. Their eyes are gleaming with joy. They're licking their lips, and spittle is drooling off their fangs. I can tell by their posturing that they have no plans to have mercy on me. There's only one thing left to do.

I close my eyes.

CHAPTER 3

I'm trying to decide what course of action I should take. Should I attack the two Russian wolfhounds with all my might and tear them apart with my supernatural strength, or should I keep my eyes close and pretend they don't see me? I squeeze my eyes tighter together. Those two terrorists have no idea how lucky they are. Then I hear a familiar voice.

"This is so positively how I like my dogs, tall, hairy, and on all fours."

I open my eyes and see Butch and Empty standing behind the imported canines. Butch is licking his lips. Empty is sticking a paw inside his mouth and making gagging sounds.

The two wolfhounds look over their shoulders at Butch and Empty. The taller one says in a thick accent "You better back off, Mack. You don't know who you're dealing with."

Butch continues to lick his lips as he and Empty walk past the strangers and stand on either side of me.

"It's a good thing for them that you showed up, Butch," I say. "I was getting ready to unleash my fury on these two clowns. There's no telling what would have happened."

Butch reaches over and pats me on top of the head with his right paw. "I know, Mixer. When you're riled, you're positively an animal."

"Where are Jim and Dandy?" I ask.

Butch replies, "Dandy wanted to finish watching Rachael make something that was delish. I insisted Jim stay home with him, and they could come together when the show is over. I positively do not want those two darlings walking the streets alone. There's no telling what they might run into in the neighborhood."

"How are they going to find us?" I ask.

Empty slaps me upside the back of the head with his paw. "They're beagles, fur breath. Following scents is what they do."

The shorter of the Russians speaks up. "You guys are in so much trouble. You have no idea the powers you're interfering with."

"Butch, I'm hungry and in need of some serious mirror time," Empty says. "Let's take these clowns out and get this over with."

Butch gives the taller of the two wolfhounds an once-over letting his eyes slowly roam all over the terrorist's body. "I love a dog who works out," Butch says. "I bet your name is Buff. Instead of taking you out, I would rather take you to the Holiday Inn Express and make yummy."

Empty sticks his paw in and out of his mouth while making some serious gagging sounds.

"How did you two know where to find me?" I ask.

Butch blows the taller of the two foreigners a kiss as he replies, "Empty saw you leave your buddy's house this morning. Knowing your habit of always finding trouble he called me, and we decided to come find you."

"How did you know where to look?" I ask. I know what is coming. I duck.

Empty's paw brushes air as his paw slides harmlessly over the top of my head. I look at him, and he grins. "Nice move."

"You better back off those yummy and Holiday Inn Express remarks," the shorter of the two Russian wolfhounds says. "We're from Alabama and dogs in Tuscaloosa don't play that game."

"Roll Tide," I say.

Before the terrorist can reply, two brown, black, and white streaks of lightning fly past the terrorists and stand on either side of Empty and Butch.

"Rachael looked delish this morning," Dandy pants. "I wish she was my buddy."

Butch gives Dandy a hip bump.

Jim looks over at the terrorists and asks, "Who are these guys?"

"They're a couple of liars," I say.

"Please positively explain what you mean by that statement," Butch replies.

"They said they're from Alabama. However, they said you guys instead of y'all."

"Good point," Empty agrees.

The taller of the two Russians points his paw at Dandy and says, "Y'all better back off. If you don't, there's no telling what will happen to the beagles if we ever catch them alone on the street."

"Oh my," Butch gasps. "You have positively blown any chance of us making yummy at the Holiday Inn Express, and I was so looking forward to a night of ruff and tough."

I hear a freight train rumbling down the distance railroad tracks. I'm surprised that the roar of the train sounds like it is getting closer. When was a railroad depot put in the Kolinsky's backyard? I realize my mistake. That's not a train. That's the war growl rumbling deep in Empty's chest.

The two wolfhounds start snarling. Butch, Dandy, Empty, and Jim snarl back.

I tell Jim and Dandy, "Don't worry. Nobody is going to mess with you while I'm around."

The snarls increase all the way around.

Both groups take a step closer toward each other.

Butch whispers out of the side of his mouth, "Mixer, would you please start snarling. My jaws are positively killing me."

I start snarling.

The two terrorists begin slowly backing out of the Kolinsky's backyard. My snarl can be intimidating.

"Butch, don't let them go. We need to finish this thing right here and now," Empty says.

The two wolfhounds spin around and take off running.

"Too late," Empty mutters. He looks over at Butch. "I have an awful feeling we made a dreadful mistake in letting those two guys get away."

I can see the worry in Butch's eyes as he softly replies, "I'm afraid you might be right, my dear friend."

Butch reaches out with his two-front paws and pulls Jim and Dandy closer to him. "I'm taking these two children home," he says. "What are you two going to do?"

Empty and I aren't worried about the two terrorists finding Butch. They didn't look that stupid. And they aren't going to try to mess with Jim and Dandy while Butch is around.

Empty looks over at me and asks, "Do you want to go to the park and check out the babes?"

"You betcha," I say. "I'm a four-legged love machine waiting to be turned on."

"First things first," Jim says.

We know what he's talking about. We gather around each other and do a group high five. We yell, "We are The Ruffians."

CHAPTER 4

Empty and I are disappointed when we get to the park. We don't see any babes anywhere. We see a couple of young mothers pushing their babies around in strollers and enjoying the morning, but that's not the kind of babes we were hoping to find. I was hoping the golden retriever would be here. Empty isn't picky. He'll settle for any four-legged babe. That boy's lack of judgment has caused him to wind up with many a dog instead of a hot babe.

We spy something short and brown hurtling across the soccer field. It looks like a bullet on wheels.

"Great Lassie in Heaven, how quaint," Empty says. "We're being attacked by a speeding hotdog."

"I bet you can kick his buns," I reply.

The speeding hotdog screeches to a stop about three feet in front of Empty and I. It's not a speeding hotdog after all. It's a brown dachshund.

"Hi," the dachshund says. "I'm Ed and I'm front Puerto Rico. My buddy and I just moved here."

"Nice to meet you Ed from Puerto Rico," I say.

Ed starts twirling in circles and yells, "I love it here. I take my buddy for a walk in the park every day. I'll go find him in a bit. I really like this town. Say, do y'all have names?"

Empty looks at me and says, "He must be from southern Puerto Rico." He looks at Ed and says, "We're part of a group called The Ruffians."

Ed stops twirling and stares at us. "I've already heard of you. The Ruffians must be something like a legend around these parts. I took out a cat named Sally the other night. Sally mentioned that she used to date a

Ruffian."

I stick my chest out in pride. I knew Sally wasn't over me. She must still be pining to feel my paws wrapped around her once more. After tasting the icing in the Mixer's bowl, Sally will never feel satisfied again. No wonder she would always scream, "You animal!"

"Sally said she went out with a dog named Mixer. He was a nerd," Ed says.

I feel my chest deflate. I hear Empty snickering beside me.

"Sally said Mixer never did anything for her catnip. She even said she could never tell when Mixer was in her litter box. She couldn't feel a thing."

I catch a glance of Empty out of the corner of my right eye. He's lying on his back and kicking all four of his paws straight up into the air. I don't think it's funny.

"Sally said that she used to have to fake it, so she didn't hurt Mixer's feelings."

Empty is laughing so hard that he has tears coming out of his eyes. I'm beginning not to like Ed from Puerto Rico.

"What's your name?" Ed asks.

"Yeah, stud muffin, what's your name," Empty roars.

So Sally wants to make up lies about my dog hood? She's only doing it because she's a scorned woman. I'm not ashamed of who I am. I will gladly shout out my name to the top of the world. I look at Ed and say, "I'm Al."

Empty slowly climbs to his feet and uses his right paw to wipe the tears away from his eyes. "I'm Empty," he says.

"Wow, I can't wait to tell Sally that I met some of The Ruffians," Ed says. "It is so cool to meet you guys. I guess I should go find my buddy and get him back on his leash. See you guys around," Ed yells. We watch Ed scooting across the soccer field.

"That boy can run," I say.

Empty doesn't answer and I glance over at him and see why. He's staring at three Russian wolfhounds standing on top of the hill by the pavilion. It looks like the terrorists have brought in reinforcements. The three wolfhounds are staring back at us. Empty licks his lips and I notice the sparkle in his eyes.

"It looks like we're going to be in a fight," I say. "I'll make a deal with you. You take the three on the right, and I'll take the none on the left."

"Love it," he replies. "I wouldn't have it any other way."

"I was hoping you would say that. I'd hate to unleash my fury in the park. An innocent might get hurt."

"You're a category-five canine."

"I guess we ought to warn Butch about the reinforcements," I say. "It's something he and the guys should know."

Empty doesn't answer as he hasn't taken his eyes off the three Russians.

I can hear the beginning of a growl rumbling in Empty's chest.

The terrorists stare at us for a few more minutes and then as one they turn around and walk away.

Empty starts whimpering.

"I guess we should go home and warn the gang," I say.

Empty nods his head up and down, looks at me, grins, and says, "You're probably right, Al."

CHAPTER 5

After Empty and I leave the park and get back to our respective buddy's homes, I decide to make use of my time and have a productive afternoon. I curl up on the bed and take a nap. I'm sleeping like a dog when the slamming of the front door brings me out of dreamland and back into reality. I know what's going on. My buddy is home from work.

"Hey, Mixer," my buddy yells. "I'm home from work." Quite the genius my buddy. Like he doesn't think that I can figure out the obvious. I should leap off the bed, rush into the living room, and leap into my buddy's arms. That's what I should do. Instead, I stand, stretch, and wiggle my hips. I look at my buddy's Oakland Raiders baseball cap lying on top of the bed stand table. I stretch out and use my nose to flip the cap off the table and onto the floor. That's going to drive him nuts.

I leap off the bed and walk into the living room. I don't see my buddy. Where's my buddy? I walk into the kitchen and stare in fear at the sight I see. My buddy is pulling a bottle out of the refrigerator. Not just any bottle, but that bottle. I cringe when my buddy closes the door to the refrigerator and reaches for a drinking glass out of the cupboard. My buddy is so intent on the bottle, he doesn't even notice me.

My buddy places the drinking glass on the kitchen's counter, unscrews the cap off the top of the bottle, and fills the glass about one-quarter full with the brown liquid. He picks the glass up to eye level, stares at the brown liquid, and then tilts his head back as he downs the drink in three quick swallows. He says, "Ah," and slams the glass on top of the counter. He pours himself another shot and repeats the process. My buddy needs help. He pours himself a third drink and slams it down like a cowboy in a Dodge

City western movie.

My buddy finally spots me and sees the disapproving look in my eyes. "Don't start, Mixer," he complains. "I had a hard day at work. The mouse came off the back of my computer, and I had to get down on my knees and crawl around on the floor to find enough space where I could stick my hand through all the wires and plug the mouse back in. Then on top of that, I almost suffered a severe paper cut when I was shuffling some papers. It could have drawn blood."

Sally eats mice, and my buddy plugs them in. My buddy may have deeper issues than I realized. I don't say anything. I look at my buddy and shake my head back and forth.

"After a hard day like that I deserve a stiff drink," he protests. He ignores the drinking glass this time and picks up the bottle. He takes three long swallows and then slams the plastic bottle down on top of the counter. My buddy defiantly stares at me. What? Am I raising a teenager?

I have to get my buddy some professional help. Lately, he's been hitting the chocolate milk way too much. Maybe I can get him into C.A., Chocolate Anonymous.

I guess my buddy is feeling the effects of all the chocolate milk in such a short period of time. He yells, "Hey, Mixer, go get your red ball, and we'll play a game of fetch in the backyard."

I stare at him.

My buddy speeds off to the bedroom. I can hear him digging through my toy chest. In a few minutes, he's back with my red rubber ball. "I got it," he yells. "Let's go."

My buddy runs out the backdoor. I walk over to my water bowl and enjoy a cool refreshing drink of water. I walk into the backyard and see my buddy standing beneath the shade of the crabapple tree waiting for me. I walk over and stand beside him.

My buddy throws the ball. "Mixer, run and fetch the ball," he yells.

I look up at my buddy and yawn.

My buddy takes off running across the backyard, picks up the ball, and runs back to where I'm standing. "Good boy," he says as he reaches down to scratch me on top of my head.

He throws the ball again. "Fetch the ball, Mixer."

I sit down and scratch at a flea roaming behind my right ear.

My buddy takes off running, again. He retrieves the ball and brings it back to me. "Good boy," he pants. "I bet you're getting tired."

He throws the ball for a third time. "Fetch, Mixer."

I lie down and sniff the grass.

My buddy stumbles across the backyard. He takes a couple of minutes to catch his breath before he picks the ball up. He half stumbles, and half crawls his way back to me. His face is red. My buddy isn't looking too good.

"That's enough exercise for one day," he gasps. "Let's go inside the house."

My buddy climbs the backstairs on his hands and knees. I look over and see Butch staring at me from his backyard. Butch is sadly shaking his head back and forth at me.

I grin.

I finally decide to go inside the house. I stop at the kitchen and am enjoying a fresh drink of water when my buddy yells, "Hey, Mixer, come check out this hot front. It's making my barometric pressure rise. Woohoo."

This sounds good. I run into the living room and look at the Sony forty-eight inch wide screen television. I stop. I stare. I see some skinny guy wearing a white shirt and plastic dark rim glasses staring back at me.

I look over at my buddy and shake my head.

"I swear that guy wasn't on the television screen when I yelled at you," my buddy says.

I give my buddy the look. He knows I'm disappointed in him.

"Mixer," my buddy pleads, "it was that lady on the screen when I yelled at you. You know the one with the big cumulus clouds. I promise."

I believe my buddy, but I'm going to let him squirm for a while. After all, dogs just want to have fun.

I spot something in my buddy's lap, which causes me to forget The Weather Channel. Cheese! I lick my lips.

My buddy sees me staring and says, "No, Mixer. You got the final piece of cheese the other time. I get the last piece this time."

I whimper.

"It's not going to work, Mixer. You always get the last piece of cheese. This slice is mine."

I walk over and place my head on my buddy's knees. I look up at him and give him the sad eyes.

"Please let me have this slice of cheese," he begs.

I sigh.

My buddy looks like he's about to cry, and then he slowly hands me the slice of cheese.

I take the slice in my mouth, run into the bedroom, and leap on the bed. I start to chew my little slice of dairy Heaven. Bleah! It's not cheddar. It's mozzarella. I spit the pieces of chewed up cheese all over my buddy's side of the bed.

He's gonna freak.

CHAPTER 6

I leave my buddy sitting in front of the television set, digging into a bowl of Blue Bell Homemade Vanilla ice cream, and hoping to find something on The Weather Channel that will make his barometric pressure rise.

The other Ruffians are already gathered in my buddy's backyard, and they don't look happy that I'm late for the meeting.

"It's positively about time you showed up," Butch scolds. "Dandy has something important to say, and he doesn't want to have to repeat himself."

"Sorry," I say.

"That's okay," Dandy replies. "There's something serious going on at the park. All the squirrels are running around and eating their own nuts."

I can't stop myself. I cross my back legs.

Empty makes a whimpering sound.

Butch looks like he's about to swoon.

"Maybe that didn't come out right," Dandy says. "I mean the squirrels are eating all the nuts that they have stored up for the winter, and they are eating any other nuts they see."

I squeeze my back legs together tighter.

"This is serious," Empty says. "If the squirrels eat up all their winter supply, then this winter there won't be any squirrels in the park with nuts."

I sit down and wrap my front paws around my back legs. I don't want to be an emergency food source for the squirrels in the park this winter.

Empty looks over at me and says, "I didn't know that you and the squirrels in the park had so much in common."

"Maybe this is the fault of the Molossus," Jim suggests.

"Is that the darling little family that moved here from Oklahoma?" Butch asks.

I'm beginning to regret the decision to drop out of obedience school. I don't know what an Oklahoma is.

"The Molossus was an ancient Greek dog," Jim says. "Their calendar runs out this year. Maybe the squirrels think that time as we know it ends with their calendar."

Empty looks over at me and asks, "Do you think Oklahoma squirrels have nuts?"

"I don't know," I honestly reply. "I don't know what an Oklahoma is."

"I saw Rachael do something wonderful with nuts on television the other day," Dandy proclaims. "She had a handful of nuts in each hand."

This sends Butch into a convulsion. I have to pat him on the back, so he can catch his breath. The patting helps him regain his composure.

"Rachael was baking a delish dessert," Dandy says, "and she put a handful each of walnuts and almonds into the dessert."

"Can we get back to the matter at hand?" Jim asks.

"What matter is that?" I inquire.

"Why are the squirrels eating all the nuts before winter?"

"Maybe it's just a fad," I say. "They might be tired of eating their nuts by now and are starting to save their nuts like they're supposed to."

"That's possible," Jim says. "Some days you feel like a nut; some days you don't."

"Has anyone considered that the terrorists might be behind this whole squirrel mystery?" Butch asks.

"Why would the terrorists care if the squirrels have nuts?" Empty replies.

"Think about it," Butch says. "If the terrorists could control the minds of animals and dry up the food chain, there would be total chaos in the animal kingdom."

"You're right," Empty agrees. "It would be chaos everywhere."

Jim and Dandy move closer to each other for protection.

I can't keep from thinking about the squirrels eating all the nuts they see. I squeeze my back legs even tighter together.

"I have an idea," I say.

"And what would that be?" Butch asks.

"I say that we don't patrol tonight."

"And, darling, why would we positively not want to patrol tonight?"

"I say we run down to Little Italy and speak to The Godfather. He always knows what's going on."

"The Godfather," Jim and Dandy whisper in awe.

Butch glances over at Empty and asks, "Have you cleared your gambling debt with The Godfather over the dog races?"

"I paid off the last of the dog biscuits last week," Empty says. "The Godfather and I are as cool as two ice cubes doing the hokey pokey in January."

We do a group Ruffian high five and set off to see The Godfather.

CHAPTER 7

The Godfather isn't Italian. The Godfather is a Hairless Mexican Chihuahua. The Godfather and his buddy live at 110 Little Italy Avenue. The Godfather controls all the shady dealings on this side of town. Most of the animals are terrified of him. Even the cats whisper The Godfather's name in hushed tones. The Godfather is constantly surrounded by his muscle. His bodyguards are four Rottweilers, and the mere mention of their names strikes fear through the hearts of the most hardened tough guys, canine or feline. The four call themselves, 'The Fang Mafia'. No one wants to cross Blackjack, Carjack, Hijack, or Slapjack.

We walk into The Godfather's backyard, and The Godfather is sitting in front of his doghouse surrounded by his four bodyguards. I'm shocked to see an additional body in The Godfather's backyard. Sally is sitting beside The Godfather, and she's resting her chin on the top of The Godfather's head. I'm not going to let Sally fall into the clutches of a criminal empire. I'm going to save her from this life of crime. I'm going to do it for her own good.

I wink at Sally and give her my sexiest canine smile.

She coughs up a hair ball and spits it at me.

If she wants to become a criminal, who am I to stop her?

"Hey, Godfather," Empty says, "Every time I see you, you're shaking like a leaf on a tree. Why don't you dog up and grow some real fur?"

"Easy, Empty," Blackjack says. "I get off work in five minutes. I would hate to have to dust the alley with you."

"Aren't you the card?" I quip.

Everyone stares at me.

"Get it," I say. "You know. Blackjack is a card game."

"Shut up, Mixer," The Godfather rasps.

"I can't believe you said that in public," Empty tells Blackjack.

"Said what?" Blackjack asks.

"That in five minutes, you're going to get off."

The four Rottweilers leap to their paws.

I push Jim and Dandy in front of me and jump behind Empty.

"Oh my," Butch gushes. "The sight of the four of you flexing your muscles and showing such aggression is positively turning me on. Me first, I plead. Me first."

Empty pretends he's shoving a paw down his throat and starts making a gagging sound.

"Show some respect, Butch," The Godfather says, "or I'll turn them loose on you."

"And I could swallow you in one bite," Butch retorts, "and you know how I love Mexican food."

The Godfather motions with his head for Blackjack, Carjack, Hijack, and Slapjack to sit down.

"We're not here for trouble," Jim says. "We're hoping you can provide us with some information. The squirrels are running around the park and eating their own nuts."

Blackjack, Carjack, Hijack, and Slapjack all groan and look sick.

"What my little friend is trying to say is the squirrels are eating up their winter's supply of food," Butch says. "Do you know why?"

"Why would I care what the squirrels in the park are doing?" The Godfather asks.

"We were wondering if it might have something to do with the terrorists running around the neighborhood. You have ears all over town. You might have heard something."

The Godfather looks shocked. "Did you say that we have terrorists running around the neighborhood? This is the first that I've heard of it."

"They're Russian wolfhounds," Jim says. "We've already had a run-in with them. We think they trained at a secret canine terrorist camp in Alabama. They mentioned Tuscaloosa."

The Godfather turns to the Fang Mafia and says, "Carjack, I want you and Hijack to start asking around and see what you can find out. If you need additional muscle, take Slapjack with you. I want you to comb the neighborhood and find those terrorists."

"If we learn anything, we'll share it with you," Butch says. "I'm hoping that you'll return the favor and share any information that you learn with us."

"I don't like you Ruffians," The Godfather says, "but I think this time we're going to have to put our differences aside. We can't let terrorists take over our neighborhood."

"Hey, Empty," Blackjack says, "this isn't over between you and me. One day, we're going to settle the score between us."

Before Empty can reply, Butch says, "Godfather, remember what I said about liking Mexican food. If anything happens to my friend, you will positively be such a small, delicious buffet."

"I'm a bad dog to threaten," The Godfather warns.

Butch snorts.

I look around and say, "Did you hear about the professional baseball bird team that went on a ten game Wrenning streak?"

Empty looks over at me, gives me a wink, and says, "Shut up."

CHAPTER 8

I spend the next day loafing about the house. I'm not in the mood to go to the park, so I spend most of the day sleeping on my buddy's bed. When my buddy left for work this morning, he'd left a nice bowl of pulled pork barbeque underneath the kitchen table for me to nibble on all day as a treat. Why he left it underneath the table, I don't have a clue. Humans. You can't live with them. You can't live without them.

Once again, I'm sleeping like a dog when my buddy arrives home from work. I'm dreaming of romping with golden retrievers in the park when the slamming of the front door brings me out of my deep, enchanted slumber.

"Mixer," my buddy yells. "I'm home."

My buddy ought to get a job in the park working as a fountain of useless information. Of course, he's home. How many other humans have a key to the front door and know my name?

I rise on all fours, give my body a good shake, and then use my nose to flip his pillow onto the floor. He's going to freak, again.

I pad into the living room and see my buddy already has the television tuned to The Weather Channel. He also has something else. That bottle of chocolate milk is sitting on his lap, and he's using both hands to clutch it like there is no tomorrow.

He averts my eyes when he sees me staring at him and uses his hands to lift the bottle to his mouth and takes three long swallows of the chocolate dairy demon. He needs help. My buddy is out of control. The chocolate milk is beginning to control his life.

My buddy finally pulls the bottle away from his lips and places the bottle back down in his lap. He seals the bottle with a brown plastic lid, and places the bottle down on the floor beside his chair. He looks so sad when he looks at me that I feel sorry for him.

My buddy needs some love. I pad over to his chair and start to give him some love. Wait a second. He doesn't need that much love. I'm not that kind of dog. I slap his knee with the back of my paw to let him know everything is going to be okay.

He gives me a little smile. "I'm sorry, Mixer," he says. "I'm going to try to cut back on the chocolate milk. I get out of control at times."

I nod.

"The electric stapler broke at work today, and I had to use a hand stapler. I used it so many times that my right hand almost started cramping. No one should have to work that hard for a living. It's not fair. Where's the fairness in life?"

I yawn. Great. I have to be a party to a pity party. That's a pity.

"I'm thinking about going to truck driving school," my buddy says.

I sit down. I don't like the way he's steering this conversation.

"We could get a job driving a truck cross country," my buddy continues. "We could pick up a couple of years' experience on the road and then come home and write songs about all our experiences. It could be our ticket to fame and fortune."

I whimper.

"Think about it, Mixer," he says as he pretends he is strumming a guitar. "Our songs would be awesome."

I collapse onto the floor. This is not going to be good.

"I'd have stayed in the right lane if you were the only one left," he sings.

I roll over on my side.

"I popped my clutch about the time your engine died."

I beat my paw against the floor.

"My baby said truckers make the best lovers. They really know how to turn on the key. That kind of hurt my feelings. I work in a factory."

I stick my paw into my mouth. The pain. Please stop the pain.

"Fifteen minutes of love in a truck stop is fourteen more minutes than I really need."

I curl into the fetal position.

"I proudly showed you my radials, and you laughed at my flat tire."

I'm howling. I can't take it anymore. I leap to my feet, run over to my buddy's chair, and grab his bottle of chocolate milk.

My buddy realizes what is happening. "No, Mixer," he screams. "Please don't do it."

I run out the backdoor with his bottle of chocolate milk.

I can hear my buddy's wails of anguish echoing through the house.

I smile.

He screams.

I'm smiling like a happy dog now. Sing about that, buckaroo.

"Mixer," my buddy wails, "Please bring my chocolate milk back. I'm sorry. I'm so sorry."

CHAPTER 9

The following night finds The Ruffians in my buddy's backyard holding our nightly meeting. Butch thinks it's a good idea if we skip patrol for a couple of nights and keep a low profile. I think he's worried about the Fang Mafia coming after Empty.

Everybody looks down in the dumps, so I decide to loosen the mood. I look around and ask, "What's a lion's favorite state?"

Everybody stares at me.

I scream, "Maine!"

Everybody keeps staring at me. They're going to be a tough audience tonight.

"You fur ball," Empty mutters.

"Play nice, Empty," Butch admonishes. "You just have your hackles in an uproar because you aren't going on patrol tonight."

Empty looks over at me and says, "Sorry." We paw bump each other.

"I think we ought to hunt down these terrorists and finish this thing," Empty continues. "I don't like hiding in our own backyard."

"Darling, we are positively not hiding. We're simply taking some precautionary measures," Butch replies.

"We need to find those Russians and take them out," Empty protests.

"Darling, you positively have got to get over your tendency for violence. Haven't you ever heard of diplomatic negotiations? If we could resolve this diplomatically, then I might still have a chance to take the taller wolfhound to the Holiday Inn Express and make yummy."

Empty sticks his paw in his mouth and starts making a gagging sound.

Butch continues, "After all, it takes a good dog to have hair on his chest and a better dog to keep that chest hair rubbed off."

Empty gags louder. I roll my eyes. Jim and Dandy start snickering.

"Besides," Butch tells Empty, "I think the Fang Mafia still has some plans in store for you. I don't trust that bunch or The Godfather."

"You, me, and Empty can take care of ourselves," I say, "but what if they do something to Jim or Dandy?"

"We can take care of ourselves," Jim and Dandy bark in protest.

Butch reaches out with his paws and pulls Jim and Dandy closer to him. He looks at me and says, "Sweetie, if that happened, then I think that I would positively go berserk and lose my peaceful ways."

Butch doesn't have a twinkle in his eyes when he says that, and when he gazes at me and Empty and we see the look in his eyes, we both involuntarily take a step backward.

Butch laughs and says, "You silly boys. I would never hurt either one of you. I love you two."

Empty and I start looking all around. I'm looking up in the night sky and trying to find the Big Dipper. Empty has taken a deep, sudden interest in the Hutchinson's television dish mounted on the side of their house. We both hate it when Butch gets sentimental and uses the 'L' word. Real dogs don't say love.

Butch laughs again and says, "Two big tough dogs, and they're uncomfortable hearing the word love. You two beat all I've seen."

Butch looks at Jim and Dandy and says, "I love you two."

They look up at Butch and reply, "We love you, Butch."

Butch looks at me and Empty and says, "That wasn't so hard was it? Now I want to hear the two of you tell each other, 'I love you.'"

I look at Empty. Empty cocks his head. I say, "I love barbeque."

Empty quickly replies, "Ditto."

"Well," Butch snorts, "I hope you two grow up one day."

"I just had a thought," Dandy says. "What if any of us are kidnapped? Who's going to read the ransom note?"

"We'll read it ourselves," Jim butts in.

"We can't," Dandy counters. "We're dogs. Dogs can't read."

Jim counterpoints, "We can't really talk either, but since this book is a work of fiction, if we can talk in it, we can read in it."

"Good point," I say.

"I'm going to take Jim and Dandy home and put them to bed," Butch says. "I suggest we all get a good night's sleep. Tomorrow is Saturday so let's spend some time with our buddies this weekend and Monday we can get back to work."

"That sounds good to me," Empty says. "I need to catch up on some serious mirror time."

We say good night and part ways. I walk into the bedroom and leap on the bed. My buddy looks so cute asleep in his Scooby Doo pajamas. I notice his head has slipped off his pillow. I ought to give my buddy a little lick on the cheek and place his head back on his pillow. That's what I really ought to do.

I stretch out over his body and use my nose to flip his pillow off the bed and onto the floor.

He's gonna freak.

CHAPTER 10

I wake up, and the sun is once again shining through the slits of the torn aluminum foil covering the window. I glance at the alarm clock and see that it's already past eight. Boy, talk about sleeping like a dog. I notice my buddy has left his pillow on the floor. So he thinks he's pulling one on me? We'll see about that.

I look over at the nightstand table by his side of the bed and see his Oakland Raiders baseball cap sitting on top of the table. I do a couple of hip shakes, walk over to his side of the bed, and use my nose to flip his baseball cap off the table and onto the floor. I love starting the weekend on a positive note.

I leap off the bed and stroll into the living room. My buddy is sitting in his plaid cloth covered recliner, still wearing his Scooby Doo pajamas, and eating a bowl of Cap'n Crunch cereal. He's also glued to The Weather Channel. I can see why. Wow. That meteorologist has a set of cumulus clouds in her skin-tight red blouse that even I'm feeling the effects of a tropical heat wave.

I walk to the kitchen for a drink of water from my water bowl. I forget about the water. I look toward the doggy door mounted on the back door and look back at my buddy sitting in his recliner and looking so peaceful. I have a plan.

I walk over to the back door and scratch the bottom of it.

"Mixer," my buddy yells. "Use the doggy door to go outside. I'm busy."

I scratch again.

I hear my buddy grumble and place his bowl of cereal on top of the coffee table. His red, plastic flip-flops make a flapping sound as he walks across the white linoleum kitchen floor toward the back door.

"I don't know why you didn't use the doggy door," my buddy complains. "It's been weeks since I've seen that weather girl, and now she might be off the air before I get back to my chair."

My buddy either needs a life or a blow up doll. Come to think of it, the blow up doll would probably become his life.

He opens the door, and I stroll outside and down the back steps. I planned on going right back in, but I see something in the backyard that catches my attention. I hear my buddy close the backdoor, and I walk over to the middle of the backyard where a light-brown toy Pomeranian is sitting underneath a pine tree. The Pomeranian lives a couple of streets over with the Ford family. Everybody calls him Truck because everybody knows that he's Ford tough. Even The Godfather leaves Truck alone.

"What's up, Mixer?" he asks.

"Ain't nothing shaking but the leafs on the tree," I say. "What's going on in your world, Truck?"

"You know me. My wheels keep on turning, and my mind keeps on burning."

"That doesn't make any sense, Truck," I say.

"You're a fine one to be talking about things not making any sense," He replies. "When was the last time you did something sensible?"

Okay, he has a point.

"I was going to tell you that Empty needs to be careful," he says. "The word on the street is that the Fang Mafia is gunning for him."

"They better not catch him," I reply.

"Mixer, even Empty can't handle four on one. The odds are too doggone stacked against him. The Godfather is pretending that he's trying to control them. He doesn't want Butch coming after him."

"If the Fang Mafia hurts Empty, there's no place they can hide from Butch. He's an animal when he's riled."

"Just tell Empty to watch his back."

"Truck, have you heard anything about the squirrels in the park eating all their nuts?"

Truck gives me a curious look when I say that. "Mixer, that's the first I've heard of it. I don't have a clue why the squirrels would be doing something so squirrelly. I'll keep my ears open and see what I can find out."

"We also have some terrorists in the neighborhood. Three Russian wolfhounds are roaming the streets."

Truck looks puzzled over that remark. "I met those three Russian wolfhounds," he says. "They seemed like pretty nice fellows. What makes you think that they're terrorists?"

"We've already had a couple of run-ins with them," I say. "Empty wants to go ahead and settle this issue with them."

"Tell Empty not to do anything rash," Truck warns. "Let me put me the word out on the street to my people and let's see what pops up."

"Sounds good," I say. "Catch you later, Truck."

"See ya, Mixer. I may see ya, but I wouldn't want to flea ya."

CHAPTER 11

I walk back inside the house, and my buddy is still sitting in his recliner, wearing Scooby Doo pajamas, and watching The Weather Channel. I notice one thing different though. My buddy has the neck of the bottle of chocolate milk clutched tightly in his right hand, and the bottle is sitting upright in his lap.

This is great. Now my buddy is drinking before noon. I'm going to have to get my buddy some help. He's not strong enough to keep walking on the wild side of life.

I give my buddy my most disapproving stare.

He glares back at me and slowly raises the bottle of chocolate milk to his lips and takes two long swallows. He carefully lowers the bottle back into his lap and uses the back of his left hand to wipe away the liquid brown mustache above his upper lip.

I might have to talk to Butch about this. My buddy needs some intervention before he crosses the Dairy River of no return. If I don't get him some help soon, he'll be traveling down a lonely path on his one way trip to Chocolateville.

My buddy stares at me with a funny look on his face. Okay, maybe the comical look is his normal look, but there's one thing stirring in the box of dog biscuits that's making me uncomfortable. He's staring at me, and I'm a dog that doesn't like to be stared at.

My buddy raises the bottle up to his lips and takes a long swallow of chocolate milk. He lowers the bottle to his lap, and uses the back of his left hand to wipe the droplets of chocolate milk off his lips. Maybe he should have used the sleeve of his Scooby Doo pajamas top as I notice he still has a pencil thin mustache of chocolate milk decorating his upper lip.

I wonder if I should let my buddy know about his chocolate, dairy mustache and decide against it. When he's this deep in the chocolate, there's no reasoning with him.

My buddy winks at me.

Great Lassie in Heaven, he's out of control. He's so far wasted in Chocolateville that he hasn't even finished the bowl of Cap'n Crunch cereal sitting on the stained oak coffee table in front of him. What kind of person would waste Cap'n Crunch in this day and age? I slowly back up two steps. What if he wants a hug? I'm not that kind of dog.

"Mixer," I've been thinking," he says.

That's great. It almost sounds like he's slurring his words, but that's not the worst thing about this situation. Is my buddy drinking because he's thinking, or is he thinking because he's drinking? Maybe I can get him to switch over to low fat chocolate milk. Something has to be done about this run away freight train my buddy calls his life. If he doesn't get a handle on his drinking problem, he's going to derail.

"I've decided against going to truck driving school," he declares.

I let out a slow breath of air. Maybe there's hope for my buddy after all. Even through the haze of chocolate milk clouding his brain he's showing some common sense.

He smiles and says, "I'm going to become an author instead."

I sit down on my butt, hard, and stare at him. I know that I misunderstood him. He said he was going to become an author. The buddy who's not right is going to try to write? I do the only thing I know what to do under the circumstances. I roll my eyes.

My buddy notices the eye-rolling and protests. "Mixer, how hard can it be? I'll write a book, send it off to a publisher, and it'll become an international best-seller. We'll go on talk shows and become rich and famous. Everywhere we go people will be swarming all over us for autographs. I'll even hook you up on a fancy date with a French poodle."

Did my buddy just say French poodle? Now I know he's lost it. This kid doesn't do international dating.

"I know what I'm going to write about," my buddy continues. "I'm going to write about love. I'm going to write a book teaching men how to pick up women."

I whimper.

My buddy doesn't notice my pain as he says, "If a man wants to pick up a lady, all he has to do is follow the simple romantic steps I'll have outlined in the book. People all over the world will be falling in love because of us. Marriage will be blossoming worldwide because I wrote a book about love. Think about all the couples who are about to enjoy marital bliss because I put writing before truck driving school."

My buddy's forgetting one thing. Marriage is the number-one reason for divorce. Couples all over the world will be coming after him to tie him up by his toes. My buddy is going to be a casualty of divorce wars.

"I've already started working on some pick up lines," he brags. "I'm going to title the book *The Cosmic Guide to Picking Up Women.*

1. *"Girl, your mother must have been an alien because you are out of this world."*
2. *"Girl, your middle name must be Comet because I can't take my eyes off your tail."*
3. *"Girl, when I look at you, I see a UFO-utterlylicious female object."*
4. *"Girl, you should be in show business because you remind me of a shooting star."*
5. *"Girl, you're so sweet that even Uranus doesn't stink."*
6. *"Girl, is your name Venus because you sure light up the sky?"*
7. *"Girl, you remind me of the moon because I sure want to explore your crater."*
8. *"Girl, we could make sweet music together because I sure want to show you my Nep-tune."*
9. *"Girl, you must work for NASA because you sure know how to booster my rocket."*
10. *"Girl, your middle name must be Space, because I sure want to explore you."*

I lie down on the floor, cover my head with my paws, and whimper louder. I have to get my buddy some much-needed help. Maybe truck driving school wasn't such a bad idea after all. After all, the trucks all have air ride seats now.

"Think about it, Mixer," my buddy yells. "I'm going to be known as the Romantic Deity."

I start howling.

CHAPTER 12

I wake up and realize that it's Sunday morning. Sunday mornings are The Ruffians rest and relaxation day. We usually hang in my buddy's backyard to chill for the day. My buddy's side of the bed is empty, so I know he's gone for a few hours. He always leaves on Sunday morning and comes back a few hours later with a bag of chopped beef barbeque sandwiches. He never tells me where he's going. Maybe that's because I'm always asleep when he leaves. Who knows?

I leap off the bed and pad into the kitchen. I glance at my food bowl. It's filled to the brim with brown chicken flavored soybean nuggets. I use my nose to flip the bowl over and watch the nuggets scatter all over the kitchen floor. Maybe one day my buddy will get the hint. Barbeque is the canine breakfast of champions, not soybean nuggets.

I stick my head through the doggy door and see the guys already scattered around my buddy's backyard. Jim and Dandy are lying on their sides, Empty is lying on his stomach with a bored look on his face, and Butch is laying on his back with his four paws stuck straight up in the air and giggling to himself. I probably don't want to know what that's all about. Maybe it's a gay thing. I'll Google it later.

I climb on through the door and walk down the three concrete steps to the backyard. I'm expecting the guys to leap to their paws with excitement because I'm finally here. It's not happening yet. My friends need some motivation.

"What do you call a baker wearing a bra?" I ask.

They all turn their heads and stare at me with blank expressions on their faces.

I scream, "A cupcake!"

They keep staring at me with the same blank faces. They're going to be a tough audience again.

Butch groans as he rolls over and stands up on his four paws, and the other Ruffians follow his lead.

"Mixer, that was positively awful," Butch complains.

"Nobody wants to hear your lame jokes this early in the morning, fur breath," Empty grumbles. "I don't know why I'm lying outside on the cold ground when I could be getting some serious mirror time inside my buddy's house. He'll be gone for a few hours. I don't even understand myself at times."

"Where do our buddies disappear to every Sunday morning?" Dandy asks. "Do you think they get abducted by aliens once a week for a few hours?"

Butch reaches out and pats Dandy on top of the head.

"They go to church every Sunday morning," Jim volunteers as he adjusts the glasses on his nose. He always has trouble with his glasses sliding down.

"Then why don't we go to church on Sunday morning?" Dandy inquires.

"Darling, dogs positively don't go to church," Butch placates Dandy as he gives him a hug.

I decide to engage with my vastly superior intelligence. I cut into the conversation and say, "I don't see why not. Dog spelled backward is God and human spelled backward is namuh. That means God likes dogs better."

Empty looks over at me and says, "Good point."

"We could start our own church," Jim volunteers. "We could use that old, empty appliance store on the corner of Fifth and Willow Streets."

"That's not going to work," I say. "The sign leaning against the side of the building says it's for whites only."

"You bait breath," Empty snaps. "The sign says *White's Appliances, The Only Store in Town.*"

"Oh," I reply. Once again, my dropping out of obedience school is coming back to haunt me. If I hadn't dropped out maybe I would have been able to read better. I'm hoping this is an important lesson for pups to learn worldwide-stay in school!

"I wonder what we would positively call our church," Butch wonders aloud to no one in particular.

"How about Paws for Prayer?" Empty suggests.

"We like it," Jim and Dandy chime in unison.

"But how are we going to get the animals in the neighborhood to know about the church?" Empty asks.

"Is this church going to be for all animals or just dogs?" I question.

"I think it should be for all animals," Jim says. "It can be nondenominational. We'll start off letting the dogs in the neighborhood know about it, and they can help spread the word to all the animals."

"Does anyone have an idea as to what would be the best way to achieve such an optimistically noble endeavor?" Jim asks.

The other Ruffians all glance around at each other. None of us have the slightest idea what optimistically means. Even Butch is looking confused.

"I have an idea," I say. "We'll go around the neighborhood knocking on all the dog house doors. We'll even knock on the ones that have a no trespassing sign outside by the dog house."

"Darling, how would we positively achieve that without getting into all sorts of trouble?" Butch asks. "I believe no trespassing means to keep off the property."

"It's no problem," I shoot back at Butch. "We'll organize ourselves into a group and call ourselves Jehovah Fleanitnesses."

"Love it," Empty says as he looks over at me.

"We think it's super-duper," Jim and Dandy yell in unison.

Butch glances over at me and softly says, "Most excellent, Mixer,"

"I suggest that we all retire to our respective buddy's homes, and give this matter a day of deep thinking and contemplation," Empty says.

Empty isn't fooling me. He's going through mirror withdrawals. He wants a chance to stare at himself all alone in the mirror for a few hours. It must be hard being a mirrorholic. Whatever you do, good or bad, is going to be a reflection upon you. Oh, well, those are Empty's problems. I have enough issues to deal with on my plate as it is. I still have to deal with my buddy's Weather Channel and chocolate milk issues, and the fact Sally is spreading rumors about me around the neighborhood.

"That might be a wise move," Butch sagely agrees. "If we are going to pull this off, it's probably going to take a lot of thought. Let me get Jim and Dandy a mid-morning snack, and start giving this situation some serious thought."

Empty looks over at me and says, "See you in the morning, Alpo breath."

We gather around, do a group high five, and yell, "We are The Ruffians."

CHAPTER 13

Monday morning. That means one thing, buffet time! Old man Mahoney at Mahoney's Meat Market always tosses the weekend's leftover cuts of meat in the alley behind his market. The leftover cuts were designed to be a buffet for any dog that was hungry. All the dogs around town scramble to be the first in line on Monday morning. The buffet serves as a local canine meat and greet.

Old man Mahoney only had a couple of rules about the buffet. No dog could take more scraps than he could eat, and whatever you took you had to finish. After all, there are starving dogs in China who would love to have the leftover scraps.

I wake up and notice something unusual about the bedroom. I can't quite place my paw on it. Then it finally dawns on me what's different about the room. My buddy has taken his pillow off the bed and placed it and his Oakland Raiders baseball cap on top of his old, antique, maple dresser. So, he thinks he's smart huh? He thinks placing his things out of my reach is going to stop me? I don't think so.

I leap off the bed and grab the end of the blue cotton blanket between my teeth. I start walking backward until I drag the blanket off the bed and onto the olive-green shag carpet. He's gonna freak.

I rush into the kitchen, grab a quick drink of water, and then I'm out the doggy door faster than you can say I'm out the doggy door.

I rush around to the gate, use my nose to flip the latch up, and take off down the street. I'm running because if I don't hurry, all the meat scraps will be gone by the time I make it to the market.

I noticed the mailman is walking down the sidewalk delivering mail to the houses on my side of the street. I hate it when I get in a doggone dilemma like this. If I take the time to chase the mailman back to his white Jeep, I might not make it to the market in time for my scraps.

I'm caught in a moral dilemma. I look at the mailman, look down the street, look back at the mailman, and look down the street again. I make my decision. I face the mailman, bark twice, and take off running toward him.

He shrieks, drops his brown leather mail satchel, and the letters he was holding in his right hand and takes off running toward his white Jeep. Look how his chubby little milky calves jiggle. He's never going to make it in time. He knows it, and I know it.

I bark three more times at his back as I'm charging him. I'm gaining with every step. He's yelling please, please, please as he feels my hot breath blowing on the back of his calves. Great Lassie in Heaven, this guy's skin is paler than his white socks.

I pull back my teeth in a snarl. I growl loud enough so he can hear me.

He screams.

I haven't had this much fun since the last time I had this much fun.

The mailman is slowing down his pace. His white Jeep is so close yet so far away.

He's only five feet away from his four-wheel sanctuary when I kick in the afterburners, sail in front of him, look up and gaze at his terrified face, stick my tongue out at him and then take off down the street in the opposite direction toward the meat market.

Okay, fun is fun, but food is a serious business, and I have to make it to the meat market before all the decent scraps are taken or I'll be stuck with nothing but scraps. Yuck.

I slow down as I see a crowd of dogs gathered around the front entrance of the alley leading behind the meat market. The wonderful aroma of two day-old meat scraps permeates the air. I can't believe all the dogs aren't rushing in to grab their meaty buffet.

I wiggle my way through the crowd and peer down the alley. There is the very good reason the dogs are afraid to go any further. The Fang Mafia is behind the meat market, and they have Jim and Dandy backed up against the red brick wall.

I know what this is all about. They're going to hurt Jim and Dandy to force Empty into coming after them. They're forgetting about Butch. It's never a good thing to forget about Butch.

Jim and Dandy are going to be toast in a few minutes, and if I go against four Rottweilers by myself, I'm going to be toast also without butter. I'm not leaving my fellow Ruffians. I notice Carjack is standing with his back legs spread a little too wide. Okay, his dog biscuits never finished baking all the way. I take off running down the alley toward Carjack. At the last second, I flip my back legs under me and slide under his body.

This might not be a treasure hunt, but look what's dangling in front of my face, Carjack's family jewels. I reach up and chomp down with his jewels between my teeth. Bleah, it's going to take four cases of Listerine to get the taste out of my mouth. Why does Butch think this is something yummy? No matter what Butch says, it doesn't taste like chicken.

Carjack doesn't say a word. His body stiffens, and he falls flat out on his side without making a sound.

I have another problem. He fell across my side, and I can't wiggle out from underneath him.

Slapjack looks at me and smiles. He tells Blackjack and Hijack to take me out, and he'll take care of Jim and Dandy.

Where's Butch and Empty?

Blackjack and Hijack have slobber dripping off their fangs as they advance toward me. It's over. My buddy is going to be left all alone and there will not be anyone to take care of him.

"Slapjack, you better back off," I hear a familiar voice say. I twist my head around and see Truck trotting down the alley toward us.

"This doesn't concern you, Truck," Slapjack says.

"I'm making it my concern," Truck replies. "Take your boys and go."

Slapjack motions with his head for Blackjack and Hijack to grab Carjack. They reach down and pull him off my body and drag him toward the entrance of the alley. Slapjack follows, and I can tell by his body motions that he's not a happy camper.

I look past the Fang Mafia, and the three Russian wolfhounds are staring down the alley. They slowly walk away without making a sound.

"Interesting," Truck says to no one in particular. "Interesting indeed."

CHAPTER 14

The word about the rumble at the meat market spread throughout the neighborhood faster than flea spray on a short hair terrier. Jim, Dandy, and I are met by Butch and Empty halfway back to our homes. I can tell by the look on Butch's face that he isn't going to be in his diva mode this morning. I can see the storm clouds rolling out of his ears.

"What were you two positively thinking," Butch screams at Jim and Dandy. "You two should have known better than to leave the house without me. You could have positively been hurt and Jim you might have broken your glasses."

"We were hungry," Jim protests. "We wanted to get to the market first to get the best cuts of scraps."

"Besides," Dandy says. "Rachael doesn't come on for another three hours, and I was bored"

"What about me?" I say. "I could have been hurt."

"It doesn't always have to be about you," Empty says. "It should invariably be about me. Besides, you don't look any the worse for wear."

"Is the word on the street true?" Butch asks. "Did you really take Carjack's dangling gardens in your mouth and nibble on the little darlings?"

"Yeppers," I say.

Butch's knees buckle and a dreamy look crosses his face as he asks, "Don't you think that they tastes just like chicken?"

Empty starts making his gagging sounds.

"Butch, are you really mad at us?" Jim asks.

Butch reaches out and straightens the glasses on Jim's face as he replies, "Sweetheart, I would be absolutely devastated if anything happened to you or Dandy. You little munchkins are my world. Please don't leave the house again without telling me where you're going."

"Save the sentimental clap track," Empty says. "We need to go find the Fang Mafia and settle this once and for all. We ought to go ahead and take out The Godfather, also."

Butch looks at Empty and says, "You leave The Godfather alone. I have plans for him. I don't want a hair on his head hurt until I've had the chance to communicate my displeasure with him."

We all know what Butch means when he says that he wants to communicate his displeasure. Someone is going to get hurt.

"Yes, sir," Empty says.

Butch looks over at me and asks, "I love you more than ever, Mixer, for coming to Jim and Dandy's aid."

"We're Ruffians," I say. "It's what we do."

Even Empty is quiet. I look over at him and see the fire dancing in his eyes.

"Are you sure that you're okay?" He growls.

"I'm fine," I say. "I just need some mouthwash."

"The Russians were also there," Dandy says.

"Why would the wolfhounds and the Fang Mafia be in the same place on a Monday morning?" Jim asks. "I need to do some musings about this."

Butch looks over at Empty and asks, "Do you think there's a connection between the two groups?"

"I don't know," Empty says. "But we need to find out."

"I don't think so," I say.

They all look at me.

"The Russians could have taken me out when I was helpless, lying beneath Carjack, but they didn't. They looked and walked away."

"It could be because Truck was there," Jim responds. "Nobody messes with Truck."

Empty looks over at me and sticks his paw out for a paw bump and asks, "Are your brains scrambled any more than normal?"

That's his way of saying he cares.

"I'm cool like an ice cube," I brag.

Empty looks over at Butch and says, "We need to find out what's going on. It's going to get violent before it gets better."

I get goose bumps when Butch softly replies, "I'm absolutely counting on it, darling. I'm absolutely counting on it."

"What's our next move?" I ask.

"We get Jim and Dandy home," Butch commands.

Empty starts to whimper.

I look at him and say, "Quit complaining and put on your big dog pants. We may be missing the buffet, but we have other things to worry about.

Besides, I know that my buddy has some Oscar Mayer Delifresh smoked turkey breast in the refrigerator. We'll snag a few slices of it. My buddy will never know the difference."

"Cool," he replies.

We paw bump.

"Let's do it," Dandy yells.

We know what he's talking about.

We gather around, do a group high five, and yell, "We are The Ruffians."

CHAPTER 15

The three Russian wolfhounds slowly stuck their heads around the corner of Peyton's Pet store and watched the retreating backs of The Ruffians.

"We're going to have to do something about those guys," the taller of the wolfhounds said. "They have a reputation for sticking their noses in business that doesn't concern them. We've planned this way too long to have The Ruffians mess everything up."

"Let's stick with our original plan," the shortest of the trio said. "Let's take one of them out. The rest of them should be in too much shock to mess up our plans."

"I like it," the taller of the wolfhounds said.

"When should we execute it? It has to be done quietly and without alerting the other Ruffians. It's going to be hunt, hit, and disappear."

"Let's plan to do the hit within the next few days," the tall leader said.

"I say we take the beagle with the glasses. He might be the easiest target to take down."

"I agree."

The two wolfhounds turned and looked at the third Russian, wearing dark sunglasses, leaning against the side of the wall.

The silent Russian spat out the toothpick hanging loose in his mouth and nodded his head. "I'll do it," he said. "Give me a couple of days to plan and the beagle will never know what hit him. It will be quick and painless for him."

"Agreed," the other two co-conspirators said.

CHAPTER 16

After Butch, Jim, and Dandy make it home to their buddy's house, Empty and I decide to stroll down to the park and check out some babes. I've never wanted to be a horse, but I'm feeling my oats as Empty and I leisurely stroll down a tree-shaded sidewalk. That little scuffle behind Mahoney's has left me feeling tougher than an egomaniac roll of toilet paper in a laxative factory. Maybe I need to go to Hollywood. Stallone can't make action-adventure movies forever. I'll be his replacement. I'll be the new action-adventure hero-Mixbo.

Empty brings me back down to earth when he asks, "Did you really bite Carjack where the sun doesn't dangle?"

"Yeah," I say while puffing out my chest. "And Butch has been lying to us all these years. It doesn't taste like chicken at all."

"I can't imagine," Empty replies. "If I want something that tastes like chicken, I'll stick to eating chicken. I can always get my buddy to go pick up a bucket of extra crispy at KFC."

"Don't be so judgmental," I say. "I heard all the stories about the night you spent behind the schoolhouse with the Doberman twins, Darla and Doris. You three ought to be ashamed of yourselves. The things y'all did on the soccer field while the lights were still on."

"I agree," Empty proudly states, "I should be ashamed, but I'm not. It's the only time I've ever been in an Alpo de Triple. The three of us made enough memories that night to outlast a cat's nine lives."

"I wonder what Butch is going to do," I say changing the subject. I don't really want to hear about Empty's love life. If he gets started on his exploits, he'll never shut up.

Empty cocks his head and looks at me with one eye while asking, "What do you mean that you wonder what Butch is going to do?"

"Well, you know how he feels about Jim and Dandy. After the stunt the Fang Mafia pulled behind the meat market, I can't imagine Butch not going after The Godfather."

Empty shakes his head back and forth and says, "You know Butch. He's not going to rush into doing something foolish. If he finds out The Godfather sent the mobsters after Jim and Dandy, after that he'll take action. If he finds out The Godfather wasn't behind it, next he'll go after the Fang Mafia. Of course, I imagine they'll do their best to steer clear of him."

Something catches my attention out of the corner of my right eye. I cringe. Across the street, K.D. Mitchell is standing in her front yard. She's holding her water hose, and once again the hose isn't hooked up to a faucet. She's just holding the green hose in her hands."

Empty senses my hesitation and says, "Relax, Mixer. It's not after eleven o'clock yet, and that's when K.D. Mitchell turns mean."

As if to prove Empty right, K.D. Mitchell smiles and starts waving at us. We both pick up the pace. Neither one of us is wearing a watch, nor are we not sure how close the time is to eleven. We don't want to be anywhere close to her when she turns mean.

"I hope that new golden retriever in the neighborhood is at the park walking her buddy," I say. "I've finally figured out a way to find out her name. I've got the perfect pick up line. She won't be able to resist the Mixer's charm and grace."

Empty looks over at me, rolls his eyes, and asks, "Okay, Grace, what's this new line you're going to use to knock her off her paws?"

I'm proud of myself. Empty is going to be so jealous that he never thought of this line. I proudly proclaim in my best cagey canine voice, "Your buddy must pick fruit for a living because you sure do have a nice pear."

"Lame," Empty mutters. "You use that line and the goldie is never going to talk to you again. For the right amount of dog biscuits, I can teach you some sure-fire pick up lines. The girls fall for them all the time."

"Okay, Romeo," I say. "Let's hear the line that's going to rock her world."

Empty grunts as he clears his throat a couple of times and says, "If you let me unleash your dreams, I'll be the dog you always wanted to collar."

I stare at him. "That's what you call a pick up line?" I ask. "That line wouldn't work in a million years. Besides, you're restricting yourself to dogs. I'm a creature of beauty that has broad appeal to all animals."

"Exactly what do you mean by that?" Empty asks with a quizzical expression on his face.

"Once I walked by a group of female pigs. They all squealed."

"That's because you were hamming it up," Empty replies.

I can't think of any snappy comebacks to his answer, so we stroll the rest of the way to the park in silence. I think what we are both wondering about was what Butch will finally decide to do.

We stand beside the bleachers overlooking the soccer field, and I could tell by the dreamy look on Empty's face that he's lost in memories. Life's not fair. Empty has memories of an Alpo de Triple with Darla and Doris Doberman, and all I have is a buddy addicted to The Weather Channel and chocolate milk. Well, I do have my memories of Sally. It's a shame that she wanted something more serious and all I wanted to do was cat around.

I'm bummed to find that Empty and I have the park to ourselves. I don't even see Ed from Puerto Rico running around. It looks like this babe hunt is going to be a total washout, and I'm hoping to make some golden memories behind the pavilion with a certain retriever. Okay, I'm hoping to at least find out her name.

Empty breaks the morning's silence by finally saying, "Great Lassie in Heaven, what a waste of time this trip was. I might as well go home and grab some serious mirror time."

I agree with him. We're wasting our time at the park this morning. "I guess I could go home and do something productive like take a nap or hide my buddy's television remote. He freaks out when he can't watch The Weather Channel."

Empty looks over at me and asks, "Why do you want to hide your buddy's television remote? He's a good buddy. Why would you want to aggravate him?"

"He drinks more when he's watching television," I say. "The chocolate milk has taken control of his life. He's powerless against the power of daily dairy liquid chocolate."

"That sounds serious," Empty agrees. "Bury his television remote in the same hole you buried his Oakland Raiders T-shirt in last summer under the crabapple tree."

I'm shocked. "I didn't think anyone saw me bury the shirt. He's still tearing the house up looking for it. Maybe I'll tell him the truth one day about where it is, but probably not. Besides, I need to get deep into the mouthwash. I think it's going to be a long time before I want chicken once again. I may not ever want chicken again."

Empty looks over at me, grins, and says, "Cluck, cluck, lover boy."

"Quit fowling my good humor with insults," I reply.

Empty grunts.

CHAPTER 17

I climb the stairs located in the back of the house and use the doggy door to enter the house. I walk into the kitchen and see my food and water bowls where they're supposed to be. I also see something that's not where it's supposed to be. My buddy is bending over and putting groceries inside the beige white refrigerator. Why isn't my buddy at work?

My buddy groans as he straightens up then turns around to grab some more groceries off the top of the kitchen counter. An alarmed look crosses his face as he sees me staring at him. He quickly turns around and slams the refrigerator's door shut. He's too slow though. I've already noticed the two half gallons of chocolate milk sitting on the top shelf of the refrigerator beside the mayonnaise and shredded cheddar cheese. This situation is worse than I thought. My buddy is now drinking doubles. It might be too late to get him into a chocolate prevention program.

"Mixer, you're home," he stammers as he stares at me like a deer caught in the headlights of a used Pontiac barreling down Highway 15 in the middle of the night.

Once again, my buddy impresses the world with his keen power of observation. I hope he has a good reason for not being at work. As if reading my mind, he begins to speak.

"The exterminator came by the office," he explains. "The smell of the pesticides was so strong that we shut the office down until tomorrow morning."

Once again, my rash decision to drop out of obedience school is coming back to bite me. I don't know what an office is. I'm not sure if I believe his story or not. Two half gallons of chocolate milk might be too much a temptation for a chocoholic. I hope he's not making the story up just so he could have an excuse to come home and start drinking.

"I'll be back at the office tomorrow morning bright-eyed and bushy tailed," he continues. His face lights up as he proclaims, "Hey, that makes me sound like a squirrel."

I think about all the squirrels running around the park with no nuts. I decide not to go there. I yawn.

My buddy grabs a twelve-ounce can of Del Monte green beans off the kitchen counter and turns around to put the unseasoned beans in the pantry. He suddenly spins around while still holding the canned green beans in his right hand and looks at me with a strange look on his face.

I cringe. I know that look. It means my buddy has mentally stumbled upon another one of his ideas which is going to enrich his life with fame and glory. What it really means is my buddy has found another way to make a goober out of himself.

"Mixer, I've decided not to become an author," he excitedly cries.

I breathe a sigh of relief. Maybe this time around my buddy is going to show some common sense. The girls on The Weather Channel would be proud of him.

"I heard at one time prison movies were the big rage at the theater," he says.

I lift my eyebrows. I don't think I like the sound of this conversation.

"Don't worry, buddy," he laughs. "I have no intention of becoming an actor and staring in prison movies."

I sagely nod my head up and down.

"I'm going to become a rap singer and sing rap songs about prison," he yells. "I'm going to go by the stage name of Butterscotch Ivory. I'll be the only person singing those types of rap songs. We're going to be rich and famous."

My mouth drops open. This probably isn't going to be good.

"Check out my dance moves," he yells, and I can see the excitement dancing in his eyes. This is so not great. My buddy is going to shake his bootie in the same place where my food bowl is located. I really don't want buddy bootie seasoning my soybean nuggets.

My buddy starts jumping around the kitchen while holding the can of green beans to his lips and pretending to sing into a microphone. I hear a dreadful racket invade my brain, and I wonder if the noise is the end of the world. Then I realize what the terrible commotion is all about. My buddy is trying to rap.

He looks at me with the sweat glistening on his forehead and hollers, "Get in the mood, Mixer. Get down like a flat tire in the bottom of a ditch."

I don't want to get down. I want my buddy to put the can of green beans away before he winds up hurting himself. Great Lassie in Heaven, Del Monte would sue us if the company saw what he's doing with their green beans. My buddy is twerking and rapping at the same time. I'll never eat green bean casserole again.

"I'm in prison and locked in a cell.
Everywhere I look, I see an ocean of males.
I had better find some inner strength and draw on the power.
I don't want baloney, toast, or Bubba in the shower.
I wonder if the cooks in the kitchen are scrambling powdered eggs.
The guy in cellblock 4-A wants me to call him Meg.
I know the armed guards are watching from the tower.
And they don't want baloney, toast, or Bubba in the shower.
I remember the time I got shampoo in my eyes.
I sat down on the floor, and I began to cry.
I curled into a ball, and I begin to cower.
I couldn't see if there were baloney, toast, or Bubba in the shower.
Every day I spend two hours in the prison yard.
Pumping iron weights and making my muscles hard.
Until that sunny afternoon when a giant gave me a flower.
I sobbed, I don't want baloney, toast, or Bubba in the shower.
I've got five more years before they set me free.
Then I don't know what will become of me.
I'll tell the probation officer looking mean and sour.
I never had baloney, toast, or Bubba in the shower.
I head down to go wash off prison sweat.
I didn't make eye contact with anyone I met.
I strip off my clothes and marvel at my power.
Then I start screaming in hysterics-I see Bubba in the shower!"

My buddy stops twerking and looks down at me with sweat dripping off the end of his nose. "Well, Mixer, what do you think?" he asks.

I walk over and look up at him.

He smiles down at me.

I hike up my right leg.

"No, Mixer," he wails. "That was my last good pair of khakis."

CHAPTER 18

The Fang Mafia sat in a semi-circle staring at The Godfather who was pacing back and forth in front of his off-white painted doghouse. Actually, three of the mafia were sitting in a semi-circle as Carjack was lying upon his side and whimpering while listening to the lyrics of the classic rock song *Poor Poor Pitiful Me,* by Linda Ronstadt, blast from somewhere deep in The Godfather's canine chateau.

Sally sat on top of the red cedar shingled roof of the doghouse with a detached look etched upon her face. Occasionally, when one of the hired muscle was brave enough to cut a glance at her, Sally would cough up a hair ball and spit it at the four-legged miscreant.

Flames of anger danced in The Godfather's eyes as he angrily rasped at his stubby tailed employees, "What was the four of you thinking? You know Mahoney's is off limits when it comes to fighting. It's a Monday morning sanctuary for all dogs. Fighting isn't allowed there. If old man Mahoney thinks his meat market is going to turn into a canine battlefield, he'll shut down the free buffet."

"We really weren't going to hurt the beagles, boss," Slapjack protested. "We only wanted to have a little fun with them. You know, push them around a little and watch them squirm."

"And what about Butch?" The Godfather growled in a scratchy voice. "If Butch thinks I sent you to the meat market to rough up Jim and Dandy, he's going to come looking for me, and you know what Butch is like when he gets his painted toenails bent out of shape. Somebody is going to get hurt, and if it's me, afterwards who's going to hire you four clowns?"

The Godfather's verbal rampage was temporarily interrupted by the screeching of Carjack yelling for his mommy.

Sally coughed up a hair ball and spat it in his direction.

"There's no telling how long Carjack is going to be out of commission," The Godfather snarled as he continued his pacing back and forth in front of his mini mansion.

"We didn't count on Mixer getting involved," Hijack griped. "We didn't even know he was there. And even if we did, who knew that Mixer had tricks up his mouth?"

"I did," Sally purred.

The Godfather glared at her, and she quickly looked away while adding, "But I was a different cat back then."

"You better remember that," The Godfather snorted. "You're my gal now and if I catch you catting around on me, then you'll be in more trouble than a litter box without kitty litter."

Sally resisted the urge to cough up a hair ball and spit it at him.

"What are we going to do about Mixer?" Blackjack asked as he inserted himself into the conversation. "After what he did to Carjack, we can't let him slide and get away without it. We have a reputation to uphold. If the other dogs quit fearing us, then we're ruined."

"Fine," The Godfather rasped as he waved his right forepaw at the air. "Just wait until the time is right and the four of you can jump him all at once. He won't stand a chance."

"You realize that once you take care of Mixer and Empty finds out about it, he's going to declare all-out war, don't you?" Sally asked in an aloof tone of voice.

"Even Empty can't take on the four of us all at once," Blackjack boasted.

A look of apprehension crossed The Godfather's face as Sally looked at him and purred, "What about Butch?"

"I'm going to have to think about it and come up with a solution," The Godfathered answered.

"I have an idea," Hijack screamed in canine joy. "I know how we can keep Butch at bay."

Blackjack and Slapjack stared at him. Carjack screamed for his mommy one more time.

"Well, are you going to tell us or just sit there all day looking like a water hydrant?" The Godfather impatiently inquired.

"After we take out Mixer," Hijack proudly stated, "we'll take out Jim as well. Send a note and his glasses to Butch's buddy's house and blame it all on the Russians. We know places to hide him where he'll never be found."

A smile lit up The Godfather's face as he slowly nodded his head up and down in agreement. "I like it. Don't rush into it though. Work out a good plan and when you're satisfied that it's fail proof then execute it."

"I'll get started on it immediately," Hijack replied.

"Now what about the other problem we were talking about," The Godfather demanded. "Have you four come up with a solution that will suit our needs?"

"Yeah, boss," Slapjack interjected into the conversation. "There's an old abandoned furniture factory south of town. No one has been inside of it for years. We think it would be perfect for our needs. We can come and go without being spotted."

"It's the perfect size," Blackjack added. "There's more than enough room inside of it to take care of our needs."

"Good, good," The Godfather mumbled as he nodded his head up and down. "You boys have done a fine job. Once this is done, you're all going to get a bonus."

"What about me, big guy?" Sally purred. "Don't I get a bonus as well?"

"Don't you worry about a thing, you foxy feline," The Godfathered crooned. "I have big plans for you. You're going to be living the high life."

"I want to go on vacation," Sally pouted. "I want you to take me to the beach, so I can lay out all day in the sun with my favorite catnip."

"Babe, when this is over," The Godfather smiled in anticipation, "I'll buy you your own beach. There won't be anyone left to challenge us."

"You're so evil, but I love it," Sally purred with her eyes half-closed.

"Well, boss, we're going to shove off and work on our plans," Hijack said. "We'll be checking back in shortly with you in case you need us."

"Take the rest of the day off," The Godfather answered. "However, first thing tomorrow morning I'll want you to find out what you can about these Russian wolfhounds that have been spotted around town. I don't like surprises, and these Russians worry me."

"When we find them, do we need to go ahead and take them out as well?" Blackjack asked. "Strangers nosing around town can't be a good thing."

The Godfather thought for a minute before replying, "No, for the time being, just follow them and see what you can find out. It might be that we can turn the situation into an advantage for us. Then you can do whatever you want to with them."

"Gotcha, boss. We haven't let you down yet."

"You better pray you keep it that way," The Godfather rasped in a menacing tone of voice. "Hired hands can always be replaced."

"You little evil thing, you're giving me goose bumps," Sally whispered in a sultry voice.

Carjack wailed for his mommy one more time.

CHAPTER 19

The Godfather enjoyed a peaceful afternoon of canine bliss. He lay stretched out on his back, with his eyes closed and his head resting in Sally's lap. Sally was daintily dipping her right paw into an opened can of Chef Boyardee Mini Ravioli and feeding The Godfather delicious tidbits of pasta stuffed with meat and tomato sauce.

"This is the life," The Godfather delightfully mumbled as a line of tomato sauce slowly dripped down his chin.

"Don't ever forget how happy I make you," Sally purred as she reached to pull out another square stuffed pasta slice of Heaven. "You'll never find anyone who treats you as well as I do. I don't see how you managed all these years without me."

"Don't you fear, my foxy feline," The Godfather answered. "I'm taking you with me straight to the top. Your every wish will be my command."

The smile on Sally's face froze, and her right paw stopped in mid-air as she observed Butch strolling across the lawn toward The Godfather's doghouse. She thought about coughing up a hair ball and spitting it at Butch, but decided to wait and see how first this new development would play out. Plus, she had no desire to be turned into a feline appetizer.

"Babes, you better open your eyes," she whispered in The Godfather's right ear. "You have company and I don't think you're going to be real thrilled about who it is."

The Godfather wiggled underneath the warm sun and buried his head deeper into Sally's furry lap. "I'm comfy," he yawned. "Make them go away."

"Well, if this isn't positively the cutest sight my adoring eyes have beheld," Butch said as he strolled up to stand in front of The Godfather. "You two are positively a Kodak moment and making memories to last a lifetime."

The Godfather's eyes snapped open.

"Please don't get to your feet on my account," Butch said. "You might as well be comfortable while we have our friendly little chat."

"What do we have to chat about?" The Godfather asked in a raspy voice as he raised his head from Sally's lap to obtain a clear look at Butch's face.

"Well," Butch replied as he pursed his lips, "we must positively address the unfortunate commotion behind the meat market this morning. I can't stress enough how displeased I am about that event. Little Dandy could have gotten hurt, and I don't want to think about how close Jimmy came to having his glasses broken by your ignorant brutes. The incident stressed me out so much that before I left the house, I painted my toenails with Dolche & Gabbana in Passione, and you know I positively don't wear a mixture of purple and pink very well. I meant to wear Butter London In Kip. That delicate pale blue seems to bring out the color in my eyes."

"The boys were just having a little fun," The Godfather stated as he stood to stare at Butch. "They were never going to actually hurt the beagles."

"Well, just so you know," Butch crooned while holding his left paw out in front of his face and admiring his painted toenails, "if Jim or Dandy had been hurt, this conversation would have been over with very quickly, and your lady friend would have to join eHarmony to find a new boyfriend."

"I'm a bad dog to threaten, Butch" The Godfather warned while pulling his upper lip back over his top teeth in a not so vicious snarl.

"Whatever," Butch snorted while rolling his eyes.

"You ought to leave, Butch" The Godfather warned. "If the boys show back up, I'm liable to forget about our agreement concerning the Russian terrorists and turn the lads loose on you. I don't think even you can take on the Fang Mafia all by yourself."

"Oh dear me," Butch gasped as he threw his right paw in front of his mouth. "You're talking about turning loose a pack of hairy, muscular brutes and letting their sweaty bodies climb all over me and forcing me to inhale the musky odor of their masculinity while they use pointy little teeth to inflict pain all over my poor, helpless body? Please do, I implore you, please do," Butch pleaded, "and if you could arrange for it to happen at a Holiday Inn Express that would make the experience so much more delicious and yummy."

"I don't like that type of language being used in front of Sally," The Godfather cautioned.

Sally coughed up a hair ball, but quickly swallowed it back down when she saw Butch glance over at her.

"Darling, you should have stayed with Mixer," Butch told her in a soothing voice.

"That sorry bucket of used flea collars dumped me," Sally retorted. "I wasn't the one who broke off the relationship. I'm a lady."

"Whatever," Butch replied.

"I'll tell the boys to leave the beagles alone," The Godfather lied. "So, I guess our business here is complete."

"Well, not quite," Butch countered. "Truck warned me that the word on the street is the Fang Mafia is going to hurt Mixer because of Mixer biting Carjack's little danglers. I was absolutely appalled when Mixer told me that they didn't taste like rotisserie chicken. Actually, I could barely make out a word the dear boy was saying with all the Listerine in his mouth. Carjack must simply practice better personal hygiene."

The Godfather inwardly fumed. Leave it to the Fang Mafia to talk over their business loud enough so anyone could hear it. Then a light bulb clicked on in The Godfather's brain. Butch only mentioned Mixer. He hadn't mentioned a word about Jim's future demise. Truck must not have heard everything. He would talk to his hired muscle about being more careful in the future when they were out talking in the streets.

"Another thing," Butch continued. "If the goon squad hurt Mixer, have you given any thought to how Empty would react? That handsome heartthrob doesn't possess the diplomatic skills that I inherited from my line of blue-blood pedigree ancestors. I'm afraid that he would simply wait until you were alone and then Little Italy would be in the quest for a new Godfather. At times, he simply gets too violent for his own good."

The Godfather took a deep breath and swallowed a mouthful of fear as he realized Butch was telling the truth. Empty would take out the mob boys one at a time, and then come after The Godfather. Okay, he would call the boys off Mixer, but the plans for Jim would still be intact.

The Godfather trembled in fear as a rumble of never-ending thunder split the morning sky, and he realized the rolling thunder was coming deep from Butch's chest while Butch's face was contorted into a mask of snarling rage with spittle slowly dripping off his fangs.

"Darling, I would prefer to end this nonsense right here and now," Butch snarled as he moved his face to within a few inches of The Godfather's visage of fear. "One quick snap and I never have to worry about my loved ones ever being hurt by you or your goons."

"Wait," The Godfather screamed in fear. "No one is going to hurt the beagles or Mixer. I promise. I'm calling a peace treaty. Please let me live, Butch."

"That's positively what I wanted to hear," Butch said as he turned around and strolled off.

Sally coughed up a hair ball and spat it in the direction of Butch's retreating back.

The Godfather peed where he stood rooted on the ground.

"I'm glad things worked out to such a delightful conclusion," Butch told himself. "As much as I love it, Mexican food positively gives me gas."

CHAPTER 20

I'm sitting in my buddy's backyard with Jim and Dandy, and we're listening to Empty complain to Butch about not taking him along on the trip to The Godfather's place.

"I can't believe you went to see The Godfather and didn't take me with you," Empty says. "You know that I have a score to settle with the mob boys."

"Darling," Butch replies, "I simply went on a peaceful journey to express my displeasure at what transpired this morning. It was a diplomatic mission, and you know as well as I do that you simply don't play well with others."

"Well, I don't like it," Empty answers. "We have terrorists doing Lassie knows what, and now the Fang Mafia is trying to play games. We should end it all right here and now."

"Sweetheart, you must calm your violent nature," Butch soothes. "We'll find out what's going on and then take the proper measures to ensure all's well that ends well."

"You should have taken my glasses with you, Butch," Jim pipes into the conversation.

"Darling, why would I have positively wanted to take your glasses with me?" Butch asks as he fondly looks over at Jim.

"Because everybody knows that you can't hurt a dog wearing glasses," Jim answers.

"He's right," Dandy joins in. "I saw that same answer on Jeopardy one afternoon when I was waiting for Rachael to come on. Television can be a very educational tool."

"Well, I will keep that in mind," Butch smiles at Dandy.

Butch looks over at me and says, "I'm appalled to learn that you don't think the danglers taste like chicken. I was so hoping you were going to expand your cultural horizons."

I look at Butch and say, "I went through both bottles of my buddy's Listerine, and it wasn't even the mint flavor."

"If the opportunity ever presents itself again, I might suggest having a little Grey Poupon Dijon Mustard on hand to enhance the palate," Butch suggests.

Empty pretends he is sticking his paw in and out of his mouth and starts making a gagging sound.

"Are we going to patrol tonight?" Jim asks to no one in particular.

"I think we should," I answer. "We haven't patrolled in a few days, and we really need to see what's going on in the neighborhood."

"I agree," Butch replies. "The neighborhood depends on us. I've heard a couple of new dogs and one cat has moved to the neighborhood, and we need to find out what type of characters they are. We have positively run into enough unsavory characters the last few days."

"I wonder what the cat looks like." I muse out loud.

Empty quits making his gagging sounds, looks over at me and says, "I thought you were interested in that new golden retriever in town. Besides, I thought you had sworn off dating cats. You would think that last psychotic feline you dated would have taught you a lesson or two."

"Sally's not a psychotic feline," Jim volunteers into the conversation. "She's a scorned woman who had her heart shredded to pieces by Mixer. She had her life's dreams shattered by Mixer's rejection. That's why she has fallen into a life of crime."

"She needs to get over it," Empty replies. "She has eight more lives to get her life's dreams to come true."

I want to get the conversation turned away from mine and Sally's past relationship, so I ask, "What do you call a dog that's never had sex?"

They all stare at me.

I scream, "A fur-gin!"

They're still staring at me. They've been a tough audience lately. Maybe I need to log onto Facebook and see if I can pick up some new jokes there.

"An elephant walks into a biker bar and orders a Shirley Temple," I try again. "One biker says, "Can you believe that?" The other biker replies, "No freaking way. I've never seen anybody order a Shirley Temple before."

"That was positively dreadful," Butch moans.

"That wouldn't have gotten a chuckle out of a laughing hyena," Empty says.

"The joke wasn't that bad," Dandy replies to Empty.

Jim joins in the conversation, by adding, as he slid his glasses back up his nose, "The logistics of that joke have me puzzled. The door would have to be one of enormous size to allow an elephant to pass through, or else we are conversing about a very small elephant which means he would be a juvenile and too young to enter a bar. All that aside, where would an elephant get money to pay for a Shirley Temple, and where would he keep such currency if he had some?"

"He would probably keep the money in his trunk," Dandy suggests.

Jim shrugs his shoulders and concedes, "I guess there is that possibility."

I look over and wink at Empty and Empty winks back. We love it when Jim slips into his solemn mode and takes everything too serious. He's just too darn cute in those moments.

"If you are through not entertaining us with your jokes, Mixer," Butch says, "I suggest we patrol the neighborhood toward the park, swing back by the school, and then patrol the other half of the neighborhood on our way back home."

"That sounds like a planley, Stanley," I tell Butch.

A dreamy look crosses Butch's face as he muses out loud, "I've never dated a dog named Stanley. I positively wonder what that experience would be like. If our relationship lasted long enough, maybe I could start calling him Stan. We could positively make yummy at the Motel Six, and definitely prove that we don't need the light left on."

Empty sticks a paw in his mouth and starts making a gagging sound.

Jim and Dandy stare at Butch.

It's none of my business. I just want a burrito.

"Oh, well," Butch says as he returns from dreamland, "If we stand here all night, we're positively not going to get any patrolling accomplished."

"You ready to patrol, Milk Bone breath," Empty asks as he glances over my way.

"I was born ready," I say. "I'm the Cupid canine and ready to let my arrows fly."

"Whatever," Butch snorts.

We head toward my buddy's fence gate when I say, "Hey, Empty, what do you call a cussing chicken?"

"I don't know," Empty replies.

"Fowl language!" I holler.

The other four Ruffians drop their heads and start groaning.

CHAPTER 21

It's strange walking by K.D. Mitchell's house and not seeing her standing in the front yard holding her water hose. I wonder if she takes the water hose inside her house at night and sleeps with it. She seems unusually fond of it.

"That's K.D. Mitchell's house," Dandy reverently whispers. "I wonder if she turns nice after eleven o'clock at night."

"What are you talking about?" Jim whispers back.

"Think about it," Dandy says in a hushed tone of voice. "Everybody knows K.D. Mitchell turns mean after eleven o'clock in the morning. If she didn't turn nice at some point, then she couldn't turn mean in the morning because she would be mean all the time."

"That's a good point," I whisper. "And why are we whispering?"

"Because," Butch whispers, "we don't know if she is the mean K.D. Mitchell right now or the nice one. Do you really want her hearing us, in case she isn't asleep?"

"I heard," Empty whispers as he joins in the conversation, "that anybody who enters K.D. Mitchell's house in the morning after eleven is never heard from or seen again."

"Might I make a suggestion which may prove useful for the situation," Jim whispers.

"Sure," Butch, Dandy, Empty, and I whisper in unison.

"Run," Jim screams.

We all take off running and don't even think about slowing down until we reach the corner of East Sycamore and Whispering Willow Avenues.

"That was close," Jim says. "Maybe we need to start using a different route on patrol."

"Darling," Butch replies while petting Jim on top the head with his right paw, "we don't even know if K.D. Mitchell was home or not. However, I agree that sometimes it's better to be safe than sorry. Now I must simply ponder on if it's true that people disappear in K.D. Mitchell's house and are never heard from again."

"Great Lassie in Heaven," Empty says. "Look what's coming down the street, Merry Christmas to me."

I look down Whispering Willow Avenue, and I see what Empty is talking about. The three Russians are walking down the center of the street like they own it and without a care in the world. I'm not sure I like the idea of foreign invaders taking over our streets.

The three Russians spot us about that time and start advancing toward our little group. I hear the echo of a deep growl rumbling around in Empty's chest.

"Empty, cool your jets," Butch tells him. "Let's see what these little darlings are doing out at this time of the night."

"If it gets physical," I say, "Butch, you take the dog in the middle. Empty, you take out the dog on the right. Jim and Dandy, you two ought to be able to handle the one on the left. I'll hang back and see if they have more reinforcements that we don't know about."

"You're a dog," Butch snorts.

The wolfhounds don't make any attempt to hide as they slowly keep advancing up the street toward us.

"This is interesting," Empty says to no one in particular. "It looks like they want to meet us. If they were trying to hide from us, they wouldn't keep walking our way."

The air is breezeless and quiet, and the blackness of the night is only broken by the overhead streetlights as the two sides slowly advance toward each other. It reminds me of a western movie where the gunfighters walk down the street and face each other. I guess I should be wishing for a poncho and a canine six-shooter, but I'm not. I'm still wishing I had a burrito.

The Russians are almost nose to nose with us when they stop, and we stop. Everybody is eyeballing each other without saying a word. I'm hoping Butch doesn't suggest that we sniff butts. That probably isn't the best way to break the ice with strangers.

The terrorists aren't saying anything, and neither are any of The Ruffians, so I decide to break the ice and see if I can get this unexpected meeting started off on a cordial note.

"What happened when the guy started drinking coffee on the trampoline?" I ask.

Everybody is staring at me.

"He got all jumpy," I scream.

Everybody is still staring at me without saying a word. Okay, so nobody has a sense of humor at the moment. Even the third Russian didn't crack a smile.

Butch purses his lips and asks the third Russian, who wasn't at the first encounter in the Kolinski's backyard, "What's your name, sailor? I positively hope it's Stanley."

"It's Ivan," the wolfhound snaps, "if it's any of your business."

"Oh my," Butch replies. "A hairy chest with an attitude, I positively feel faint. I think that I'm going to call you Capitol One because I would love to see what's in your wallet."

"Knock it off, Mack," the tallest of the Russian says. "I've told you before that dogs in Tuscaloosa don't play that game."

"What do you guys want?" Empty asks as he cuts into the conversation. Okay, so maybe Empty is never going to win a Mr. Personality contest.

"We've heard that you guys have been asking around about the squirrels in the park eating all their nuts," the tall Russian replies. "It's none of your business why the squirrels in the park don't have nuts any longer. You five need to quit playing rent a cop before you get into trouble. You don't have any idea the powers you guys are messing with."

"Why don't you enlighten us," Jim bristles at the tall one.

"I feel enlightened every time I see Rachael on television," Dandy dreamily says.

Empty reaches over and pats Dandy on the top of his head.

The third Russian advances a step toward Dandy with a scowl upon his face, but is stopped by the sound of Butch's voice breaking the night air, "I positively wouldn't do that, darling," Butch croons. "I might know how to use yum yum to make things feel all better, but please don't take my yum yum fetish as a weakness. I also know how to make things never do yummy things again. When I break something, it's positively beyond repair."

"Back off, Ivan," the tall Russian orders. "There's not going to be any trouble tonight. We can always settle with these buffoons another time."

"Buffoons?" Jim yells. "Why don't you try knocking my glasses off my face and see how things turn out for you."

Ivan backs off, but I don't like the way he keeps looking at Jim.

"You've been warned," the tall terrorist tells Empty. "It's the only warning y'all will get. Do the smart thing and stay away from things that are none of your business."

The wolfhounds turn around and start walking away in the opposite direction without saying a word. Wow. I bet all Russians aren't that rude.

"Butch, we're going to have to settle with these guys one day," Empty growls.

I get chill bumps down my spine and my tail curls up when I hear

Butch's soft response, "I'm counting on it, darling. I'm positively counting on it."

CHAPTER 22

I get home, and I'm surprised to see two things. My buddy is home and there's a bag of Dyson's dog food sitting on the floor and leaning against the kitchen counter. Dyson is the most popular dog food in town. It's also the most expensive. My buddy can only afford to buy it for me as an exceptional treat. I'm exceptional, so that explains why he bought me a bag. What I don't understand is why my buddy is at home instead of that place called work?

He sees me and says, "Hi, Mixer, guess who's home? I didn't go to work today. Today is my birthday, so I'm going to stay home and party like a rock star. I've invited all my friends to drop by for a pulled pork barbeque sandwich, ice cream, and a slice of chocolate birthday cake."

Did he say pulled pork barbeque? I look at the kitchen table and see an aluminum pan covered by a foiled top. I can smell the delicious aroma of pulled pork barbeque emitting from the pan. My day just got better.

I look on top of the kitchen counter, and I see three birthday cakes, a case of Pringles potato chips, several packages of hamburger buns, and three gallons of chocolate milk sitting beside some red plastic drinking cups. I already know that Blue Bell ice cream is in the freezer.

"Whenever my friends get hungry," he says, "they can stop by for some food. It's going to be a daylong celebration."

Okay, I get it. My buddy is happy he's celebrating his birthday. If he thinks the pulled pork barbeque is going to last all day he's about as crazy as any human. I'm worried about the three gallons of chocolate milk. I hope my buddy is planning on sharing the milk. I don't want to have to put him in rehab because he couldn't control his chocolate milk obsession.

That's for me to worry about later. Right now, all the activity has made me tired as a dog. I just want to hop up on the bed and catch some shut-eye. I walk into the bedroom and leap on top of the bed. I see my buddy's pillow lying on his side of the bed. It's his birthday. I should leave the pillow alone on his big day. I use my nose to flip the pillow off the bed and onto the floor.

I can't find a comfortable spot on the bed, and I toss and turn for a couple of hours. I can't get the pulled pork barbeque out of my mind. I leap off the bed and walk into the living room. I see my buddy sitting on his sofa sipping a tall glass of chocolate milk. I look into the kitchen and see that none of the snacks have been moved. I look over at my buddy.

"It's only noon," he explains. "All my friends are at work. I'm sure they'll be dropping by during their lunch hour for some food. I even rented a karaoke machine. We can all sing and eat sandwiches and cake."

My buddy looks so happy. I'm beginning to have some bad thoughts about how this day is going to turn out. I walk into the kitchen for a long drink of water out of my water bowl. I push a kitchen stool against the table. I hop on top of the stool and pull the lid off the pulled pork barbeque. Thank you, Mr. Pig, for your selfless sacrifice to my stomach.

I eat all the barbeque that I can handle and leap off the stool. I grab a quick drink of water and walk back into the living room. I look at my buddy. He beams a smile at me. I don't beam back and walk into the bedroom and climb onto the bed. I curl up on the bed and grab a few hours of sleep.

I wake up from my nap and leap off the bed. I walk into the living room and see my buddy still sitting on the sofa. I look in the kitchen and see one of the gallon containers of chocolate milk is empty. I was worried about this. All the chocolate milk is proving to be too much of a temptation for my buddy.

I notice all the other food on the kitchen counter is still untouched. I look over at my buddy.

"It's only five o'clock, Mixer," he says. "I'm sure all my friends will be coming over for some birthday food after they get off work."

I shrug my shoulders and walk into the kitchen. The kitchen stool is still standing in the same place by the table. I climb back on the stool and start on my second helping of pulled pork barbeque. I eat until I absolutely can't take another bite.

I awkwardly climb off the stool and waddle over to a corner. I'm too stuffed to even think about making it to the bedroom. I curl up in a ball in the far corner of the kitchen, and I'm asleep the second I close my eyes.

I awaken a few hours later. My mouth feels as dry as my buddy's sense of humor. I stumble over to the water bowl and drink water until I feel like I'm about to explode. There's no way I'm going to make it out the doggy door in this condition. My buddy is going to have to open the door for me, so I can attend to some personal business.

I waddle into the living room, and my buddy is still sitting on the sofa. I can see the beginning of tears in his eyes. I look up at the clock. It's after midnight.

"It's over, Mixer," my buddy says. "My birthday is over and not one single person in the world stopped by for some birthday food. Nobody called me on the phone to wish me a happy birthday. I didn't even get one single birthday card in the mail."

I really need my buddy to open the backdoor, so I can attend to my personal business. However, I see the pain in his face and hear the hurt in his voice.

I look at my buddy, and the pitiful look on his face is heartbreaking.

I have a decision to make. I make it. I forget about the personal business. My buddy needs me. My buddy needs a hug. I walk over to the sofa and give my buddy a slap on the knee with the back of my paw.

That ought to help!

CHAPTER 23

I wake up the following morning, and I noticed that the other side of the bed is empty. I guess my buddy has gone to that place he calls work. I felt so sorry for him last night. He was so depressed about nobody stopping by the house to help celebrate his birthday that he couldn't take one final look at the girls on The Weather Channel before he went to bed.

Maybe I need to stop picking on my buddy so much. It's time to show him some love. It's not his fault that he has a problem with chocolate milk and a germ fetish. He needs more support and understanding. I use my nose to flip his one-hundred percent polyester fiber pillow onto the floor. I'll start being more understanding tomorrow. He's going to freak.

I give my hips a couple of shakes like any self-respecting dog would do, leap off the bed, walk into the kitchen and much to my surprise my buddy has left me a treat. The water bowl is filled with clean, fresh water, but the food bowl is filled with pulled pork barbeque instead of brown chicken flavor soybean nuggets. Now I feel bad about his pillow laying on the bedroom floor, but not that bad as I scarf down a couple of bites of the pulled pig to get my morning started off with a squeal.

I squeeze through the doggy door and walk down the steps to the backyard. I was hoping to spot some hot babes taking an early morning stroll down the street. What I spot is The Godfather sitting and shivering underneath the crabapple tree.

This I can't figure out. Why is The Godfather sitting in my buddy's backyard, and I wonder where the Fang Mafia is hiding as I quickly look around the yard.

"Mixer, quit being paranoid," The Godfather rasps in that voice of his.

"I made the boys stay down the street by the stop sign. I wanted the chance to talk to you alone."

Wow. The Godfather wants to talk to me alone. That's never happened before. I think about telling him a joke to break the ice, but I know from experience that he doesn't have a sense of humor. I feel the need to make him feel welcome though. I get an idea.

"The oven's turned off, so the chicken ain't baking.
You're welcome here, but quit your shaking.
You're sitting in a spot where I buried a bone.
And when you leave I'll say doggone."

The Godfather stares at me with a blank look on his face and asks, "What was that noise? I've never heard anything like it before."

"It's canine rap," I proudly say. "I got the idea from my buddy. If I ever get tired of being a superhero, I'm going to start a rap band. I'll call it Mixer and the Woofers."

"Whatever," The Godfather says as he rolls his eyes.

"Godfather, is there something I can do for you?" I ask.

"No," he replies while shaking his head. "There's nothing you can do for me. I'm The Godfather. However, there is something I can do for you."

I look over The Godfather's head and through the chain-link fence. I can see Butch sitting in his buddy's backyard with a perplexed look upon his face. I know Butch is wondering why The Godfather is in my buddy's backyard. I'm wondering why The Godfather is in my buddy's backyard. I feel better knowing Butch is awake and about. If the Fang Mafia should show up and decide to start a fight, Butch probably needs to be here to pull me off them. At times even I don't know my own strength. I'm an animal when provoked.

"I'm all ears," I tell The Godfather.

"Mixer," he rasps, "You don't have to worry about the boys coming after you. I've forgiven you for the incident behind the meat market. As far as I'm concerned, it's all water under the bridge. I've already told the guys you're off limits."

His goons start the fight with Jim and Dandy, and I'm the one being forgiven. Okay, I'll pass that one on to Jim and see if he can figure it out.

"Thanks," I say, "but what about Empty? Blackjack keeps making threats about him. You know that Empty isn't going to back down."

"If Empty keeps jacking his jaws about me, I'm not responsible for what happens to him," The Godfather angrily spits out. "As of right now, we aren't interested in any of you Ruffians. It's a clean slate as far as I'm concerned."

"Thanks. I'll pass that on to Empty."

"We all need to work together," The Godfather continues. "We need to find out who these Russian terrorists are and what they want. It's going to take our combined forces working together to keep our neighborhood safe."

I'm not saying that I don't trust The Godfather, but I don't trust The Godfather. I look over his head again, and I see Butch is no longer in his buddy's backyard. There's a reason for that. Butch is sitting right behind The Godfather.

"What about Sally?" I ask. "Does she forgive me too?"

"Pal, you can forget about Sally," The Godfather declares in a loud voice. What happened to his rasp? I'll pass that on to Jim as well. Jim's going to have a busy morning.

"Sally is my gal now," The Godfather continues. "I'm going to give her the life of luxury that you never could."

"I don't want her back," I quickly say. "This Mixer needs to be free to blend in with the world and spread his love. I'm a lean, mean mixing machine."

"I don't care about your love life," The Godfather snaps. "I'm just here to let everybody know that we all have a truce."

I look over The Godfather's head and see Butch crossing his eyes and sticking his tongue out at The Godfather's back.

I try to keep a straight face as I tell The Godfather, "I think that's a great idea. We have to find out what the terrorists are up too before none of the squirrels have any nuts left."

"I agree," The Godfather confirms. "The squirrels have to have their nuts."

Butch is now marching around on his hind legs behind The Godfather's back and using his front paws like he's playing a trombone. I wonder what he had for breakfast.

"What about Butch?" I ask.

"What about Butch?" The Godfather arrogantly questions. "Do you think that I'm afraid of Butch? Everybody talks about how bad Butch is. I'm not afraid of Butch. Butch is simply still around because of my good nature. It would only take one snap of my finger, and Butch would be no more. In fact, if the day ever comes, I might do the dirty deed myself. I'd probably enjoy it. I'm a bad dog to mess with."

"I wouldn't let Butch hear you say that," I advise.

"I repeat," The Godfather snaps, "I'm not afraid of Butch. If Butch was here right now, I would have him groveling at my feet."

I can't help myself. I start snickering.

The Godfather looks furious at my laughing and then realization sets in as his face drains of all color. "He's behind me, isn't he?" The Godfather whispers.

"Positively," Butch mutters in The Godfather's ear.

"How much did you hear?" The Godfather whispers again.

"Darling, I heard everything," Butch says. "If you plan on bumping me off why not do it now, but I have to admit that groveling thing sounded kind of kinky."

"Butch?" The Godfather asks.

"Yes, honeybunch," Butch replies. "What do you want to tell me, and I hope you remember how much I love Mexican food."

"Bye," The Godfather screams and takes off running out of my buddy's backyard.

Butch looks at me and says, "Well, that was positively fun."

"We'll have to do it again one day," I say.

Butch grins and we high five each other.

CHAPTER 24

"What's all the commotion about?" Empty asks as he uses his muscular hind legs to push off the ground and bound over the chain-link fence. "I was into some serious mirror time when all that yelping interrupted my concentration. I swear it's getting so a dog never has any alone time around here anymore. All that screeching sounded like somebody's tail got caught in a hot waffle maker at a pancake breakfast on a Tuesday morning."

"That was The Godfather," I say. "He dropped by this morning to tell me howdy-doo."

Empty did a double take at the mention of The Godfather's name. "Why did The Godfather drop by to tell you howdy-doo?"

"He wanted to let me know that the Fang Mafia wasn't going to come after us. The Godfather is declaring a truce, so we can all try to figure out what the Russian terrorists are doing here. We're going to combine our resources."

"The Godfather wants a truce?" Empty incredulously asks.

"Yes sirree and skippity-doo-dah."

"So the Fang Mafia isn't going to start trouble with us?"

"Nope."

"They're not going to corner me and try to beat me up?"

"Nopers, just quit talking bad about The Godfather."

"I'm not going to be in a fight?"

"Not unless you get married."

"Well, crap," Empty says.

"Darling," Butch cuts into the conversation. "You know that we can't trust The Godfather. I don't know what game he's playing, but I'm sure that you'll get the opportunity soon to engage your brute force in the physical confrontations that you have come too dearly enjoy far too much. The world would be a better place that instead of fighting all dogs should get together and make yummy. Make yummy not war."

Empty sticks his paw in his mouth and starts making a gagging sound.

"Where are Jim and Dandy?" I ask changing the conversation.

"The little darlings are currently fighting over the television remote," Butch drawls in an exaggerated southern accent. "There's an all-day Rachael marathon on and Jim wants to watch The Animal Planet. The little honey bugs look so cute when they get into a ruckus over the remote. Not that it happens very often."

"How are they going to decide who gets the remote?" Empty asks.

"When I left the house, they were doing rock, scissors, and paper," Butch replies.

"Now let's get to the million-dollar question," Empty says. "The Godfather was here for a reason. We need to find out that reason. For all we know, the Fang Mafia and the terrorists are working together."

"You have a valid point," Butch replies. "They could be working together, but I don't think so. We can't trust either side, and we simply must find out what's going on."

The dropping out of obedience school has come back to bite me again. I don't know what a valid is. I make up my mind to go back to school and get my diploma.

"I could ask Truck if he heard anything," I offer. "If there is anything going on out in the streets, Truck will know about it."

Butch taps his paw on his teeth as he's thinking and finally replies, "That's a good idea. Talk to the little darling and see what you can find out. Any information would be useful at this point. There are some shady forces at play here."

"I think we need to go to the park and see if we can find any squirrels with nuts," Empty says. "They might be able to shed some light on the subject."

"You know the squirrels aren't going to talk to us," I complain. "Would you talk to somebody that chased you back up a tree every chance he got?"

"Okay, fur breath," Empty replies. "You might be right about the squirrels not talking to us, but we could still check the park out."

Empty's not fooling anybody. He wants to scout for some babes. It's not a bad idea. The Mixer of love is ready to do a little blending as well.

"Good idea," I decide. "We might be able to pick up a clue."

"Are you coming with us?" Empty asks Butch.

"I'd love to," Butch responds, "but with The Godfather showing up here this morning, I think that I better watch over Jim and Dandy. I don't want to leave them alone, and I positively know that I'm not going to be able to pull them away from the television set until later this afternoon."

Butch looks aghast when I belt out of the blue, "My cousin Henry didn't have any nuts, and he wasn't even a squirrel."

Empty crosses his rear legs and sits down, hard, as he asks with a sick look upon his face, "What happened?"

"His buddy told him that they were going to go get some ice cream. They wound up at the veterinarian instead. All Henry remembers after that is waking up, and his danglers were gone. He hasn't been the same since."

"That's absolutely dreadful," Butch whispers. "That would ruin a yummy life."

"I don't date dogs with danglers," Empty says.

"I do," Butch beams.

Empty, once again, starts making his gagging sounds.

"Oh grow up," Butch fusses.

"I want to date that new golden retriever in the neighborhood," I say.

"It's not going to happen," Empty smirks.

"Why not?"

"Because you're not a professional baseball player."

"Why do I have to be a professional baseball player to date a golden retriever?"

"Until you become one, she's out of your league."

Butch looks over at me and says, "Pooh and rubbish, Mixer. If you have your eyes set on that golden retriever, you go for what you want. Empty's trying to discourage you so he can make his play for her. You know he's a dog when it comes to romance."

I look over at Empty and ask, "Would you really do that?"

"You betcha," he replies with a smile.

"All's fair in love and war," I admit. "There are plenty of hot babes waiting for the Mixer to fold in some love in their lives."

We high five each other.

"Children," Butch mutters under his breath.

CHAPTER 25

The Fang Mafia left the shadow of the stop sign they were standing under and started walking up the street when they saw The Godfather running toward them.

"Look at the little guy go," Slapjack marveled. "I didn't know he had it in him."

"Be careful what you say," Hijack warned. "If The Godfather hears you calling him little, you'll be sleeping with the fishes tonight. You know how sensitive he is about being short."

"I wonder if fishes really sleep," Carjack inquired in a high-pitched falsetto voice.

"Forget about the fishes," Blackjack said. "Amigo, I wonder if your voice is ever going to return to normal. You sound like Sally after she's had a rough night."

"It's not my fault," Carjack protested. "My danglers are still sore from where Mixer bit them. I didn't realize his jaws were so powerful."

"Nobody's blaming you," Hijack piped into the conversation. "I'm surprised that you're up and walking around so soon. Once I tripped on a curb and hit my danglers, and it was three days before I felt like moving."

"Forget about the danglers," Slapjack admonished. "We need to find out how the meeting went with The Godfather and what we need to do."

"You're so right," Blackjack agreed. "It's going to be fun to double cross The Ruffians and be done with them once and for all."

"I want one to be the one that takes care of Mixer," Carjack said. "After what he did to me, I should be the one that gets to take him out."

"Are you going to bite his danglers?" Hijack inquired.

"Not with two bottles of catsup and a jar of Tabasco Sauce," Carjack replied. "I'm not that kind of dog."

"Forget about danglers," Blackjack warns. "Let's see what The Godfather has to say."

"How'd it go, boss?" Slapjack asked as The Godfather finally wheezed his way to a stop in front of them.

"It went perfect," The Godfather panted. "Mixer swallowed the whole story. He thinks everybody is going to work together to take care of those Russian terrorists."

"Are we actually going to try to find out what the Russians are doing?" Blackjack inquired. "So far they haven't bothered us any."

"I don't care what those guys are doing," The Godfather snapped. "They can take over the whole neighborhood as far as I'm concerned. All I want is everybody's nuts."

"You sound like Butch," Hijack quipped.

Hijack looked away and started intently studying the antics of a mockingbird in a pine tree when The Godfather glared at him.

"We've been working on our plan to take out Jim," Slapjack interjected into the conversation to divert The Godfather's attention away from Hijack.

"Okay, Mixer swallowed the story," Blackjack said. "However, the million-dollar question is will the other Ruffians buy it as well?"

"I think they will," The Godfather rasped. "I sounded so believable that I almost bought it myself, and I knew it was a lie."

"What about Butch?" Hijack asked as he rejoined the conversation. "Did you happen to see Butch while you and Mixer were talking?"

"No," The Godfather lied. "Butch wasn't anywhere around, so I think he'll fall for it when Mixer tells him that we all now have a truce."

"Give us a few more days to perfect our plan, and we'll make the move to take Jim out of the picture," Slapjack said.

"Wonderful," The Godfather glowed. "When you take Jim out of the picture make sure you leave his glasses behind so the other Ruffians will think they'll see him again. Say in the note that when Jim is returned, he'll be able to get his glasses back."

"Great thinking, boss," Carjack said. "If they think they're going to get him back, they'll let their guard down, and we can take out another Ruffian."

"I've been thinking about that," The Godfather said as he used his right hind leg to scratch at a flea playing behind his right ear. "When we take out the second Ruffian, I think it should be Butch. Since Empty and Mixer always hang together, we'll have to take them out at the same time. With Butch out of the way that should make the task a little easier."

"And then we take Dandy out, and The Ruffians are no more," Slapjack boasted with an expression of eager anticipation.

"Plus, we have everybody's nuts," Carjack added.

"When this is over, I'm going to take Sally on a vacation," The Godfather said. "Indulge her with some fancy catnip. I might even put indoor/outdoor carpet in her litter box. She's going to be rolling in the life of luxury."

"What are we supposed to be doing while you and Sally are on vacation?" Carjack inquired.

"I'm going to give you boys a well-deserved vacation," The Godfather rasped. "But first, we have to take care of The Ruffians and our other business at hand."

"No problem there, boss," Blackjack added to the conversation. "After this is all taken care of and vacation is over, do you have any future plans for us or your empire?"

The Godfather's face illuminated with joy as he rubbed his front paws together and proclaimed, "We're going to take over the China neighborhood. I don't get along with the Shar Pei that runs things over there. It'll be fun to take over his neighborhood."

"We're going to have to be careful," Hijack warned. "Most of those Chinese dogs know dog fu, so they're going to be hard to take down in a fight."

"We can take them," Blackjack added with an air of smug self-satisfaction. "I don't even think the Chinese dogs want to mess with the Fang Mafia. We might be a small crowd, but everybody knows that we're still the mob."

"I've always wanted to date one of those chow chows," Carjack added to the conversation. "Something about their eyes just makes me want to yank my leash."

"There is something about those Chinese dogs that grab your attention," Slapjack agreed.

"You can have all the Chinese dogs you want after we take over," The Godfather said, "but first we have to take care of our current business. We've stood here yammering long enough. Let's go home. Sally promised that she would have some mini beef raviolis waiting for me."

The Godfather and the Fang Mafia started laughing and walking back to Little Italy. As they did, Ivan the Russian terrorist walked from behind the side of a house and stared at their retreating backs.

Truck walked around from the side of K.D. Mitchell's house and stared at the back of the terrorist.

CHAPTER 26

The three Russians met in an alley behind Robinson's Retail Rodeo Shoppe to discuss their future plans and the best way to proceed.

"I'm going to have to step up the plans," Ivan told the other two terrorists. "It appears the Fang Mafia is going after the same target that we're going after."

"Why would the Fang Mafia be going after the beagle?" the taller of the other two asked.

"It looks like there's some bad blood between the two groups," Ivan explained. "It means that I'm going to have to move my schedule up. If the Fang Mafia neutralizes the beagle before I do, it's going to mess our plans up."

"Well, whatever you do, hurry up," the shorter of the wolfhounds snapped. "I'm ready to get this over with and go home. I'd kill for a bowl of shchi and a kolbasa link."

"Quit thinking with your stomach," Ivan reprimanded. "The timing is going to be very important. I'm only going to get one shot to make this happen, so everything has to run smoothly. If I miss the hit, we won't get a second chance."

"I shouldn't have to remind you, comrade, that if you fail in your duty, there could be some severe consequences," the taller of the two Russians said. "You were brought in because you are a specialist and supposed to be the best at what you do."

"Don't worry about me," Ivan retorted. "You two better concentrate on doing your jobs or the severe consequences could be falling on your heads and not mine. Besides, I don't even know your names. I don't take orders from nameless comrades."

"There's no need to know our names," the taller of the two wolfhounds snapped. "You were brought here do a job and be in and out of this mission. Names aren't important."

"That's telling him, Vicktor," the other terrorist yelled.

"Boris, you idiot," Vicktor screamed. "Now he knows my name."

"Who are you calling an idiot?" Boris retorted. "Now he knows my name as well."

"Doggiemen," Ivan soothed. "I'm afraid the tension of the moment has frayed some nerves, so let's all calm down and keep a cool head."

"You're right," Vicktor agreed. "We have our assignments to worry about. Snapping at each other over trivial matters is counterproductive."

"How are you going to take the beagle out?" Boris questioned.

"The less you know about that the better off you will be," Ivan replied in a secretive voice.

"That's a good idea," Vicktor suggested. "If we don't know, we can't tell."

"Failure is not an option," Ivan voiced as he reached down into a brown bag sitting on the ground and pulled out a pizza roll.

"Are those Totino's pizza rolls?" Boris and Vicktor asked in unison while licking their lips.

"They are," Ivan proudly pronounced. "Doggiemen, I salute you."

CHAPTER 27

I use the doggy door in back of the house and walk into the kitchen to grab a drink of water. I can hear the television blaring in the living room, so I know that my buddy is home. I wonder what kind of mood he's in. That birthday fiasco hit him pretty hard. I'm not sure he's ever going to get over it. I decide there's only one way to find out, so I walk into the living room to check on the status of my buddy.

My buddy must have seen me out of the corner of his right eye because as I walk into the living room, he spins around to face me with his hands hidden behind his back. It's too late. I already spotted that glass of chocolate milk he was holding. Now he's trying to hide his drinking problem from me. I'm going to have to figure out how to deal with this denial stage he's going through.

I stare at him.

"Mixer, I don't have anything behind my back," he stammers.

I squint my eyes in my best Clint Eastwood impersonation.

"I wouldn't hide chocolate milk from you. I'm not that kind of a buddy," he says.

My stare is getting intense now.

"Mixer, I'm sorry," he says as he pulls his hands from behind his back and shows me the Mason jar he uses as a drinking glass. The glass is filled about one-quarter full of chocolate milk. Okay, he's not drinking doubles, but he still lied to me.

"I promise that I'm going to try to cut back on my chocolate milk. I'll switch over to iced tea and bottled water. Will that make you feel better?"

Okay, if he can do that, I'll let him have chocolate milk on occasion, but not every day. I think of all the money he's going to save from not spending so much of it on his liquid chocolate obsession.

I nod my head at him.

"Mixer, look over at the television," he blurts out. "They have a new girl on The Weather Channel. She's pretty hot."

Now he's trying to change tactics to steer the conversation away from the chocolate milk. I glance at the television to indulge him. Whoa! My eyes pop open and my tongue drops out of my mouth. The Weather Channel does have a new weather girl and talk about some high cumulus clouds. I feel a tropical heat wave wash over me while I'm staring at her. If chocolate wasn't bad for dogs, I'd grab a double shot of my buddy's chocolate milk just to calm my nerves. I don't know what dog she belongs to, but I bet he sleeps in the bed with her every night. Wow!

"Mixer, I have some wonderful news," my buddy cries out.

I reluctantly turn my head away from the television set and look at my buddy.

"The reason no one showed up for my birthday party was because I put the wrong date on the invitations. Sometimes I can be such a silly goose in a gaggle of geese walking in circles on the ground. When I realized that I'd put the wrong date on the invitations, I started laughing so hard all my co-workers thought that I'd gone honkers. Do you get it? Not bonkers, but honkers since I was talking about geese."

My buddy just gave me an idea. Since he's talking about geese, I turn my head to take another gander at the television set. There's a commercial on. Talk about a major league bummer. I wasn't through doing my clouds study.

"Sometimes I think that I should be a standup comic," he says.

If this conversation doesn't improve, I'm going into the bedroom and take a nap.

"I've been doing some more thinking," he continues. "I think the time has come that we need to have you fixed."

I spin around, cross my rear legs, sit down hard on the worn-out shag carpet, and give my buddy my best you've got to be kidding look. I may not be a pirate, but my family jewels are staying in my treasure chest.

"We wouldn't call it that," he exclaims. "We'll call it a snip party and make a whole day out of it. We'll go to the vet early in the morning, get the snipping down, and when you wake up, we'll come home and have cake and ice cream."

I growl.

"Mixer, don't take it that way," he pleads. "It's going to be for your own good. I'll even use it in my Butterscotch Ivory routine."

I growl louder.

My buddy bends over and places the Mason jar with the chocolate milk in it on the floor and starts dancing around the living room and rapping.

"His name is Mixer because he doesn't look like a Chip.
I may take him to the vet for a little snip.
They'll put him under, and he'll have a dream.
Then we'll come home for cake and ice cream.
We won't tell him what's going on.
He'll never realize that something is gone.
And if he doesn't notice the stiches.
I'll never tell him why he has the itches.
I'll buy him a fish tank and fill it full of guppies.
Then he won't think about why he can't make puppies.
Between the cake and fish, we'll have so much fun.
It'll be for his own good in the long run.
Once he gets used to being that way.
He'll probably thank me profusely one day.
That'll be two little problems he'll have gone.
I might reward him with a big ham bone.
He'll thank me for the day we took a little trip.
And the vet grinned and smiled and went snip snip."

"See, Mixer," my buddy says after he quits dancing. "It's going to be a big hit for the Butterscotch Ivory routine. Your snip is going to make us famous."

I'm getting worried. He looks serious. I need to think of something.

My buddy smiles at me.

Inspiration strikes.

I uncross my rear legs, stand up, and walk over to the Mason jar sitting on the ground. I lift my right leg above the glass jar.

"No, Mixer," my buddy yells. "Please don't do it. I won't ever bring up a snip party again. I'm sorry. I'm so sorry."

Good buddy. I knew that he would see it my way.

CHAPTER 28

I leave my buddy sitting in his recliner eating a bowl of Lucky Charms cereal out of a red plastic bowl and watching The Weather Channel. I know he's hoping the new weather girl will make another appearance. I think about telling him that her shift is probably over, and she won't be back on television until tomorrow. That's what I think about doing. Instead, I keep my mouth shut and don't tell him anything. Who am I to take away a person's dreams?

I walk into the backyard, and the other Ruffians are already gathered for our nightly meeting.

"What's up?" Empty asks.

"I sent a female tornado chaser a picture of myself," I reply.

"What happened when she saw it?" Dandy asks.

"She was blown away," I answer.

"That was positively cheesy," Butch fusses.

"I like to watch Rachael make dishes with cheese," Dandy dreamily says.

"Cheese was first made around four thousand years ago," Jim pipes in. "It's interesting, because no one is exactly sure what person is the one that created cheese. It could have been created on purpose, or it could have been an accident."

"You spend too much time watching educational television," Empty says. "You ought to get a mirror and take a break from all the television you watch. I find that looking at me is a lot more enjoyable than looking at a television screen."

"I could watch Rachael all day," Dandy says as he joins in the conversation.

Butch reaches over with his right paw and pats Dandy on top of his head.

"I'm just saying the kid needs more recreational time, and what could be more recreational than looking at yourself in the mirror," Empty protests.

"I think that it's positively dreadful that you would try to sway the child from his educational studies," Butch admonishes. "Being self-centered is not necessarily a good way of life for a dog."

"You're the one who gets his toenails painted," Empty counters.

"Whatever," Butch snorts.

I butt into the conversation by saying, "I've got problems, which mean we may all have problems."

"What are you babbling about, leather leash breath," Empty says.

I look over at Empty and he holds out his left front paw for a paw bump.

I look around, take a deep breath, and say, "My buddy can't control his chocolate milk drinking anymore. I've caught him lying to me. Plus, he was trying to hide his glass of chocolate milk from me, so I couldn't see it."

"I absolutely hate it when you catch a buddy in a lie," Butch moans. "You think you have spent all this time raising them right, and then they disappoint you."

"You could have made that statement just as easily without the adverb abuse," Jim fusses at Butch. "At times I don't know what I'm going to do with you."

Butch clucks his tongue at Jim and says, "Darling, I absolutely could have restrained from adverb abuse, but it positively gave you an excuse to share your knowledge of proper language, so in effect, I have furthered your education."

We all watch Jim try to come up with a snappy comeback. He finally gives up and tells Butch, "Appreciate it."

Butch looks over and winks at Empty and me.

"Have you tried hiding his chocolate milk?" a solemn Dandy asks.

"It wouldn't do any good," I reply. "He would buy more when he left to go to work. As far as I know, he may keep a bottle of chocolate milk in his desk drawer at work."

"That would only work if he had a refrigerated desk," Jim says. "I can't imagine a buddy drinking lukewarm chocolate milk. I imagine it would make him sick if he drank too much chocolate milk that wasn't refrigerated."

"If that's the case," Dandy asks, "how can our buddies drink lukewarm chocolate milk and get sick, but then turn around and drink hot chocolate?"

I look over at Empty and Empty spreads his paws wide in front of his body. He doesn't have a clue how to answer Dandy's questions any more than I do.

"Darling," Butch coos while lovingly looking at Dandy, "after you have brushed your teeth and said your prayers, I'll explain the difference between hot chocolate and a dairy product."

"Thanks, Butch," a happy Dandy replies.

"This is even worse than when Sally had a drinking problem," I say.

"I didn't know Sally used to have a drinking problem," Empty says with a curious look on his face.

"Oh, yea," I tell him. "I used to catch her drinking out of the toilet all the time. It took a lot of hard work, but I finally broke her of the habit."

"Mixer, do you see the irony in what you said?" Jim asks. "You saved Sally from her drinking problem then turned around and left her, leaving her in a life of spiraling tragedy."

I look over at Empty and ask, "What's an irony?"

"Beats me," he says.

"Well, we're all here for you, Mixer, to support you in any way, we can," Butch adds.

I look around, and all the other Ruffians are nodding their heads at me. I almost get misty.

"What's the other problem you were talking about?" Empty asks.

I take a deep breath, look around and say, "My buddy is unwell. For all I know, it might be contagious and your buddies might be indisposed also. I hope there's a cure for it."

"What kind of sickness?" Dandy asks with saucer eyes.

"He has the snip disease," I say. "He was talking about taking me into the vet and have me snipped. He wanted to have a snip party with cake and ice cream. If the disease is contagious, your buddies will want all of you to be snipped as well."

Empty immediately drops to the ground, curls up in the fetal position, and starts groaning.

Jim and Dandy hug each other and start trembling in fear.

Butch looks aghast. "That is dreadful," he cries. "If we're snipped, then we won't be danglers, we'll be danglees."

"Worse than that," Empty moans from his fetal position, "we'll be dangless."

"Dang," I say.

"Okay," Empty says as he slowly rises from the ground. "Everybody keep a close watch on your buddies. If they start acting like they have the snip disease, get out of the house and seek cover. Stay in hiding and we'll eventually find you."

"What's wrong?" I ask Butch in an alarmed voice when I notice that he's about to faint.

"I was thinking," He whispers, "that if all the male dogs are snipped, I'll have to make yummy with boneless, skinless danglers, and I don't like broiled chicken."

"Stay strong, brother," Empty barks out. "Stay strong."

We gather around, do a group high five and very shakily yell, "We are The Ruffians."

CHAPTER 29

The neighborhood is quiet, so we decide to patrol around the park and see if we can spot any unusual activity. I notice that we're walking slower than normal as we keep our hind legs close to each other. I know why. We're all thinking about the snip disease. If we keep our legs close together, it will be hard for anyone to get to our danglers. Even Butch has his hind legs close together as we walk. I guess even he's not immune to the fear of the snip disease.

We're walking across the soccer field on the north end of the park when we see two figures, in the distance, walking our way. Because of the night's fog, it's hard to make out who they are. They're too small to be the terrorists or members of the Fang Mafia, so none of us are particularly worried. Okay, I'm not particularly worried. Butch and Empty don't worry very much and with Butch close by, Jim and Dandy don't have much to worry about either.

We pass the soccer field for the high-school soccer team when I recognize the two figures. I'm surprised to see them in the park at this time of the night.

"Look, it's Truck and he's walking a hotdog," Jim exclaims.

"That's not a hotdog," I say. "That's Ed from Puerto Rico."

"He's from southern Puerto Rico," Empty adds. "He says y'all."

"Hee haw," Butch joins in. "I positively love a southern accent. I dated a treeing walker coonhound from Tennessee, and he absolutely sounded so adorable when he would start baying during yummy."

Behind me, I can hear Empty making some gagging sounds.

"What's up?" Truck asks as he and Ed walk up.

"The clouds in the sky," I say. "We're doing our patrol and decided to check out the park. Nothing is happening in the neighborhood."

"Wow," Ed says. "Are all of y'all The Ruffians? I can't believe that I'm finally getting a chance to meet all of you at once."

"Charmed, I'm sure," Butch flatters.

"Great Lassie in Heaven," Empty mutters under his breath behind me.

"You must be Butch," Ed says with awe in his voice.

"In more than one way," Butch shoots back.

Behind me, Empty's gagging sounds are getting louder.

"Wow, you're famous," Ed gushes. "Everybody has heard of you. Even Truck says that no one messes with Butch."

"When they do mess with me, I prefer it be at a Holiday Inn Express," Butch replies in his best flirting voice. Empty almost splits my eardrums as his gagging sounds grow in intensity.

"You're out of luck, Butch," Truck says as he joins the conversation. "Ed has a girlfriend. He met her while walking his buddy at the park."

"She is wonderful," Ed boasts. "She's new in town. She's a golden retriever. I'm glad I met her before another dog stole her heart. I think that we're in love."

I feel crushed. The golden retriever I had my heart set on is taken. All that time I spent watching her shake her hips was for nothing. I should have made my move when I had the chance. Now she belongs to Ed from Puerto Rico.

Behind me Empty's gagging sounds have changed to a low snickering. "You got beat out by a hotdog," he gloats.

I start thinking of ways to get even with Empty. Most of my thoughts I have to quickly dismiss as I'm sure they're illegal in two or three counties in Mississippi and all of California.

"We're Jim and Dandy," Jim and Dandy say in unison to Ed.

"Wow," Ed babbles to Jim and Dandy. "I can't believe that I have now met all The Ruffians. I've already met Empty and Al."

"Who's Al?" Dandy asks.

"I'll tell you later," I quickly interrupt.

"Are you the one that likes to watch Rachael cook?" Ed asks Dandy.

"I am," Dandy replies. "I think she's delish."

"I do too," Ed oozes. "I watch her every chance I get."

"Well, maybe one day you can come over to the house and we can watch her together" Dandy enthusiastically offers.

"Then we can watch The History Channel and make a whole day out of it," Jim adds.

"That would be neat," Ed replies. "I'll bring the dog biscuits."

"This is so positively adorable," Butch says. "I love seeing people make new friends. Friendship is the ties that bind people together."

"We're not people. We're dogs," Empty points out.

"Whatever," Butch retorts.

"I'm showing Ed the best places in town to go to and the ones to avoid," Truck explains. "I'm also letting him know which dogs he should avoid and which ones are okay to be friends with. I've already warned him about The Godfather and the Fang Mafia."

"The Godfather sounds like he's somebody I don't want to mess with," Ed somberly says. "I'm not looking for trouble. I just want to take my buddy for walks in the park and spend time with Goldie. That's my girlfriend's name."

I don't like Ed bringing up my future girlfriend whom I'm never going to have. Maybe Ed should move back to Puerto Rico. Goldie should be involved with a lean, mean, love mixing machine and not a hot dog. Besides, I already know I have better buns than he does.

"Speaking of The Godfather, have you heard any news on the street?" I ask.

Truck shoots me a look and says, "I'll stop by your place in the morning. We need to talk, but there's no reason to bring Ed into it."

"Gosh," Ed oozes as he looks at us. "Are y'all on a case or something?"

"Darling," Butch says. "When you can be yummy like nobody's business, it translates to that I'm always on something."

Jim and Dandy start snickering.

Empty's making gagging sounds again.

"Well, it was wonderful to finally have a chance to meet all of you," Ed says, "I guess I should get back home though. I don't like leaving my buddy alone too much. There's no telling what kind of trouble he could wind up getting into."

"I'll walk you home," Truck volunteers. "I need to be getting back to the house myself."

"See you in the morning," I tell Truck.

"You take care of yourself Ed from Puerto Rico," Butch says. "It was nice to meet you."

"Same here," Jim and Dandy say in unison.

"See y'all," Ed replies.

Empty looks at me and says, "You can always try to get Sally back."

He ducks when I swing my paw at his head.

CHAPTER 30

I wake up the following morning to the sounds of The Weather Channel playing on the television in the living room. I'm surprised by that. My buddy usually turns off the television when he goes to that place he calls work. I look around the room and see what I can flip on the floor. It looks like my buddy has Mixer proofed the room. Everything is out of my reach.

So my buddy wants to play this way. I'll accept the challenge. I use my nose to flip his pillow onto the floor and give my hips a couple of shakes. I hop off the bed and let all four paws land on my buddy's pillow. That ought to teach him to start a germ warfare with me.

I walk into the living room, and I see why The Weather Channel is playing on the television. My buddy is sitting in his recliner, wearing Spiderman pajamas, and eating a bowl of Lucky Charms cereal. So he decides not to go to work and doesn't even inform me of his decision ahead of time. I don't like this. This spontaneous decision of his is going to mess up my routine. I'll have to do some thinking about this and decide what his punishment will be.

"Mixer," my buddy yells when he sees me. "Good morning. I decided not to go into work today, so we can spend all day together."

So my buddy thinks I can't figure out he didn't go to work on my own. I think all that chocolate milk he's been drinking is causing him to be mental. I'll have to keep my eyes on him.

"I have to run to the bathroom," my buddy tells me as he places his cereal bowl on the coffee table in front of his recliner. "I don't want you to mess with my cereal while I'm gone."

This is great. A grown man wearing Spiderman pajamas who's addicted to The Weather Channel is telling me not to mess with his toasted oat pieces and colored marshmallow's shapes floating around in a bowl of milk.

As soon as I hear the bathroom door click shut, I reach over and take a couple of laps out of the cereal bowl. What do you know? My buddy is using whole milk over his cereal. That deserves another couple of laps. Okay, I'm done. My buddy will never know the difference.

I walk into the kitchen to check out my food and water bowls. The water bowl is filled with fresh, clean water. The food bowl is filled to the brim with Dyson dog food. I'm going to be eating well today.

I decide to go ahead and go outside and see if Truck has shown up yet. As I'm crawling through the doggy door, I hear my buddy yelling, "Mixer, thank you for not messing with my Lucky Charms." I'm almost tempted to go look up the golden retriever and see if I can steal her away from Ed. I don't know why, but for some reason, I'm feeling magically delicious.

I spot Truck sitting under the crabapple tree with a bored look on his face. I wonder how long he's been waiting. I really wasn't expecting him this early.

"Mixer, what's up?" he asks as he spots me walking up.

"The ceiling in the kitchen," I say.

"You ought to have your own hour on The Comedy Channel," he says with more than a hint of sarcasm. I decide to ignore the sarcasm.

"Did you get Ed safely home last night?" I ask.

"Yeah, he's a good kid."

"He's a walking hotdog who steals females away from deserving dogs," I counter.

"Ed didn't steal Goldie away from you," Truck says. "You should have made your play for her when you had a chance. It's not Ed's fault that you decided to drag your paws on the field of love. Love isn't an egg timer. You can't always wait the full three minutes before you decide to check out the water. Besides, you need to take Sally back. If she keeps hanging around The Godfather, she's going to come to a bad end. I hardly recognize her anymore. You need to save her from herself. She's her own worst enemy right now."

"She hates me," I point out. "That might make it a little hard to rekindle the spark in the mixing bowl. She's going to have to accept that once you've been mixed by the Mixer in the romance pantry your life is never going to be the same again."

"You're a dog," Truck says.

"Last night, you acted like you didn't want to talk about The Godfather, in front of the hotdog from Puerto Rico," I say changing the subject.

Truck looks around as if checking out the neighborhood for eavesdropping ears before replying with, "There's no reason for Ed to be involved in any of this, but the word on the street is that something big is going down, and it involves you Ruffians."

Okay, if Truck was trying to get my attention, it worked. "What is it that's exactly to be going down?" I ask.

Truck shakes his head back and forth as he replies, "I don't know all the details, but the word is something very big is going to happen soon. I don't know if it involves all you guys or maybe just one or two of The Ruffians."

"I'm going to have to let the other guys know about this," I say. "If any of us get hurt, you know how Empty is and Butch will be unstoppable."

"That's why I'm telling you now," Truck agrees. "You guys need to stay together all the time, and I'll have my contacts on the streets keep their eyes and ears open."

"I wonder if the Russian wolfhounds have anything to do with this?" I ask almost more to myself than Truck as I wonder out loud.

"That's what puzzles me," Truck responds. "I spotted one of the Russians following the Fang Mafia the other day."

Now I'm puzzled. "Why would the Russians be following the Fang Mafia?"

"I don't know," Truck admits. "As soon as I find out more I'll let you know."

"Thanks, Truck," I say.

"I'll be in touch," Truck responds as he starts to walk away. "See ya, Mixer, I wouldn't want to flea ya."

I know the other Ruffians are probably still asleep, unless Empty is up snagging mirror time. If Empty could find a way to marry himself, he would.

I decide to check on my buddy, and grab a power nap before I fill in the other guys on what all Truck had to tell me. In fact, with my buddy taking off from work, I probably won't be able to fill them in at all until our nightly meeting.

I walk in the living room and I'm surprised to find that my buddy isn't sitting in his recliner, but a full bowl of Lucky Charms cereal is sitting on the coffee table. My buddy is probably in the bathroom again. It's a shame he can't use a tree like I do.

I don't want my buddy to get sick from eating too much food for breakfast, so I quickly lap up the milk and all the contents in the bowl. Hey, I'm a magically delicious cereal killer.

I walk into the bedroom, and just as I leap on the bed for a nap I hear my buddy yell from the living room. He doesn't sound like he's in his happy place.

"Mixer!"

CHAPTER 31

I wake up from my power nap and lay in bed for a few minutes. I must have needed a nap more than I care to admit, because I swear once I crashed out, I slept like a dog. I hear the sounds from The Weather Channel floating in from the living room, so I know my buddy's still home. It looks like we're going to have a buddy party.

I stand up in the bed, yawn, give my hips a couple of shakes, and leap off the bed to walk into the living room. My buddy is still in his Spiderman pajamas, but instead of eating cereal, he's holding a book in front of his face.

I'm surprised to see my buddy reading a book. Maybe he's reading a self-help book on how to escape the strangling hold chocolate milk has on him. I read the title of the book. Nope, he's reading *Crewel Work* by Natalie Alder. The title doesn't sound like a self-help book.

I guess my buddy senses my presence, because he lowers the book away from his face and smiles. "Look, Mixer. I'm reading a cowboy romance book. By the time I'm through reading it, I'll know all about romance. That's going to really help me out when I get a girlfriend one day. My girlfriend will be amazed at all the romantic things I know."

My buddy thinks he's going to get a girlfriend one day. Jim was right. This book really is a work of fiction.

I cringe when I see my buddy fold over a page in the book as he closes it and places the book in his lap. He should use a bookmark. I hate to witness book abuse.

"Mixer, we're going to have so much fun today," my buddy continues. "To start with, we're going to remove all the labels off the canned vegetables in the kitchen. Then we're going to see if we can paste the labels back on the right can without knowing what's in the can. If we mess up and paste the incorrect label on the inaccurate can, think about how funny it's going to be when we cook."

I debate on whether to pack my collar and leashes and run away from home.

He claps his hands together and shrieks, "Imagine we think that we're opening a can of canned baby carrots, and a big wad of spinach dumps out instead. Wouldn't that be so funny? It's going to be so much fun that I should try to sell the concept to Hollywood as a game show. Can you imagine peas coming out of your can when you think you're holding stewed tomatoes? Oh, Mixer, we're going to have so much fun playing paste the can."

My buddy needs his can kicked.

"Then we're going to go get some ice cream in a cone," my buddy says.

My ears perk up. Ice cream is a good thing. Ice cream is a very good thing. Maybe my buddy doesn't need his can kicked just yet.

"And you know what we're going to do when we order our ice cream at the drive-through window?" my buddy asks.

I cock my head sideways.

He starts slapping his knees with the palms of his hands and screams, "We're going to say we want it in *waffle cones*, because we haven't had breakfast yet. That's going to be so funny. We should have done this a long time ago."

I drop my head and stare at the floor. I'm not sure that I'm going to survive the buddy party. My buddy may be going to a buddy party of one.

"And then we can go to the park and take a long walk. We'll walk and walk until we can't walk anymore. When that happens, we'll stop walking."

I look back up at my buddy. The park sounds like a good idea. It'll give me a chance to see if I can notice anything amiss, and to see if the squirrels are still eating all their own nuts. Besides, if I play my cards right and wear my buddy out, he'll go to bed early, and I won't have to worry about him interrupting The Ruffians meeting tonight.

"I bought some special clothes to wear to the park," he tells me. "I'm going to look so good in them. Do want to know what I bought?"

I shake my head no back and forth. He tells me anyway.

"I actually bought some skinny jeans," he brags. "When the babes see me wearing them, I'll be the chick magnet that Kentucky Fried Chicken used to fantasize about."

I slowly start backing away from my buddy. This conversation is taking a turn to the weird side. My buddy wearing skinny jeans while walking through the park eating soft-serve ice cream out of a waffle cone, and trying to look like a chick magnet. Great Lassie in Heaven, I wish the mothership would come back and take my buddy away to whatever planet he came from. My buddy's an alien. That has to be the only explanation.

"And you probably think that's all the fun we'll be able to have in one day, don't you?" my buddy gleefully yells.

I hope so. I know that dogs just want to have fun and all that, but this is getting ridiculous. My buddy has way too much time on his hands.

"Oh no, no, no," my buddy hollers. "Do you know the cardboard roll that comes inside a roll of toilet paper? I've been saving those, and when we get back home, I have a special game we can play. You're going to love it."

I lie down and cover my ears with my paws.

"Do you know what we're going to do?" he asks.

The paw trick isn't working. I can still hear him.

"I'll hide them all throughout the house, and we will race each other and see which one of us can find the most cardboard rolls. Every time we find one, we have to race to the bathroom and drop it in the wastebasket and yell 'Stinker'! The first one to yell 'Stinker' five times wins. It's going to be so much fun. Though I realize you will have to bark 'Stinker' instead of saying it."

I roll over on my back and stare at a water stain on the off-white painted ceiling. I have to think of a way to get out of this buddy day. Running away from home seems my only option.

"I might even sell the idea to Mattel toys," my buddy prattles on. "They can advertise it as the game that is so much stinking fun to play."

I roll over and stand up. It's time to break the news to my buddy that this buddy party isn't going to happen. He's grown. He'll get over it.

"Do you know why I'm looking so forward to our special buddy day?" he earnestly asks with wide eyes.

I stare at him.

"Mixer, it's because you're my best friend in the whole world. As long as I have you, I have everything I want or need."

I'm getting misty eyed. It must be allergies.

"Mixer, I love you," he says.

I sigh and walk into the bedroom to grab my dog collar and leash. There's nothing wrong with my buddy. At heart, he's a good buddy.

CHAPTER 32

"Did I positively see your buddy wearing skinny jeans this afternoon?" Butch asks at our nightly meeting in my buddy's backyard.

"Yup," I reply. "He wanted to wear them on a walk through the park and become a chick magnet. They turned out to be a chick repellant."

"I positively wish they would make skinny jeans for dogs," Butch drools. "I would be a chic canine fashion legend."

"Yeah, yeah," Empty cuts in. "Let's get to the important stuff. Did your buddy score with a babe at the park?"

"He ate a Baby Ruth candy bar," I say. "Does that count?"

"Those are good," Dandy says. "But I'm not sure they're as sweet as Rachael."

"Actually, it's a confectionery product," Jim joins in as he pushes his glasses up on his nose. "It was originated by the Curtiss Candy Company in Chicago. The company originally had a candy bar called Kandy Kake, which was made into the Baby Ruth candy bar."

Once again, the dropping out of obedience school is coming back to bite me. I don't know what a Chicago is.

"The sweetest thing I know is my reflection in the mirror," Empty brags.

"You're too modest," I tell Empty. "We need to do something to build up your confidence and self-esteem."

"Boys, boys, let's not quibble," Butch warns. "We all positively know that I'm the sweetest thing walking around on four paws."

"I'm sweet too, aren't I, Butch?" Dandy nervously asks.

"Darling," Butch gushes. "You and Jim are absolutely so sweet that I should nickname you two, Honey and Sugar. You two are my world and don't you ever forget that."

"That's sweet," I tell Empty.

"Ditto," he replies.

I clear my throat while looking at each member of our little gang and say, "I have something not so sweet to say. I talked to Truck this morning. The word on the street is that something big is going down, and it involves us."

You can hear a flea drop a pin during the ensuing silence.

Finally, Empty shuffles his paws and says, "Define what you mean that it involves us. What involves us and who is going to involve us?"

Jim again pushes his glasses back up on his nose, nervously looks around, and says, "This confrontation that is apparently going to garner our attention could be the work of the terrorists or the mob. We know we can't trust The Godfather."

"I hope it doesn't happen when Rachael is on," Dandy stutters. "She's making dishes using a Hibachi grill, and I don't want to miss any of the recipes."

"Darling," Butch drones. "Did our dear little friend, Truck, have any specifics to share or is all this general information?"

"It's all general information," I tell him. "Truck said that he was going to have his contacts on the street keep their eyes and ears open. He did mention that he spotted one of the wolfhounds spying on the Fang Mafia."

"Why would a terrorist organization be spying on the mob?" Empty asks.

"That's interesting," Jim muses out loud. "Two diverse organizations that possess no affection for us might be engaging in covert operations against each other."

Empty looks at me and says, "Translate."

"We don't know what dog the flea is biting," I reply.

"Gotcha."

"I wonder if it would do any good to have another chat with The Godfather." Butch asks to no one in particular.

"Bad move," Empty warns. "If it is the mafia after us, we don't want to tip our hand. If it's the terrorists after us, we don't want to share any information with The Godfather that he could use against us."

"You're right, my dear friend," Butch agrees. "However, I must admit that I'm hoping it's the Fang Mafia and not the Russians, who have decided to threaten our little family."

"Why would you want that?" I ask in surprise.

"Because I have positively never sniffed butts or made yummy with a foreigner," Butch admits. "I think the experience would be absolutely delightful."

Empty starts making loud gagging sounds.

Butch looks over and Empty and says, "You and your partner in crime must simply grow up one day."

"We are grown," Empty replies. "We're just conservatives."

"I'm not a conservative," I deny. "I'm an independent."

"Whatever," Butch snorts.

"I think we should put off the political debate until a more proper moment," Jim advises. "We need to start making some contingency plans."

"As least you know that you're safe," Dandy tells Jim.

Once again, Jim pushes his glass back up and asks, "Dandy, what makes you think that I'm safe? I'm as much a Ruffian as anybody here."

"Because everybody knows you can't hit a dog wearing glasses," Dandy points out.

"I say we go over to Little Italy and take out the Fang Mafia," Empty blurts out. "If it turns out that we're wrong, then we know to go after the terrorists."

"Calm your penchant for violent activities," Butch warns. "We need to keep a cool head and not go off with our Milk Bones in an uproar. This isn't the first time others have been less than pleased with us. Remember when that gang of toy French poodles tried to take us down a couple of years ago. That was quite the surprise attack."

"Yeah, they were fast little suckers," I say.

"Not fast enough," Empty pipes in.

"I think we should skip patrol tonight," Butch cautions us, "and let's all do some serious thinking about this unpleasant situation."

"You might be right," Empty agrees. "If we aren't careful, walking around in the dark could get us ambushed. We need to find out who's behind this."

"When the time comes to fight are you going to be ready?" Empty asks Butch.

Butch rubs his toenails on his chest while replying, "You can absolutely count on it darling. I'm afraid my talent for breaking things will positively come into play."

"Let's do it," Dandy says.

We do a group high five and yell, "We are The Ruffians."

CHAPTER 33

I walk into the backyard to meet Empty. Empty and I decided the night before that we would go to the park this morning and see if we could pick up any useful information. Butch thought it was a great idea, but he was going to stay behind with Jim and Dandy in case there was any trouble in the neighborhood.

I look over at the spot beneath the crabapple tree and see the spot isn't empty. The spot is filled with a body, a girlish body, a Sally the cat womanly body. I wonder why Sally is sitting in my buddy's backyard and then inspiration strikes me between the eyes. I know why Sally is here.

Evidently, Sally has never gotten over me. Her journey in the Mixer's mixing bowl of love was unforgettable. Even being with The Godfather can't replace the treasure she felt while with me. I'm priceless, but she's still trying to find a way to buy my affection. It's probably the only thing in the world she truly wants.

I feel sorry for her. She's chasing a dream that can't come true. I'm the pot of gold at the end of the rainbow which must be shared with all. I'm desirable. I'm wonderful. Everybody wants to ride on the Mixer's love train. I am dog. Hear me bark.

As I'm walking toward the crabapple tree, I noticed the bags underneath Sally's eyes. Wow, she must have really got deep into the catnip last night. Being with The Godfather must not be all that it's cracked up to be. I remind myself to let her down easy. She's now a fragile creature with a shattered heart, but she's still yearning for the dream of being with me. I can see the desire and longing in her feline eyes as I approach. I need to think of the nicest line I can conjure up. It has to be delicate and caring. It has to be dripping with compassion.

I stop walking, look at her, and say, "You look horrible."

She coughs up a hairball and spits it at me.

I duck.

"You still don't know how to talk to a lady," she says.

This is great. My buddy thinks he's going to get a girlfriend and Sally thinks she's a lady. I feel like my life is getting very complicated.

"You're not a lady." I point out. "You're a cat."

"Whatever," she hisses.

I'll give her credit for one thing. She does a great Butch impression.

"Does the mafia Godfather know that you're over here with The Godfather of Romance?" I ask. I mentally give myself two shakes of a happy tail for that line.

"The Godfather doesn't own me," she growls. "I come and go as I please and where I please. Nobody tells me what to do."

"Would you please tell me what you're doing here," I say.

Sally arches her back and purrs, "What's the matter? Do two old friends have to have an excuse to get together and enjoy a conversation?"

I point out the obvious. "We're not friends."

"What makes you say that?" she purrs again.

"Because you hate me, or have you forgotten that?"

Fire flashes in her eyes as she hisses, "That's because you dumped me, you jerk."

"We've already been through all that," I reply. "The other animals were never going to accept our relationship, and it would have been unfair to the kids."

"There wouldn't have been any kids," she growls in a high screech. "I was on the pill."

"Well, now you're with The Godfather," I point out, "so it's useless to cry over spilled Milk Bones. It's time you moved on."

"Do you really think I'm still clinging to you and hope we get back together?" she asks. "Bud, I moved on a long time ago. The Godfather treats me like a lady."

"You don't understand," I say. "You need to move on because you're standing under the tree, and I really need to use it."

"That's it," she spits out. "You always thought of yourself before you thought of me."

I'm rocking back forth on all four paws. I really need to use the tree.

"At least The Godfather cares about my feelings," she purrs. "He's a real man."

I leave that line alone. I need to think of a way to move this conversation along. My eyes are beginning to water. I really need to get to that tree.

"You still haven't told me why you're here," I say.

"Okay, I'll tell you why I'm here," she hisses. "I don't know what's going on, but the rumor is something big and bad is about to happen to The Ruffians. If it's only going to happen to one of you, I hope it's you."

"What does The Godfather have to say about all this?" I ask. "Or is The Godfather the one behind all the rumors?" I'm hoping that she'll slip up and unintentionally provide some useful information. I'm also hoping that she'll move. I really need to use the tree.

"The Godfather doesn't tell me his business, and I don't ask," she retorts. "And you better be careful about spreading rumors. The Godfather will send the Fang Mafia after you."

"Truck has already told me about the rumor of somebody coming after us," I answer. "So, if you dropped by to see me tremble in fear, all you did was waste some time."

"Then why are you trembling," she sneers.

She's right. All four of my legs are trembling. If I don't get to that tree soon, I'm going to have an accident.

"I wanted to personally tell you. If you are the one somebody is after, how happy that will make me feel. Nobody dumps me and just walks away."

This is beginning to be weird. I'm standing in my buddy's backyard and arguing with another dog's cat. I don't think that happens a lot to other dogs.

I blow her a kiss.

She coughs and spits another hairball at me.

I need to think of a way to get her to leave, and then it comes to me.

"What do you call a dog driving a car?" I ask.

She scrunches up her face in confusion and says, "I don't know."

I scream, "Dogmatic!"

She arches her back as she stands, "I'm leaving on that one. I always hated your cheesy jokes. I don't know why you bother to keep telling them."

"I have a million more," I tell her.

"Keep them," she hisses as she swipes the air with her claws in my direction.

I watch her walk away. She still knows how to put the kitty sway in her hips.

I turn back to the tree and for the first time this morning, I feel relieved.

CHAPTER 34

"I can't believe you invited Sally to your buddy's backyard," Empty says while we're strolling toward the park.

"I didn't invite her," I protest. "When I walked out into the backyard she was already there. If you had shown up a few minutes earlier, you could have run her off."

"No, doggy wee," Empty replies while shaking his head back and forth. "That's your girl. I don't get involved in other couple's fights."

"We're not a couple," I protest again. "She wanted to let me know that if anything happens to The Ruffians she hopes I'm the one that gets it."

"Well, I kind of agree with her," Empty says while cutting his eyes at me.

"I can't believe you hope I'm the one that gets it," I say. "I thought we were pals."

"We are," Empty exclaims, "and I hope none of us get it. However, better you than me. I have a brand new mirror that I haven't broken in yet."

"You're such a dog," I reply.

"Woof weef and brush your teeth," he replies without bothering to look at me again.

"We might be in trouble," I tell Empty.

"I know we're in trouble," he shoots back. "Either the terrorists or the Fang Mafia has it in for us, and we don't know which side. It could be both sides for all we know."

"That's peanuts compared to the trouble we're in now."

"What are you babbling about, fur breath?" he asks with a quizzical look on his face as he takes a glance my way.

"Look straight ahead, but don't make eye contact," I tell him.

Empty sees what I'm talking about. K.D. Mitchell, wearing a Hello Kitty housecoat, is standing in her front yard holding her green water hose. Once again, it's not hooked up to the outside faucet. She's just standing there holding it in her hands and staring at us.

"Is it after eleven o'clock?" Empty whispers without turning his head.

"I don't know," I whisper back.

"What do you think we should do?" Empty whispers in an even lower tone of voice this time. "Do you think we should turn around?"

"Too late," I state. "She's already spotted us. Just keep walking straight ahead and don't make eye contact. We don't want to be in a doggy pot pie tonight."

Empty and I use baby steps to advance down the sidewalk until we are even with K.D. Mitchell. We cut our eyes toward her and she's glaring at us.

"This is beginning to freak me out," Empty admits.

"Me too," I whisper. "Just keep walking. We're almost past her house."

We're both holding our breaths as we keep advancing down the sidewalk. We're finally far enough past her house, and we both sneak a look behind us. K.D. Mitchell is still glaring at us. She hasn't moved her body, but her head is twisted all the way around as she stares at us.

"Whoa," Empty declares. "I never want to see anything like that again. Can we please pick up the pace? I'm not going to feel safe until we're off this street."

"I think that we're safe now," I tell Empty. "But I agree. Let's not waste any more time getting to the park."

We enter the south end of the park by the clusters of baseball fields and are surprised to see a group of young human children playing softball on one of the smaller fields.

"That's odd," Empty says, "I wonder why those children aren't in school?"

"I'm with you on that one," I agree. "Education is very important. If those kids don't develop learning skills at a young age, they might never ever get a proper education."

"Look at those gym shorts they're wearing," Empty says. "I bet their students at the elementary school a couple of blocks away, and this is their physical education time."

I know what I'm talking about when I say it's important to develop learning skills at a young age. I dropped out of obedience school, and once again it has come back to bite me in the tail. I don't know what a gym is.

A couple of the young human children spot us, drop their little ball gloves to the ground, and start running toward us while screeching with joy.

"Great Lassie in Heaven," Empty grumbles. "Hasn't anyone ever taught those kids not to run up to strange dogs?"

"We don't bite kids," I respond.

Empty shoots me a look of frustration and says, "I know that, you know that, but those kids don't know that."

"Good point," I say. "We could take off running. Those kids would never catch us."

"Good and bad," Empty disagrees. "We take off running and those kids might think it's fun to chase dogs, and that's a great way to get bit or hurt."

"What if we walk slowly away?" I suggest. "The kids will know that they're not chasing us, and hopefully their teachers will teach them dog etiquette."

"Good thinking," Empty says. "You ready to go?"

"Wait," I slowly say. "Look what's chasing after those kids as best he can."

Empty sees what I'm talking about. A young human on crutches is trying his best to keep up with his little friends.

I see a human adult in blue shorts and a white T-shirt chasing after the kids and yelling for them to stop. The little humans aren't listening to him.

"He's never going to catch them in time," Empty observes. "Let's wait here until he gets the little humans gathered up."

Two boys and one girl run up to Empty and me and throw their arms around our necks as they start petting us.

"Wag your tail," I whisper to Empty out the side of my mouth, "and look friendly."

"Sorry," he whispers back. "I forgot the proper park etiquette."

The kids are petting Empty and me and giggling. Empty loves the attention. Of course with his ego, the show of attention is right up his alley.

"I wonder what their names are?" the little girl asks her friends.

Before they can respond, the grown human in the blue shorts runs up while yelling, "Kids, get away from those dogs. You never run up to a strange dog."

"We wanted to pet them, Mr. Parkinson" the little girl protests.

"I know," Mr. Parkinson replied. "But no matter how handsome a strange dog may look, you never run up and start petting one. They may bite or they might be sick. You never know."

"I'm the handsome one he's talking about," I whisper to Empty out of the corner of my mouth.

"Fat chance," Empty replies.

"Children," Mr. Parkinson continues in a placating tone. "If you want to pet a dog, always ask the dog's owner first if it is permissible."

"Great Lassie in Heaven," Empty whispers. "This guy is delusional."

"I can't believe he thinks humans own dogs," I respond in a hushed tone.

"What do you think we should do about it?" Empty asks.

"I think we should bite him."

"Good idea," Empty agrees.

"C'mon, children," Mr. Parkinson says with a trace of impatience in his voice. "We have to gather up our equipment and get back to the school so you won't be late for your next class."

The three kids give us one last hug around the neck as they back away to join the blue shorts seriously needs a mental examination human. Just as the three kids rejoin their teacher, the young human on crutches finally walks up.

"No, David," Mr. Parkinson says. "You have to turn around. It's time we returned to the school."

"I want to pet the dogs," the young human named David stutters.

"That child is special," Empty says.

"All children are special,"

"You know what I'm talking about, fur breath."

I nod my head up and down.

"Please, just one pet," David stutters again.

"No, David," Parkinson says in a more forceful tone. "Turn around and head back toward the ball field."

"I'm going to bite that guy," Empty says.

"I won't stop you," I respond.

Empty and I both see the tears on David's face streaming down his cheeks as he uses his crutches to slowly turn his little body around and start making his way toward the ball field.

Empty looks over and me and says, "C'mon."

We both walk on either side of David and stay right beside him as the three of us walk back to the ball field together.

Empty and I look up at little David's face. He's smiling all the way back to the ball field.

CHAPTER 35

Empty and I watch the little humans gather up their softball equipment and trudge toward the direction of their school. A light-blue van is parked in the parking lot behind the aluminum bleachers directly behind the home plate. Parkinson helps David into the van, and I notice how gentle he is with the child.

"Maybe Parkinson is having a bad day," I tell Empty. "He was gentle with David when he was helping him into the van."

"That's possible," Empty agrees, "but I still should have bitten him."

"You need to work on your people skills," I tell him. "You're not a very good people person."

"I'm not any kind of people person," he counters. "I'm a dog."

"Moot point," I reply.

Empty arches his eyebrows as he asks, "Where did you learn the word moot?"

"I'm a dog of many talents," I proudly state. "I've got a vocabulary where most dogs just have arfs, barks, and bow-wows."

"Whatever, fur breath," Empty responds. "Let's walk on over to the pavilion and see if anything is happening there. If nothing else, it will give us a good field of vision to observe the park. There has to be a reason the squirrels are acting so squirrelly."

This is a perfect time to spout out one of my legendary one-liners, so I look at Empty and say, "Okay."

We're walking across the east soccer field when a squirrel runs in front of us across the halfway line. The squirrel's cheeks are bulging out because of the two large pecans in its mouth. The squirrel spots Empty and me and spits his nutty treasures out on the Bermuda grass, and sprints for the safety of a nearby pine tree.

"That's weird," Empty observes. "Why would a squirrel go to all the trouble of stuffing his mouth with nuts, just to spit them out in the center of a soccer field?"

"Butch says some male humans do the same thing in the park when the sun goes down," I reply. "Maybe the manly humans are squirrelly as well."

Empty starts making a gagging sound.

We keep strolling toward the pavilion, and nothing catches our attention until we spot a group of squirrels chattering and chasing each other underneath the sanctuary of a group of oak trees. That strikes us as odd since squirrels are solitary creatures and don't usually play well with others. Then we spot the reason. The squirrels are gathering up all the acorns they can find. The squirrels spot Empty and me and spit out all the acorns in their mouths and scurry up the oak trees. The limbs and leaves of the oak trees finally quit shaking as the squirrels settle down in hiding from Empty and myself.

"This isn't making any sense," Empty says. "Every time a squirrel spots us, it spits out its nuts. Why would they do that?"

"I'm that irresistible," I brag.

I'm waiting for Empty to come back with a sarcastic retort, and I'm surprised when all I get is silence out of him. I glance his way, and I see why he didn't respond. He's staring at Ed from Puerto Rico, Truck, and Goldie the golden retriever walking in front of the concession building.

"I can't believe a hotdog is walking your girl," Empty snorts.

"Now I should be the one that kicks his buns," I say.

Goldie stops long enough to eat the leftover popcorn from a discarded popcorn bag lying on the ground. Ed and Truck patiently wait while she consumes her popped delight.

"You couldn't afford her anyway," Empty says. "She likes takeout."

"I wonder why Truck is spending so much time with Ed?" I ask. "Truck's never been the kind of dog to socialize in the park."

"Let's go ask the happy little cowpokes," Empty responds.

"Make sure Goldie doesn't make a spectacle of herself," I tell Empty. "If she gets too close to me, she will probably lose all self-control. I'm irresistible. Most females simply refer to me as the light switch."

Empty narrows his eyes as he asks, "Why would they call you the light switch?"

"Because they can't wait to turn me on and never want to turn me off," I brag.

"You have some serious delusional problems," Empty replies.

I shoot back with, "I don't spend all my free time staring in the mirror."

"With your body, I don't blame you," Empty counters.

Okay, score one for Empty. I'll let him think he's won this battle of wits.

Empty surprises me by saying, "Let's not go talk to them. Let's follow them from a distance. Something doesn't seem to be right with this picture."

Goldie finally finishes wolfing down the popcorn like a dog, and she, Ed, and Truck walk around the corner of the painted blue cylinder block concession building.

"It didn't take her long to finish off the popcorn," I say as much to myself as to Empty. "I thought she would have been a daintier eater."

"You never can tell about females," Empty wisely says. "Just when you think that you have them figured out, they change the rules."

"For two dogs that are supposed to be a couple, Ed and Goldie weren't walking very close together," I say while showing off my supernatural power of observation.

"You have a point," Empty agrees. "She doesn't have a whole lot of wiggle in her hips."

"Maybe she's two-timing Ed with Truck," I declare.

"But that would mean she's three timing you," Empty counters.

"She hasn't one timed me yet," I point out. "I'm the fur-none in this scenario."

Empty's ears lean forward as he asks, "What's a fur-none?"

"A dog that's not getting any loving."

"Agreed," Empty agrees.

Empty and me walk around the side of the concession building and are surprised to see the mysterious trio are nowhere in sight. It's like the park swallowed them whole.

"They must really be in a hurry to get to wherever they're going," Empty says. "We weren't that far behind them."

"Unless they spotted us and decided to hide until we leave," I concede.

"This keeps getting weirder and weirder," Empty answers. "We might as well go home and have a Ruffians meeting to discuss this."

"I'm anxious to see what Butch thinks about all this," I admit.

About that time, a gray fox squirrel runs around the corner of the concession building and skids to a stop when he spots Empty and me. The squirrel spits out a mouthful of nuts at mine and Empty paws and takes off running in the opposite direction.

I look at Empty and say, "This place is nuts."

CHAPTER 36

We're all sitting under the crabapple tree in my buddy's backyard, and discussing the strange things going on at the park.

"Let me get this straight," Jim says as he pushes his glasses back up on his nose. "Every time the squirrels would spot you and Empty they would spit their nuts out of their mouths."

When Butch hears this, his legs buckle and his eyes take on a dreamy gaze. Dandy quickly reaches out to steady him, so he doesn't fall over.

"Rachael does wonderful things with nuts when she's making holiday desserts," Dandy says. "I love seeing all the different things she can do with nuts."

"There's a difference," Empty points out. "She's cooking. At the park, the squirrels would stuff their mouths with nuts, and then spit them right back out."

That's more than Butch can handle as his eyes completely glaze over, and he collapses to the ground with a soft thud on the grass.

"Sorry, Butch," Dandy apologizes. "I was trying to keep you steady on your feet."

Butch doesn't even hear Dandy as he dreamily mutters, "I remember the first time I put nuts in my mouth and finally spit them back out."

Empty starts shoving his paw in and out of his mouth while making some serious gagging sounds.

I look over at Jim and Jim shrugs his shoulders as he says, "He'll snap out of it in a moment. These trips down memory lane never last long."

"I can't figure out what the squirrels in the park are doing," I tell him.

"That is a mystery," he muses. "The squirrels should be storing nuts for their winter supply as well as consuming them in their daily diet to maintain the nutritional need their bodies would still require to operate daily."

I hate it when Jim impresses the world with his enormous vocabulary. I'm definitely going back to obedience school and get my diploma. I don't know what a daily is.

"Rachael says that you can cook a meal full of nutrition in under thirty minutes," Dandy pipes in. "I think that's pretty impressive."

"That's very impressive," Jim agrees while nodding his head up and down. "A delicious meal doesn't have to be a time-consuming event. The time-consuming should be saved for the devouring and enjoying the prepared culinary delights."

I look over at Empty who says, "You got me. I don't have a clue what he said either."

"You two should positively expand your horizons," Butch states as he slowly climbs back to his feet. "If only you two would embrace it, there's so much more to see in this world than you realize. Vast cultural experiences are waiting to be embraced."

"I'm not embracing anything," I flatly say.

"Glad you're finally back from dreamland," Empty snaps at Butch.

Butch stretches his body and sighs as he glances at me and Empty. "I simply don't know what I'm going to do with the two of you."

"Butch, are you okay?" Dandy asks with a worried look in his eyes.

"I'm fine, darling," Butch coos while patting Dandy on top of the head. "I simply got lost in the moment and memories past."

"Do you have any thoughts on the squirrels?" Jim asks Butch.

Butch shakes his head back and forth while replying, "I'm positively at a loss just as the rest of you as to why the squirrels are behaving so badly."

"I wonder if the Russians could be behind this?" I ask as I look around at the other Ruffians. They look at me like they're trying to decide if I might be on to something.

"Let's not forget The Godfather," Empty warns. "He might be behind it, or it could be the Russians, or they could be working together."

"Or it could be the squirrels are just nuts," Jim says.

'True that,' Dandy happily yaps.

"We can't spend all our time concentrating on the squirrels," Empty warns while scratching behind his left ear with his left rear paw. "We have other things to worry about as well."

"Are you talking about the big thing going down on the street concerning us?" Jim asks while peering over the top of his glasses.

"Actually, I was talking about the fleas still being terrible at this time of year," Empty grumbles, "but, yeah, we can't forget that somebody has a bad dog biscuit in for us."

"I can't imagine anyone wanting to hurt me as adorable and loveable as

I am," I brag. "I'm sure that one day I'll win the nomination for dog of the year."

Dandy rolls his eyes as he replies, "Mixer, after what you did to Carjack, I think you have every reason to be as wary as the rest of us. I can't imagine him taking his dangles being bitten lying down. He's going to try to get even at some point."

"But lying down is the best time to have your danglers bitten," Butch croons. "And, Mixer, I positively can't believe you didn't enjoy the musky lingering taste enhancing your palate. I thought for sure that you would think it tastes like rotisserie chicken."

Empty starts another round of gagging sounds.

"Actually, that's not exactly what I was talking about, Butch," Dandy says.

"I can't believe you said that," Jim fusses. "You're getting as bad as Butch in abusing adverbs. Proper grammar is important, and I wish you two would remember that."

"Oh, pooh," Butch snorts. "I've abused things a lot worse than adverbs."

"All this talking isn't accomplishing anything," Empty scolds turning his concentration to the back of his right ear. "We need to hit the streets and take some action instead of waiting for trouble to come to us."

"But, darling," Butch replies, "we've yet to determine to which unsavory characters we need to be leery of. We can't throw the pup out with the bath water."

"Actually, Empty has a valid point," Jim says while staring daggers at Dandy as if blaming him for his own adverb abuse. "Sometimes a good offensive is the best defense."

"Haste makes waste," Butch counters.

"My buddy makes hasty pudding," I quip.

Empty takes a swipe at my head with his right paw and mutters, "You need to get serious, fur breath. This isn't the time or place to talk about your buddy's cooking."

"Can I have some the next time he makes it?" Dandy requests in a serious voice.

"You bet your flea collar and rabies vaccinations you can have some," I tell him. "I'll save a special bowl of it just for you."

"Thanks, Mixer," Dandy happily yaps while doing a little dance.

"Well, darlings," Butch declares. "We all need to go check on our buddies. We won't patrol tonight. Instead, we'll have a down night to rest and relax."

We gather around for a group high five and yell, "We are The Ruffians."

CHAPTER 37

I climb the back steps and use the doggy door to enter the house through the kitchen. I peer into the living room and don't see my buddy sitting in his recliner and watching The Weather Channel. Okay, that's not the first time that it's happened, but still it definitely isn't the norm.

I check out my food and water bowls. The water bowl is filled with clean, fresh water. The food bowl holds a surprise. Lying on top of my chicken flavored soybean nuggets are five fish sticks laid out in a neat row. My buddy must have recently taken the fish sticks out of the oven because they're still warm. I lean my nose forward to sniff the rectangular little logs of fish. I quickly pull my head back in surprise. I recognize the scent of the fish sticks. I can't believe that my buddy has left five Mrs. Paul's fish sticks in my bowl for a treat. If he's willing to break out the good stuff, something really big must be happening.

I decide to leave the fish sticks for a midnight snack and stroll into the living room. The television is set to The Weather Channel, even if the sound is turned down low. I check out the weather girl talking about the low front moving across The Great Plains. She's great. Her cumulous clouds are really rising inside that tight, low-cut, dark-blue silk blouse that she was poured into. Wow.

I know that it's not polite to stare, so I take one last glance at her and start ambling toward the bedroom. A nap is beginning to sound like a pretty good plan about now.

I stop in the hallway and stare at the bedroom. The door is closed. The door to the bedroom is never closed. I wonder what's going on. I'm beginning to feel uneasy about this unexpected development. No buddy in the living room and I can't get into the bedroom. I walk to the door and use my front right paw to scratch the faded white paint on the door frame.

"Mixer, is that you?" my buddy yells from inside the bedroom.

I want to ask him how many other dogs would be scratching on the bedroom's door, but I don't feel like stating the obvious. So I don't say anything.

Then my super-charged brain kicks in, and the wheels start spinning like a Chevrolet pickup truck on an iced slick road outside Butte, Montana, in January. Why does my buddy have the door to the bedroom closed? What is he doing in there that he doesn't want me to see? When did my buddy start thinking that was his bedroom? I'm stuck with all those questions and no answers. If I had known humans were so difficult to raise, I would have thought long and hard about getting one. I'm not playing anymore. I want answers. I scratch on the door frame again, but this time I scratch harder. That should get his attention.

"Give me a few more seconds," my buddy yells. "Mixer, I have a big surprise for you."

Okay, this is good. I like surprises. I wonder what it could be. It's not my birthday, and it's too early for Christmas. Maybe my buddy has me a female Irish setter in the bedroom. I start getting excited. I've always been a sucker for redheads.

I see the doorknob steadily turn and the door creaks on its hinges, and it's leisurely pulled open a few inches. I hear the patter of running feet and the creaking of the bed's box springs as a body makes the soft sound of someone jumping on the bed. I'm getting excited. My buddy must have the bed ready, and the covers pulled back. I swell my chest out. I wonder what the Irish setter's name is. I think that I will call her Ilene. That sounds like a fitting name for a gorgeous redhead.

"Mixer, come on in," my buddy hollers.

I use my nose to push open the bedroom's door and stroll inside to find my Irish soul mate of unbridled love. I look around the room. There's no Irish setter in the room. I look at the bed. There's no Irish setter in the bed. There's a buddy in the bed. My buddy is standing in the middle of the bed wearing nothing but a sizeable pair of non-woven fabric diapers. Rather my buddy has taken several pairs of diapers and used Scotch tape to tape them together to form one huge diaper. My buddy is also holding a fourteen-inch cast-iron skillet above his head in his right hand. I sit down, hard.

"How do you like it?" my buddy yells as his cheeks are flushed red with excitement and his eyes twinkle with happiness. "I finally figured out a way to become rich and famous. I'm going to become a professional wrestler. This is going to be my wrestling outfit. I'm going to be billed as The Pampered Chef."

I close my eyes and groan.

Unable to keep the glee out of his voice, my buddy yells again, "Do you get it? My wrestling trunks are made of Pampers diapers and some cooks use a cast-iron skillet, so that's how I came up with my ring name of The Pampered Chef. We're going to be famous. I imagine that I'll be wrestling on Pay Per View events all the time. I wonder how much that pays?"

I groan again. Of all the buddies in the world, I had to get the one whose light switch might not exactly be wired up to the electricity. I don't have a good feeling where this is going. My buddy is the column writing, rapping, author, and wrestler. I need to check the refrigerator. I have a feeling my buddy has gotten deeper into the chocolate milk than normal.

"Look at this," my buddy hollers.

I open my eyes and look.

My buddy is holding a pillow against his side in a headlock. "I'm going to call this move the puree," he chortles.

I shake my head back and forth.

"And look at this move," he screams as he moves the pillow in front of his body and leaps into the air and down on the bed with the pillow flattened underneath his stomach.

I groan louder.

"That's going to be my finishing move," he feverishly yells. "I'm going to call it the griddle, because when I put that move on an opponent they'll be well done."

My buddy needs help. My buddy needs help more than I'm able to give him. My buddy needs help more than anybody can give him.

"Check out this move," he pants, as he leaps to his feet and reaches down to snatch the pillow off the mattress. "This is how I'm going to throw my opponent over the top rope."

My buddy's feet slip out from under him, and he lands on his back on the mattress with the pillow landing on top of him. Great, my buddy is getting beat up by sixty-five percent polyester and thirty-five percent cotton twin pillow.

My buddy pushes the pillow off to one side and leaps to his feet again while grabbing the fourteen-inch cast-iron skillet with his right hand. I'm sensing something bad is about to happen.

"This is how I'll celebrate all my victories in the ring," he cries as he starts to swing the cast-iron skillet in circles above his head.

Great Lassie in Heaven, I notice something I don't want to see. Every time my buddy swings the skillet in a circle above his head, a piece of Scotch tape pops off his diaper. Slowly but surely his large diaper starts popping off his body one piece at a time.

I look up in time to see the skillet slip out of my buddy's hand and crash against his forehead with a resounding clank. My buddy's eyes roll toward the back of his head as he silently falls backward and off the other side of the bed and onto the floor.

I walk around the bed and see my buddy lying on the floor in his tattered diaper with the skillet lying by his side. I think about waking him, but change my mind. He's probably going to be knocked out all night, and that will mean I get the whole bed to myself.

I leap up on the bed, walk around in a circle a couple of times, and curl up for a nap. Naps are good.

I hear my buddy's ragged snoring on the floor beside the bed.

Mixer-one. The Pampered Chef-zero.

CHAPTER 38

I wake up the following morning to the dulcet sounds of The Weather Channel playing on the television set. I look over the other side of the bed and grimace when I see my buddy still lying on the floor with a large, black and blue goose bump in the center of his forehead. If my buddy ever wakes up within the ensuing year, he's going to be in for a long day.

I leisurely pad into the kitchen and check my food and water bowls out of habit. I spy the five fish sticks left over from last night. Leftover fish sticks are awesome, so I wolf them down before I remember to say grace for my food. I admit it. Sometimes I have all the table manners of a dog. It's something I'm trying to correct, it just hasn't happened yet.

I top off my fishy breakfast with a long drink of water. My buddy is going to complain about all the water sloshed out all over the floor and having to mop. Come to think of it, my buddy probably won't even know who he is when he wakes up.

I glance around the kitchen to see if there is anything to capture my interest. There isn't anything that I can see, so I head toward the doggy door to go check out the backyard. I'm almost to the exit when I spin and walk back toward my food bowl. I look at the bowl filled to the brim with chicken flavored soybean nuggets instead of Dyson dog food or barbeque. I flip over the bowl and watch the nuggets scatter all over the linoleum floor. If my buddy is going to have to mop, he might as well sweep also.

Satisfied with my morning work, I use the doggy door to go to the backyard and greet the day. The backyard is vacant, and I don't see activity in any other backyards. Butch and the boys are probably still asleep, and if Empty is awake, I'm sure he's deep into his mirror time.

I don't even see Sally Baggy Eyes strolling down the street. Maybe she's finally given up catting around all night and getting deep into the catnip. The Godfather might have put a stop to that. If I had known that she was going to turn to a life of crime after I broke up with her, I would have probably still broken up with her. I can't blame her for taking the breakup as hard as she did. If I broke up with me, I would miss me too.

Whoa. I see some activity on the street that I hadn't noticed before. Goldie the golden retriever is walking down the street. She doesn't seem to be in any hurry to reach any particular destination as she's stopping to smell all the bushes and flowers in the human's front yards. I wonder why Ed isn't with her. *Ed!* He's not with her. This is my chance to make my move and dazzle her with my wit and charm.

I race around the crabapple tree toward the gate leading to the side yard. The gate is open. My buddy must have forgotten to close it the last time he took the waste container to the curb for the trash collectors to empty. Way to go, buddy. I owe you one.

I streak out the gate like a dog streaking out of a gate, and pretend that I'm a Mixer 747 as I fly down the sidewalk. If I hurry, I ought to be able to intercept her at the stop sign on the corner. I see K.D. Mitchell is already standing in her front yard and holding her green water hose. It's not after eleven o'clock yet, so I know I'm safe. She hasn't turned mean yet.

I streak to the stop sign and see that I've made it in time. Goldie is still three houses down the street and daintily nibbling the leftover contents of a pizza box lying beside an overturned large, green garbage can. That girl does love her takeout food. I guess she's one of those who figure it's cheaper to eat out than eat at home for one.

I stand there beside the stop sign gasping and trying to catch my breath while staring at Goldie. I can't believe how beautiful she is. Her coat is shining in the light of the early morning sun, and she chews her food like a real lady.

I need to think of a line that's going to sweep her off her paws. After experiencing the elixir of Mixer, Goldie will never give Ed from Puerto Rico a second look. I admire her grace as she slowly makes her way up the sidewalk while using her tongue to wipe away traces of tomato sauce from her lips.

A look of puzzlement crosses her face as she sees me standing beside the stop sign. I know what's causing it. I feel sorry for the kid. She's probably shaking in her paws at the thought of being so close to me. The intimidation factor must be overbearing. She knows she's about to get mixed up in Mixer's world, and it's probably all she ever wanted since the first time she laid her gorgeous brown eyes on me. She winds up with Ed because she figured I was out of her league and untouchable. She's going to be putty in my paws. I have my line ready.

She stops a few feet away from me while smiling and says, "Why, hello."

"You have nice ears," I say. That ought to do the trick.

Her smiles widens as she replies, "Thank you. I've seen you around the neighborhood, but I've never caught your name."

"I'm Mixer," I say with more than a little pride. "I've guessed you've heard of me."

"No," she replies while shaking her head back and forth, "I'm sorry, but I'm afraid I haven't. Is there any reason I should have heard of you?"

So she wants to play hard to get. I've heard that a lot of blondes are like that. Two can play that game. I'll play hard to get myself. That'll teach her.

"I'm part of a group called The Ruffians."

Goldie's eyes widen in amazement as she gasps, "I have heard of The Ruffians. You guys are like something of a legend. It's an honor to meet you."

That's it. She's all mine. She just doesn't realize it.

"I saw you, Truck, and Ed walking in the park yesterday," I say. "I was there with my pal Empty. We were killing some time there."

"Oh, okay," she smiles as her eyes sparkles like, well, two sparklers. "Truck has been showing Ed and me the sights. He's really a sweet dog."

"Ed seems like a good dog too," I say. I keep the part about him looking like a hotdog to myself. I'm not sure how serious Goldie is about him.

"Why, thank you," she laughs. "He's a good dog and a lot of fun to be around. Things clicked after we met, and now we're going steady."

There it is. The ultimate challenge laid out in front of me. I'm going to have to use some tact here. It's time to make my move with a line she can't resist.

"Now that you met me," I say, "I guess you're ready to drop that walking hotdog and become my girl. I won't mind if you and Ed stay friends."

Her beautiful eyes narrow as she stares at me, and then she laughingly says, "I thought you were serious about calling Ed a hotdog, but I think you were only joking. Yes, he does favor a hotdog in a way, but we are very happy together, and I could never leave him for another dog."

I'm glad Empty's not here to see my rejection. I would never hear the end of it.

"Mixer, it was so nice to meet you, but I need to be on my way," she says.

"Okay, I'll see you around the neighborhood."

I watch her as she walks away with swinging hips.

Wow. Bow wow!

CHAPTER 39

I watch Goldie walk away, and she's putting way more swing in her hips than is necessary. I know why. Being so close to me must have been torture for her. I'm the all-beef Mixer burger that she pretends she doesn't want, because she has to go home to a hotdog.

I decide that maybe it's time to head back home and check on my buddy. It was nice having the bed all by myself last night, but I don't want him to sleep all day. After all, my water bowl will need a refill, and I can't reach the faucet.

I watch the mailman's white Jeep slowly creep up the street toward me, and the mailman glares at me as he passes by. Okay, two can play that game. The next time I will bite him, although I have a feeling, his chubby, hairy pale calves aren't going to taste like chicken either. As crazy as this world is getting it won't be long until nothing tastes like chicken, including chicken. That's when I may run a fowl of the law.

I take my time walking back to my buddy's house. There's no hurry. I'm pretty sure that he still hasn't wakened yet, and my water bowl was still half filled with water. I see K.D. Mitchell standing in her front yard, holding her green water hose two houses down and across the street. Birds are flying low and circling around her head. K.D. Mitchell is smiling at the birds. I know why. It's not after eleven a.m. yet, so K.D. Mitchell hasn't turned mean. The birds are chirping and singing as they fly around her head, K.D. Mitchell is whistling, and I'm confused. I'm no longer sure if I'm in a fiction book or a Disney movie. I'll ask Jim about it later.

I spot something else out of the corner of my left eye. Ivan the Russian wolfhound is standing on the sidewalk across the street from me. He's staring straight ahead like he's not paying any attention to me, so I know he's paying attention to me. I wonder where he came from. I look all around, but I don't see the two other terrorists.

I'm wondering if Ivan wants me to dog up, and have us go one on one with each other. It would be the biggest mistake he ever made. When I'm enraged the animal in me comes out.

I take three quick steps forward and stop. Across the street, Ivan did the exact same thing. I back up two quick steps and stop. Ivan does the same, but keeps staring straight ahead.

I stick my left paw out and hold it in front of my body. Ivan does the same. This is getting ridiculous. He's imitating every move I make without making eye contact. I must have him quivering in his paws.

I wag my tail five times in rapid succession. Ivan keeps staring straight ahead. I should have known that he wasn't a tail wagger.

I can't figure out what he's trying to accomplish unless he's trying to distract me. Bingo, the light just went off in Mixer's brain. Good boy. I look back over my left shoulder and see the other two terrorists quietly sneaking up on me.

I may get my buddy to change my name to Gherkin because right now it's looking like I'm in a pickle. I can't go backward and if I try to go forward Ivan has a perfect angle to cut me off. I don't want to say that things aren't looking good for me, but things aren't looking good for me.

I could wait until the three Russians all get within hearing range and use my exceptional ability to tell jokes, and make my escape while they were laughing uncontrollably and in no shape to pursue me. If it was after eleven a.m., I would lure the three foreigners into K.D. Mitchell's front yard and let the mean K.D. Mitchell make dog stroganoff out of them.

I come up with a brainstorm in the middle of a perfectly good sunny morning. I close my eyes and mentally summon all the other Ruffians to my side. Hey, if it can work in a movie, it can work in a book. I open my eyes and look around. It didn't work.

I glance back over my right shoulder again and see the wolfhounds have measurably closed the gap between us. I also notice that Ivan is slowly angling across the street toward me. For a really good-looking dog, this isn't looking good for me.

I look straight ahead and see one of the most beautiful sights I have ever seen. Truck is walking down the sidewalk toward me, and he has muscle with him. Ten light-brown toy Pomeranians are following behind him and gazing intently at the three Russian wolfhounds.

You've never known fear until you face down a pack of toy Pomeranians headed your way. I guess the Russians felt the same way because all three slowly turn around and start walking off in the opposite direction.

I watch as Truck and his rolling band of four-legged muscle come to a stop a couple of feet away from me. Those wolfhounds got off lucky. I was about to go postal on them.

"What's up, Mixer?" Trucks asks.

"The sun," I reply. Truck looks around me as he watches the backs of the Russians growing smaller in the distance and says, "It looks like you were about to be the guest of honor at a party you weren't even invited to."

"It's a good thing you showed up," I answer. "I was about to become their worst fleamare. You probably saved their lives."

"I'm sure I did," Truck dryly replies. "How come you're out all alone without the other Ruffians? I would think you guys would all be sticking together for the time being."

"I saw Goldie out walking," I admit. "I thought it would be nice to properly introduce myself to her. My momma raised this dog to be a gentleman."

Truck arches his eyebrows as he asks, "You know she is Ed's girl, right?"

"I wasn't trying to steal her away from Ed," I lie. "I wanted to be polite and say hi to her." I cross my tail behind my back and add, "My intentions were honorable. Now, what are you doing on this side of town so early in the day?"

"Me and the boys were out killing some time. It's been a slow week for street news. I tell you what. We'll walk you safely to your buddy's house in case the wolfhounds should decide to double back."

"Hey, Truck," I ask. "What did one egg say to the other egg beside the frying pan?"

"I don't know," Truck says.

"Omelet let you go first," I holler.

An ocean of groans escape from the milling band of Pomeranians.

"That's probably your corniest and lamest joke yet," Truck groans.

"Thanks. I wasn't expecting a compliment this early in the day."

Truck jerks his head toward the sidewalk behind him and says, "C'mon, let's get you home before you try to think of anymore jokes. Besides Butch would eat me alive if he found out I was around with the boys and still let something bad happen to you."

"Butch likes you," I protest.

"He also likes hamburgers, but he still eats them," Truck points out.

Okay, maybe Truck has a point.

We walk back to my buddy's house in silence, and once we make it safely there, Truck breathes a sigh of relief. I guess he was really serious when he said, if anything happened to me on his watch, Butch would eat him.

"Thanks, a lot, Truck," I say.

"See ya, Mixer. I wouldn't want to flea ya."

I walk around to the back of the house and use the doggy door to enter the house. I walk into the living room and see my buddy sitting in his recliner and still wearing his tattered diapers while watching The Weather Channel. A large black and blue lump is located in the center of his forehead.

He spots me and weakly whispers, "Mixer."

I stare at him and wait.

"I don't want to be a wrestler anymore."

Good boy!

CHAPTER 40

I wake up from a well-deserved nap and look around the room to see if I can spot anything to flip over onto the floor. I change my mind, stretch, and shake my hips instead. My buddy has been through enough lately and there's no sense in adding to his pain. After all, I'm not an animal.

I leap off the bed and pad into the living room. My buddy is asleep in his recliner, but the sounds of The Weather Channel are still blaring from the television set. I take a glance at the screen and do a double take. The sight of the weather girl talking about the severe weather passing through Minnesota is almost enough to send my blood pressure through the stratosphere. I know that I would never kick her out of my kennel for eating dog biscuits.

I look at my buddy and noticed the swelling on his forehead has diminished, but the black and blue bruise is now tinged with yellow. I have a feeling that my buddy is going to have every color of the rainbow decorating his forehead before he finally heals from his latest misadventure. I'm tempted to give him the nickname, Skittles, but decide against it. My buddy would never catch on to the meaning behind the name. He doesn't possess my above smarter than your average St. Bernard intelligence.

I notice something else about my buddy. He has a glass pint bottle of chocolate milk wedged between his body and the chair's armrest. The bottle is three-quarters empty. This isn't good. My buddy is now using the addicting, brown liquid to hide his pain. I'll deal with him later about this new development. Waking him up now is going to be next to impossible.

I continue on my journey and stroll into the kitchen. I check out my food and water bowls. The water bowl is filled with clean, fresh water, and the food bowl is filled to the brim with dried nuggets. I sniff the not very enticing nuggets, and use my nose to flip the bowl over and watch as the nuggets scatter all over the kitchen floor. If my buddy is going to insist on filling my food bowl with dog food instead of barbeque, he could at least use Dyson's dog food instead of the cheap stuff. I think all the chocolate milk is beginning to affect his decision-making skills.

I crawl through the doggy door and walk down the steps into the backyard where the other Ruffians are already gathered.

"It's positively about time you showed up," Butch says. "We have a lot to talk about, and we can't do it if you lollygag in your buddy's house."

I ignored the scolding and look at Dandy while asking, "What do you get when you cross a priest with a cell phone?"

"I don't know," Dandy honestly answers.

I scream, "Ring around the collar!"

"Great Lassie in Heaven," Empty mutters.

"That was dreadful," Butch moans. "I don't know where you come up with these jokes."

"It wasn't that bad," Dandy pants. "In fact, I thought it was kind of funny. I'm going to tell it to Jim. I bet he doesn't know the answer either."

"Thanks," I tell Dandy. "Why isn't Jim here?"

"There's a special about humpback whales on Animal Planet and the little darling didn't want to miss it. I couldn't deny the little angel the chance to continue his education," Butch explains without dwelling on the matter.

So one more reason pops up and reminds me that I have to go back to obedience school and finish my education. I don't know what a deny is.

Butch stares at his toenails and asks, "Does this 'Warm Yummy Pink' shade of toenail polish make my butt look big?"

I don't know what to say, so I don't say anything.

Empty starts making his gagging sounds.

"Any shade of toenail polish will look good on you, Butch" Dandy says.

"Why thank you, darling," Butch says as he reaches out with his left paw and pulls Dandy close to him.

Empty and I look at each other and shrug our shoulders. We know better than to get involved when Butch is having a bonding moment with his children.

"I talked to Goldie this morning," I tell Empty. "She seems like a nice girl."

Empty furrows his eyebrows as he glares at me, "You know better than to try to steal another dog's girl. There are plenty of Pepperidge Farm Goldfish crackers in the bag. You don't need to be reaching for the cracker that's already taken."

"I wasn't trying to steal anything," I lie. "I saw her walking down the sidewalk and thought it would be a perfect time to introduce myself. I'm a gentleman."

"Yeah, right," Empty snorts.

Dandy joins in by saying, "Empty, you have to admit that Goldie is prettier than a bullfrog eating a turnip in a bingo hall on a Tuesday night."

"I'm not saying she isn't pretty," Empty explains. "I'm saying she's already taken."

I can't believe this is coming from a guy, who's a dog when it comes to trying to score with babes. I decide to change the subject.

"I saw the three terrorists in the neighborhood this morning," I inform the group.

Empty's face immediately gets serious as he asks, "Did they try to hurt you?"

"You care," I tease.

"Don't push it," he warns.

Empty looks over at Butch and asks with hope in his voice, "Can we get violent now? The terrorists are showing up in the neighborhood regularly. I can't see where that is a good thing. I say we settle this once and for all."

"Darling, before we make a move we need to find out exactly who has been making threats against us. It wouldn't do us any good to attack the wrong force," Butch patiently explains.

Dandy looks up and Butch and says, "I'll fight too."

Butch wraps both of his paws around Dandy, pulls him close to his chest, and croons in his ears "I know you will, my sweet little floppy ears, but you're the tracker in our little group, and we positively can't have you getting hurt."

Empty and I look over at Butch and Dandy and smile. I know that we're both thinking the same thing. We're both wishing we had a camera because this is a Kodak moment.

"Speaking of which, how did you get away from the wolfhounds," Empty asks me in a curious voice. "I can't imagine you taking on three trained professional terrorists by yourself."

"Truck and some of his boys happened to be in the neighborhood, so the Russians backed off," I say. "You know that nobody wants to tangle with Truck."

"That's odd," Butch muses. "It's rare to find Truck and his gang of misfits on this side of town in the morning. I wonder what prompted him to come this way."

"He said he was checking things out," I clarify. "I think he's worried about this rumor that something big is coming down."

Before Butch can answer, a baying Jim burst out the backdoor of his buddy's house. He makes a beeline for the chain-link fence and takes a flying leap when he is about three feet away from it. Butch reaches over the top of the fence and grabs Jim's red leather collar in his mouth and pulls him over the top of the fence into my buddy's backyard.

"That special about humpback whales was awesome," an excited Jim pants to Butch.

"I'm glad you enjoyed yourself," Butch smiles as he gives Jim a hug.

Jim looks over at Dandy and says, "I left some buttered popcorn pushed under the pillows on the couch. If you want it, you can have the rest of it."

"Thanks," Dandy says in appreciation. "That'll give me some snacks to enjoy when Rachael comes on."

"Those two are so polite," Empty observes.

"That's because I raised them right," Butch brags.

"I don't know if I can make the patrol tonight," I say. "My buddy hurt himself, so I might need to stay around the house and keep an eye on him."

"What did he do this time?" Empty asks with an amused look on his face.

"He hit himself in the forehead with a cast-iron skillet," I snicker.

Jim and Dandy break into a round of giggles.

"That is dreadful," Butch sighs. "Your buddy is a good buddy, but he is absolutely accident prone. It's a wonder he doesn't stay in a body cast."

"Let's do it," Jim says without correcting the adverb abuse.

We know what he's talking about.

We gather around, do a group high five and yell, "We are The Ruffians."

CHAPTER 41

The Godfather paced back and forth in front of his doghouse glaring at the Fang Mafia sitting in a semi-circle in front of him. He would stop pacing long enough for Sally to pull a bite of original Armour Vienna Sausage out of the 4.6 ounce aluminum can and feed it to him. Occasionally, when taking a break from the pacing, he would linger long enough to lick the sausage's juice off Sally's claws, which caused her to purr in feelings of absolute contentment and joy.

"I give you guys one job to do, and you still haven't gotten it done," The Godfather snarled. "How hard is it to take out one glasses wearing beagle and hide the body where it will never be found? It's not like I'm exactly asking you to discover The Fountain of Youth."

"The hard part is trying to catch him alone," Blackjack protested. "When he's not in his buddy's house, he's always surrounded by the other Ruffians."

"Why don't we take out Mixer?" Carjack inquired. "He has a habit of running around the neighborhood by himself. He would be an easier target."

"I do the thinking around here," The Godfather snarled, "and I want the beagle with glasses taken out of the picture."

"Simmer down, boss," Hijack interjected into the conversation. "We'll get the job done, so don't blow a gasket. We have to do this hit, so it can't ever be traced back to us."

"Three days," The Godfather rasped. "I want the beagle taken out within the next three days. If you can figure out a way to place the blame on the Russians, it will make it so much the better. Our plans are almost complete. We're within two weeks of owning all the animals in this town. Once we have that squared away then you guys can go on vacation."

"Are you and Sally going to go on a vacation as well?" Slapjack inquired.

The Godfather didn't immediately answer as he took the time to lick the sausage's juice off Sally's paws.

"Purr," she growled. "Are those your ears standing up, or are you glad to see me?"

"I've got special plans for you, babes," The Godfather whispered in her ear. "We'll go to the beach, lie around in the sun for a few days, and cat around to your heart's content."

"Purr," Sally growled in contentment through half-closed eyes. "You sure know how to treat a lady. I can't wait."

The Godfather turned around to address Slapjack. "Sally and I are going to go to the beach for a few days. After all this planning, we need a vacation as well."

"What if the wolfhounds are still hanging around when our business is complete," Hijack asked. "We don't know the reason they're in town."

"I haven't thought about that," The Godfather admitted as he looked over his right shoulder to give Sally a seductive wink.

"That's not a problem," Blackjack retorted. "We'll take out the Russians and blame it on The Ruffians. Jim's the brains behind that outfit, and with him gone, they'll be unable to figure out a way to prove they're innocent."

"You're forgetting one thing," The Godfather reprimanded Blackjack. "When this is over none of The Ruffians will be around anymore either. They'll be with their good pal, Jimmy Boy."

"You're right," Blackjack replied as a wicked smile played on his face. "When this is over, we'll be done with those clowns for good."

"I sure would like to get even with Mixer," Carjack complained. "After what he did to me, it doesn't seem right that he gets by with it."

"Get over it," Hijack retorted. "Mixer got in a lucky bite, but you have to look at the big picture. Our dreams of owning a criminal empire are within our grasp. We have enough on our paws without you looking for revenge."

"Nicely worded," The Godfather said in an approving voice. "We've put entirely too much work in this thing to blow it now. Mixer will get his with the rest of The Ruffians. You're going to have to be content with that."

"After we take out Jim," Slapjack warned the others, "if Butch figures things out and puts two and two together, he'll be coming after us."

"I hope so," Blackjack admitted. "I've wanted to settle with Empty for a while now. There's never been enough room in this town for the both of us."

"Do you think you can take him one on one?" Carjack asked. "Empty's a pretty tough guy, and he really knows how to handle himself in a fight."

"Oh please," Blackjack snorted. "Does a dog bark at a mailman? Besides, I have an idea I want to run by all of you."

"It better be a good one," The Godfather cautioned. "You know that I don't like anyone doing the thinking around here but me."

"I think that you'll like it," Blackjack warily replied.

"Well, be like a bad piece of bubblegum and spit it out," Hijack snapped.

Blackjack looked at the assembly, cleared his throat and said, "We all know that Truck gets along with The Ruffians, but he's been known to pull off some shady deals of his own. He'll do anything, and I mean anything for a dog biscuit. Since The Ruffians trust him, why don't we bribe him with a couple of pounds of dog biscuits to lure Jim to an isolated place, and that's when we take out the Brainiac beagle."

"I'm not sure about that," Carjack replied while scratching underneath his chin. "What if Truck says no? Then what's to prevent him from telling Butch?"

"If Truck says no, you take him out on the spot," The Godfather snapped. "There's four of you and only one of him."

"Yeah, but we are talking about Truck," Slapjack uneasily replied.

The Godfather looked at his hired muscle with an incredulous look on his face. "Are you telling me that four grown Rottweilers can't take care of one toy Pomeranian?"

"Under normal circumstances, yes," Slapjack retorted. "But, Truck isn't normal circumstances. I think we can pull it off, but we'll have our hands full."

"What if Truck agrees to the deal, but after the hit has gone down, he decides to blackmail us for more dog biscuits, so he won't tell Butch?" Carjack asked.

"It doesn't matter," The Godfather growled. "Truck will be a tool. Once a tool is no longer needed you get rid of it. Either way it goes, Truck can't be allowed to live. If he decides to help and setup Jim, it would make your job a lot easier, but then he has to be disposed of."

The Godfather looked at Sally and took another bite of Vienna sausage before saying, "My dear, we might have to utilize your feminine wiles to set Truck up."

"No problem, I love to hear a dog squeal. You should remember that from last night, you animal," Sally purred.

"Woof," The Godfather passionately replied.

Blackjack rubbed his paws together and said, "This town is finally almost all ours."

CHAPTER 42

Boris, Vicktor, and Ivan, the three Russian wolfhounds, sat in an alley behind Baker's Bakery munching on a discarded bag filled with left over pastries.

"This is pretty good," Boris mumbled around a mouthful of jelly filled donut. "But I don't know why someone doesn't invent a chicken liver flavored donut."

"You ought to try these bagels," Ivan stated. "They're the best bagels I've had in a long time. I wish I had some cream cheese to spread on top of them."

"You have bigger things to worry about than cream cheese," Vicktor said while glaring at Ivan. "The man wants to know why you haven't taken out the beagle yet."

"Man?" Boris questioned without a confused look in his eyes. "Since when did a dude get involved in our business?"

"It's a figure of speech," Vicktor snapped. "Man, Top Dog, the Big Kahuna, you get the picture. The word is coming down from the top that they want the hit to happen immediately if not sooner. The beagle was supposed to already be out of the picture."

"I've run into an unexpected dilemma," Ivan explained. "I'm having a hard time finding the target alone which is making the hit almost impossible."

"No excuses will be accepted," Vicktor snapped. "I'm giving you no more than three days to execute your task. You're supposed to be the best specialist around. If it's not accomplished in less than three days, you will suffer severe consequences. Time is of the essence and remember when in

Rome."

"Take snapshots with your cell phone and post them all over Facebook," Boris interrupted while finishing the sentence for him.

"I'm not talking about social media," Vicktor barked in frustration.

"I've think that I've come up with a solution," Ivan slyly replied. "I'm going to need a local accomplice, somebody that the beagle trusts."

"What do you have in mind?" Vicktor asked with apprehension in his voice.

"That toy Pomeranian named Truck is friendly with The Ruffians. If I can bribe him to lure the target out into a secluded spot, then I execute the hit."

"And why would Truck agree to aid you?" Vicktor asked while taking a large bite out of an apple fritter.

"It appears that Truck operates in a lot of gray areas," Ivan explained while looking to see if there were any more bagels in the discarded white bag. "I've picked up that his weakness is dog biscuits. If we could bribe him with the proper amount of dog biscuits, I think we could turn him against The Ruffians, but it's going to be expensive."

"Ah, I see where you're going with this," Vicktor agreed. "You're talking about using Milk Bone dog biscuits."

"Correct," Ivan said while nodding his head up and down. "If I'm to pull this off, we're going to have to use the good stuff to turn him."

"What if Truck turns down the offer or yet, accepts the offer and sells us down the river by telling The Ruffians?"

"Then we eliminate Truck from the picture," Ivan calmly stated. "It's not like we're going to hang around this town forever."

"It has to be done within three days," Vicktor firmly insisted.

"Now that I have a clear plan of action, I see no issue with that deadline," Vicktor said with a ring of assurance in his words.

"Good luck, comrade," Boris interjected into the conversation.

"Here's something that I haven't told you before," Vicktor told Ivan, "if you conclude the business at hand in the set amount of time, I'm authorized to present you with a bonus.

Ivan kept quiet as he stared at Victor and waited for him to finish his offer about a bonus.

Vicktor leaned forward and confidentially whispered, "I'm authorized to present you with a box of Little Debbie Oatmeal Crème Pies."

A look of ecstasy and triumph crossed Ivan's face as he said, "Consider it done. I'll do anything for a Little Debbie."

"To victory," Boris and Vicktor replied in unison.

CHAPTER 43

I use the doggy door in the back of the house to enter our cozy little abode and stroll into the kitchen to see if there is anything new and exciting happening there. I check out my food and water bowls. I don't see any earth-shattering events happening in either one of them.

I look through the open doorway and see my buddy sitting in his recliner and watching The Weather Channel. That's nothing new and exciting, but I do smell something that is new and exciting in the living room.

The tantalizing smell drifting from the living room and teasing me like a mailman on the other side of the fence wearing blue spandex shorts can only mean one thing. My buddy must have stopped by the Catfish Cattle Café and rounded me up a plate of fried catfish for supper. I'd recognize that wonderful smell anywhere.

I stroll over to the doorway and sit down as I stare at the Styrofoam platter sitting on top of the coffee table. I don't have to look inside the tray to know what wonderful bounty that culinary treasure chest contains. It will contain three catfish fingers fried to a golden-brown hue, three golden-brown hush puppies, a compartment filled with creamy coleslaw, two sliced dill pickles, one slice of onion, and a slice of white bread. Sitting beside the tray is a 16 ounce red plastic cup. I'm hoping my buddy brought me home a glass of sweet iced tea. I lick my lips.

My buddy looks over and sees me staring at my supper and defensively holds his hands out in front of him as he cries, "No, Mixer. The last time I brought home a plate of catfish fingers you got all the fish, and I didn't get any."

So my buddy thinks I'm not going to get the catfish. He doesn't know how close he is to getting his bohonkus kicked.

I stare at the Styrofoam platter and lick my lips.

"No, Mixer," he cries again in a pitiful voice. "You don't know how rough of a day I had at work. The janitorial service didn't show up, and I had to put a new plastic liner in the wastebasket in my office all by myself. As I was taking out the old trash bag, a piece of paper with coffee stains on it almost touched my hands, and I have no idea where that coffee had been."

I start to tell my buddy that if the coffee stained paper was in the wastebasket in his office, then it was probably his piece of paper and coffee. Instead, I keep my mouth shut. I'm going to let him figure that one out on his own. Besides, it really doesn't matter. I don't know what an office is. It's probably something I don't need to know.

My stomach growls and I lick my lips as the delicious fragrance of my supper teases my nostrils with its enchanting scent.

My buddy notices and whines again, "Mixer, no. I'm having the catfish. After I eat, I'll get you a hotdog. How does that sound?"

A hotdog? Does my buddy think that I'm a cannibal? His issues are running far deeper than I ever thought was possible. He might be beyond help.

He suddenly leaps to his feet and yells, "Since I'm not going to be a professional wrestler anymore, I'm going back to being the rapper Butterscotch Ivory. I'm going to record the first ever rap song about catfish. It's going to be so different that it will make us rich and famous."

I know what my buddy is trying to do. He's trying to distract me. He really isn't going to rap about a catfish. His ploy isn't working. I'm still going to get those fish.

My buddy starts rapping.

"I'm a little catfish, and I swim.
Whatever I do, I do on a whim.
I eat all kind of stuff on the lake's muddy floor.
Then I pat my little fishy stomach and eat some more.
I'll never go out with a fisherman on a date.
I don't want to wind up on his cousin's plate.
He tries to entice me with a new shiny lure.
He'd have better luck trying to hook manure.
I'm a handsome little fellow with an awesome fin.
I can catch any female fish with my watery grin.
I'm looking at a cricket floating on a hook.

He's looking kind of bored and reading a book.
I'm swimming in circles and watching the boats above.
The fisherman wants to pick me up, but I'm not feeling the love.
Maybe I'll swim back down to the lake's muddy floor.
Find a cute female crappie and try to score."

My buddy quits rapping and stares at me with his cheeks flushed with excitement and a drop of sweat hanging off the tip of his nose while yelling, "How did you like it, Mixer? Wasn't that an awesome rap song? Butterscotch Ivory is going to be famous."

I don't reply and I resume staring at the Styrofoam platter.

"I'll even tell jokes in between the songs," my buddy babbles in a voice that is entirely too bubbly and cheerful.

I look at my buddy and wait.

"Mixer, what do you call a fish on top of a television set?" he asks.

I keep waiting as I see no point in replying.

"A channel cat!" he giggles. "Do you get it, Mixer? A catfish is a fish, and a television has channels and there are some catfish known as channel cats. Wasn't that joke incredible?"

I yawn.

My buddy bends down and unfastens the top of the Styrofoam platter. He straightens back up and points his right index finger at me and sternly states, "I'm going to go wash my hands while my supper is cooling. I don't want you to mess with the food."

I can't believe he pointed his finger at me like I'm a dog. His bohonkus is in more trouble than he realizes.

I watch my buddy walk down the short hallway to the bathroom and close the door behind him. When I hear the sound of running water from the faucet, I walk over to the coffee table and start nibbling on the first catfish finger. Great Lassie in Heaven, this fish is good.

I hear the water stop running as my buddy turns the faucet off and the creaking of the doorknob as he turns it to open the door. I'm not worried. My buddy will open the door halfway and close it again to rewash his hands. He's terrified of germs on a doorknob. I can't believe my buddy is afraid of his own germs. This will happen three times.

I hear the bathroom door click shut for an additional time and listen to the sound of running water. I start devouring my second little taste of Heaven. I glance over at the reservoir filled with creamy coleslaw and run my tongue over the top of it. My buddy will never know the difference. The coleslaw hits the spot, and I'm not normally a cabbage eating dog.

I listen to the sound of the bathroom door opening and clicking shut for the third time. When my buddy opens it for the fourth time, he'll use a towel to touch the doorknob.

I use my nose to push the sixteen-ounce plastic glass of tea off the coffee table and onto the floor. I watch as the lid pops off and crushed ice and a light-brown liquid spill out from the cup. I bend over and enjoy a few laps of the liquid. The drink is exactly what I hoped it would be. It's hard to beat sweet iced tea when eating catfish. The two go together like fish and tea.

I hear the bathroom door open again, and take one more lick over the top of the coleslaw, and wolf down the third catfish finger. I snatch up a golden-brown hush puppy as I turn around and streak for the doggy door. My buddy doesn't need three hush puppies. Two ought to be plenty for him.

I'm halfway through the doggy door when I hear my buddy wail in anguish, "Mixer!"

CHAPTER 44

Truck was a worried toy Pomeranian. Both the Fang Mafia and the Russian wolfhounds approached him with the offer of two pounds of Milk Bones dog biscuits to lure Jim into a spot where he could be taken out with a minimum of a fuss.

Truck eagerly accepted the offer of both groups, and now he was the proud owner of four pounds of Milk Bone dog biscuits. Truck knew he was going to have to keep a low profile after the malicious deed was performed. The group he betrayed would surely come looking for him, and he wasn't sure if he was even safe from the side he helped. They could easily double cross him as well. Truck decided that he was going to have the toy French poodles stay close to his side for a while. It might be wise to even bring the miniature Pinschers out of retirement.

Truck felt a twinge of guilt at the thought of betraying The Ruffians. He'd always liked Jim and insisted that when the hit happened, he didn't want to see it. Both sides readily agreed to his demands. There was no reason for him to actually see the deed being done as long as it was successfully executed, and Jim eliminated from the picture.

Even with his reputation as being a bad dog to mess with, Truck still felt a twinge of apprehension as he thought about how The Ruffians would react. Dandy would probably be filled with too much grief at the loss of his lifelong friend, but the other three would be berserk and filled with rage and the desire for revenge.

Truck's body involuntarily trembled at the thought of Butch going in berserker mode. Truck knew what Butch was capable of when pushed past his breaking point. Empty was no bargain either. Egomaniac or not, he was a pure fighting machine when roused. Truck idly thought of Mixer. For all of Mixer's corny jokes, he was no slouch when it came to taking care of himself when pushed into a corner. He and Empty were pretty much inseparable, so more than likely they would be working together to find who was responsible for taking out Jim. Butch would be with them at times, but he doubted that Butch would stray too far from Dandy.

Truck shrugged his shoulders and observed the white clouds idly drifting by in a blue sky. There was nothing he could do about it now. Four pounds of dog biscuits had already been delivered, so backing out of the deal was out of the question.

Truck would keep a low profile until things calmed down. He would also keep the toy French poodles close by as reinforcements.

Truck reasoned to himself that he could always play the Fang Mafia and the Russians against each other, and if push came to pull, he could betray them to The Ruffians. Butch would handle the matters from there on out.

Truck decided that if he played his cards right, he would come out of this situation smelling like a rose. He'd been in more precarious situations than this.

Truck took off walking down the sidewalk toward Jim's buddy's house. The wheel had already been set into motion, and now he had a beagle to set up.

CHAPTER 45

All The Ruffians are sitting in my buddy's backyard underneath the crabapple tree, and trying to decide where we want to patrol tonight. Empty wants to patrol around the schoolyard. I want to patrol closer to our homes. In case there was a possibility that we could spot more strangers in town, Jim and Dandy want to patrol close to The Godfather's neighborhood. Everyone is pleading his case with a strong position.

Butch is the only one not joining in the argument. He's sitting under the crabapple tree and staring off into the distance with a dreamy look on his face. None of the guys mind because Butch looks like he's enjoying being in his happy spot. And when Butch is merry that means nobody is getting hurt.

I turn back to face Empty and resume the argument when Butch idly says to no one in particular, "It's time I got another steady boyfriend."

Empty immediately doubles over and starts making gagging sounds while making a motion of shoving his paw in and out of his mouth like he's trying to throw up.

Jim pushes his glasses back up his nose and says, "Butch, I thought that you were through being in relationships."

"Yeah," Dandy pipes in, "why do you want another boyfriend when you said serious relationships are too straining to work out."

"Because," Butch yawns, "I positively didn't get a gift on Valentine's Day last year, and I absolutely don't want to go through that anguish again."

Butch is such a diva. He always worries about the wrong thing.

"I didn't realize you got upset about not getting a Valentine's gift," I say. "It looked like it didn't bother you last year. After all, you never mentioned it."

"I don't want flowers or a chew toy," Butch quickly clarifies, "but nothing says yummy like a male hairy paw on your tummy."

Empty's gagging sounds grow in intensity.

"I'm not sure that I'd really want to get gifts on Valentine's Day," I tell Butch. "I can see where you might get something that you don't want."

A look of puzzlement crosses Butch's face as he says," I'm not following your line of logic, Mixer. Valentine's Day is to show your loved ones how much you care, and it's a special day of love and romance. How could you positively not want to receive gifts on an exceptional day such as that?"

"That's what I'm talking about," I stress. "I especially don't want to receive anything on that day. What are the initials for that special day of romance?"

"VD," Dandy excitedly yips.

"Bingo," I yell.

A look of horror crosses Butch's face as he gasps, "I sure don't want that to be given to me on Valentine's Day, but I'm not sure if dogs can catch a venereal disease."

Okay, he has me there. I don't know what a venereal is.

"Actually, we can," Jim points out while letting his glasses drop down to the ground by his front paws. "Dogs can catch Canine Herpes, Canine Brucellosis, which also can be transmitted to humans, and Canine Transmissible Venereal Tumors. Practicing safe sex also applies to dogs. The safest way to keep a dog safe from sexual diseases is to have a dog de-sexed."

When Butch hears that he drops straight to the ground in a dead faint. Empty curls up in a ball on the ground and starts groaning. I sit down and tightly clinch all my legs together. Nobody is going to have this cowboy de-sexed. Dandy takes off running in circles around the crabapple tree while yelping in canine horror.

"That is horrible," Empty groans in a loud terrified voice.

"You can't stay curled up in a ball on the ground forever," Jim admonishes Empty.

"Yes, I can," Empty yells. "Yes, I can."

"I have an idea," I say. "Let's change the subject."

"Yes, darling, let's positively do," Butch whispers in a weak voice as he awakens from his faint and slowly stands on wobbly legs.

Dandy stops his running around the crabapple tree and stares at us with his mouth hanging open and drops of saliva dripping off the end of his tongue.

"Well, what do you guys want to talk about," Jim asks as he retrieves his glasses from the ground. "I'm certainly open to a new topic of conversation."

"Do human mothers breast feed their babies the same way dogs do?" Dandy gasps. "I've always been curious about that."

We all look at Jim. If anyone knows the answer to that question, it will be him.

Jim clears his throat as we all stare at him with rapt attention.

"Some mothers prefer to use a bottle when feeding their babies," Jim orates. "However, a lot of mothers prefer to breastfeed their child. Once the process begins, it's best to continue for two years because a baby needs whole milk until the age of two, and a human mother's milk is whole. After that, it is up to the mother to determine when to stop breastfeeding her child. Although, there are some human mothers who quit breastfeeding their child after a few months."

A vivid image of Ms. Kolinsky sunbathing in her backyard runs across my brain like a fox chasing a rabbit on a Saturday night. I wish I was her baby. I'd gladly wear a diaper for two years. Wow.

"What if the mother has more than one baby?" Dandy asks in a curious voice.

"Good question," Butch and Empty respond in unison.

"That's why human mothers have a dual feeding machine in front," I quickly answer before Jim can start in with a long discussion.

Jim glares at me as he firmly states, "That's not exactly how I would have answered the question, but I guess it serves the purpose of answering Dandy's question."

Okay, Jim's not thrilled that I interrupted his educational seminar he was holding tonight, but he's a grown dog. He'll get over it.

"We still have to decide where we're going to patrol tonight," Empty says as he looks around at the other four of us.

"Why don't we patrol around the school grounds and the neighborhood tonight, and tomorrow night we can patrol close to The Godfather's neighborhood?" Butch suggests.

I look surprised as I look at Butch. "I didn't think you heard a word we were saying earlier," I say. "You were off in your happy place doing whatever jolly thoughts you do there."

"Darling, I always hear and see what's going on around me," he croons.

"I believe you," I say.

We paw bump.

CHAPTER 46

The argument about where we should patrol turned out to be a waste of time as we wind up patrolling in the park. Butch wants to check out the small pond at the south end of the park and see if we can spot the squirrels doing anything fishy.

The only sounds in the park were a light breeze rustling the leaves on the trees and the pitter pattering sounds of our paws crunching on the gravel path. It's almost eerily quiet compared to the laughter and sounds accompanying the park during daylight hours.

I turn my head and tell Empty, "There's nothing like a stroll in the park at night when you're in the company of good friends."

"You can say that again, and you better not," Empty warns as he replies without looking at me.

I ignore the warning and ask him, "Why are good friends like hemorrhoids?"

"I'm afraid to ask," he grimaces as he turns his head to look at me.

"Because sometimes they're a pain, but they'll always be there for you in the end," I answer. I'm waiting for the guys to break into a round of thunderous applause.

I don't get any applause, but Butch groans, "Mixer, that was so positively cheesy. Are you sure you aren't from Wisconsin?"

"It wasn't that bad," Dandy says. "I've heard you tell a lot worse."

"It's funny about jokes," Jim blurts out. "I was watching a documentary on one of the television channels about how jokes affect one's mood. A joke doesn't necessarily make a person feel better. A lot of the success of a joke depends upon the mood of the audience."

"I wasn't telling it to a person," I remind Jim. "We're dogs."

"That's true," Jim agrees. "I keep forgetting that a lot of the documentaries I observe on television are dedicated to the inferior breed."

"He's talking about humans," Dandy tells Empty.

"I know," Empty smiles as he affectionately pats Dandy on top of his head.

"Well, this is a disappointment," Butch states as we finally reach the pond. "There aren't any squirrels out. I was hoping that we might find a hint which would help answer some questions."

"Maybe they're afraid," I volunteer the information to Butch.

Butch crinkles his forehead and asks, "Why would the squirrels be afraid to be out walking and playing in the park at night?"

"If I didn't have any nuts, you wouldn't catch me out here alone either," I explain.

"He has a point," Empty says as he joins in on the conversation.

"I wonder where those male humans are that usually come to the park when the sun goes down?" Jim muses. "I haven't seen any of them out either."

Butch starts sputtering and trying to catch his breath when Dandy says, "Maybe they're not here because all the squirrels ate their nuts as well."

"It's okay, big guy," Empty says as he pats Butch between the shoulder blades and tries to help him regain his breath.

"I had a visual I never had before," Butch admits. "It's one I hope not to have again anytime soon."

"What now?" I ask. "No squirrels at the pond kind of put a damper on this idea."

"Let's check out around the concession building," Empty suggests. "You never know who or what you might find in that area of the park at night."

"Maybe we can find some popcorn or the remains of a hotdog lying around," Dandy says in a hopeful tone of voice. "This patrolling has worked up my appetite."

"Darling," Butch says as he lays a paw on top of Dandy's head, "I've positively told you time and time again to never accept food from a stranger."

"Cut him some slack," Empty says. "The walking has made me hungry as well. I wouldn't turn down a bucket of extra crispy chicken about now."

"We can all grab a snack when we get back to our buddies' homes," Butch scolds. "Right now, now we're on a business trip, and we need to take it serious."

"I seriously want to eat too," I say as I look at Butch. "All this talk about hotdogs, popcorn, and chicken has made me hungry as a dog."

"Children," Butch mutters under his breath to himself. "You do everything to raise them right, and they still want to argue with you."

"Well, we aren't accomplishing anything by standing around here and flapping our gums," Empty admonishes. "Let's get busy."

"Hold on a sec," Jim says as he sniffs the air. "The wind has shifted and I'm picking up a familiar scent."

Jim looks over at Dandy and asks, "Do you smell it as well?"

Dandy raises his head, closes his eyes, and takes a deep breath. He opens his eyes as he looks at Jim and says, "I'm picking up three different scents, but I know the one that you're talking about."

"Well, are you going to fill the rest of us in?" I ask. "Quit making things so spooky."

Jim looks at me and says in a solemn voice, "Sally's here in the park, and I don't think she's with any members of the Fang Mafia. I'd recognize their scent anywhere."

"This is getting interesting," Empty says as he looks at Butch. "I say we go find Sally and see what she is up to."

"Positively," Butch replies.

"The wind is blowing toward us, so we should be able to sneak up on them, as long as we keep quiet. Maybe, we can listen to them without them knowing we're here."

"Great plan," Butch says. "Jim and Dandy, you two lead the way. We'll walk in the grass beside the path, so we don't make a crunching sound on the gravel."

"I think we should keep our voices to a low whisper," I add. "We need to make as little noise as possible."

Jim and Dandy lead the way with their noses stretched out inches above the ground as they quietly and slowly lead us toward our quarry. It doesn't take long to realize they are directing us toward the concession stand. This is working out better than I expected as the concession stand was our original destination.

Jim and Dandy stop just before the outside water fountain by the maintenance shack and stare straight ahead toward the blue cylinder block building which serves as the concession building. We all can see Ed, Truck, and Sally walking in front of the building. We aren't close enough yet to hear what they are saying, but they're all talking with each other in an animated conversation with lots of body gestures.

"This is interesting," Empty whispers in my ear. "Why isn't Sally with The Godfather and Ed with Goldie? And why is Truck hanging with them?"

Before I can answer a loud blood-curdling scream splits the silence of the night, and I watch Ed, Sally, and Truck break into a run around the corner of the concession building.

I look back at Butch and ask, "What was that all about? Why did you scream?"

"I think I stepped on a worm," Butch shrieks. "I stepped on something and it was icky and gooey, and wiggly. I positively can't stand worm yuck on the bottom of my paws."

Oh wow. The fiercest dog around these parts, and he's afraid of a worm. I make a mental note to never take Butch fishing.

"Well, they're gone now," Empty dejectedly says. "We may never find out what those three were talking about."

"I'm sorry," Butch apologizes. "I have half a mind to find that worm and settle up with him. What's he doing crawling around at night?"

"Doing worm things," I tell Butch.

"Well, we might as well call it a night and head home," Empty says. "I still have time for a midnight snack and some serious mirror time."

"It's okay," Jim and Dandy tell Butch in unison. "We still love you."

"I love you too, darlings," Butch replies as he hip bumps both of them.

Empty looks at me and inquires," "I wonder what your girl is up to?"

"She's not my girl anymore," I remind him.

"Well, let's go home, lover boy," he says while taking a playful swing at my head.

"Hey, Empty," I say.

"What?"

"Why did the chef go to the gym?"

"I don't have a clue."

"She wanted to whip some eggs into shape," I yell.

Empty groans all the way home.

CHAPTER 47

I use the doggy door to enter my buddy's house expecting to find my buddy asleep in the bedroom. Of course, I stop first to check out my food and water bowls. There's no earth-moving event happening in either one of them.

I pad into the living room and see that my buddy is going to save me the trip from walking into the bedroom. He's sitting in his recliner, watching The Weather Channel and eating a Butterfinger candy bar. Bits of chocolate and pieces of the flaky peanut butter center are scattered all over the front of his Scooby Doo pajamas.

I'm not happy with this discovery. I've raised him to always get eight hours of sleep at night, and I definitely don't like him eating sugar at bedtime. Now with this unexpected sugar-high, I'll never be able to get him to fall asleep.

He finally notices that I'm standing in the doorway observing and picks up the remote control in his left hand, and mutes the weather forecast blaring from the television set. He's looking at me like he's trying to decide if he's going to be in trouble for being up so late. He had better be happy that I'm in a good mood.

"Mixer," he says with an innocent look on his face, "I couldn't get to sleep, so I'm still wide awake. That's what happens when you can't fall asleep."

That's my buddy. He's the fountain of obvious information. He ought to know by now that I'm a dog that doesn't like the obvious being stated. It drives me crazy every summer when he comes into the house and tells me, "Mixer, it sure is hot out there today." I always want to tell him that I figured that out four hours ago when it was ninety-five degrees in the shade, but since I hate responding to the obvious, I never say anything.

"I've been thinking, Mixer," he continues. "I need an alternate plan in case my career as a professional rapper doesn't work out."

I sit down and drop my head between my knees so I can stare at the floor. My buddy has been thinking. I can see where nothing good is going to come out of this.

"I'm going to get a second job as a standup comedian," he says, and I can hear the pride in his voice. "I'm going to use the stage name The Knock Knock Cuckoo. I'll be the only comedian in the business telling knock knock jokes on stage."

I raise my head up and stare at him. My buddy is staring back with a goofy grin plastered all over his face. Great Lassie in Heaven, he's serious about this.

"Check out this joke," he chortles. "Knock knock."

I know. I'm supposed to say who's there, but I'm not sure I want to hear this, so I keep my mouth shut. My buddy answers for me.

"Who's there?" he hollers.

I yawn.

"Who?" he yells.

I roll my eyes.

"Who who?" he screams.

I take the time to pass a little gas. My buddy's never going to notice. He's in the zone.

He spreads his arms wide and bellows, "Who who said the owl."

I lie down on the floor and sigh.

"Do you get it, Mixer?" he asks while bouncing up and down in his recliner and slapping his hands on his knees. "Who said the owl because owls say who. I'm going to actually say who on stage. People are going to go crazy."

My buddy has lost it. He needs help. He needs intervention from a knock knock master. No, on second thought he needs intervention from a realist. I'm dealing with Russian terrorists, and my buddy wants to be a knock knock celebrity.

"Hey, boy, do you want to hear another knock knock joke? I have a million of them," he says with way too much excitement in his voice.

I growl.

"Okay, maybe one joke is enough for tonight," he agrees. "I know that you're so proud of me. If you could talk, you would probably say how proud you are of me."

I close my eyes and sigh. I would tell him that I can talk, but he might not believe me, so I don't say anything.

"Oh, Mixer, Mixer, Mixer," he stammers while flapping his right hand in the air toward me. "I thought of another one. You have to listen to this one. You're going to love it."

I give him my best you have got to be kidding look.

"Knock knock," he says.

I stare at the floor again. I'm not sure how much longer that I'm going to be able to take this. I'll never let him eat sugar before bedtime again.

"Who's there?" he giggles.

I watch a baby cockroach crawl between my front paws. I'm tempted to squash him, but I change my mind. If I have to listen to this, he has to listen to this. He looks up at me and rolls his eyes. I agree with him. Crawl free, baby cockroach.

"Willie," he cackles.

Great Lassie in Heaven the torture is never going to end.

"Willie who?" he snorts.

My mind is made up. I'm definitely peeing in his slippers when he goes to sleep.

"Willie tell another knock knock joke," He roars.

I'm ready to face the Fang Mafia or the Russian terrorists. There's nothing they can put me through that can be more tortuous than what my buddy is putting me through.

"Isn't that so funny?" He roars again. "I'm going to dress in a lemon colored jumpsuit and carry a plastic yellow hammer and aluminum trash can lid on stage. I'll bang the hammer against the lid, and everybody in the audience will yell knock knock. I bet they even give me my own reality television show, and you're going to be in it as well."

I can't take anymore. I walk past him and head to the bedroom. Tomorrow morning I'm planning on going down to the Plaza Pizza joint. The guy who always empties the trash at the pizza joint usually will be outside with a few slices of pepperoni to pass out to any dogs that might be hanging around. I'm going to see if Empty wants to tag along. Until we figure out what is going on, it's probably not a good idea to be roaming the streets alone.

I stand in the hallway staring into the bedroom, and I can't believe what my eyes see. Happy Birthday to me! My buddy's favorite pair of maroon slippers are lying on the small dark-blue natural fiber rug beside the bed. This would have probably been a good night for him to wear the maroon slippers instead of his Scooby Doo house shoes. His Scooby Doo shoes would have been safe from my wrath.

I walk over to the slippers and raise my right leg. It feels like Niagara Falls is flowing.

From the open doorway I hear my buddy cry in anguish, "Mixer."

CHAPTER 48

I wake up and the only sound I hear in the house is the gentle whirl of my buddy's Whirlpool washing machine. I look over the side of the bed and see his maroon slippers are gone from the dark-blue rug. Well, now I know what's in the washer going around and around. With my buddy's phobia about germs I'm sure he used way more laundry detergent than was needed.

I stand up, give my hips a couple of good shakes and leap off the bed. I walk into the living room and see a white plastic Star Wars cereal bowl sitting on the oak coffee table. I walk over and look into the bowl. I'm surprised to see that the bowl is still half full. I sniff to see if it's anything I might be interested in snacking on. The smell of Kellogg's Frosted Mini Wheats invade my nostrils. Normally, I might be interested, but this morning I'm not in a frosted mood.

I walk into the kitchen to check out my food and water bowls. The water bowl, as usual, is filled with clean, fresh water. I look over my food bowl and see a slice of American cheese lying on top of my chicken flavored soybean nuggets. So my buddy left me some soybean ala mode. I have to admit to myself that it was a thoughtful gesture. I wolf up the slice of cheese and wash it down with a long drink of cool water. The slice of cheese was good, but it had a slight soybean flavor aftertaste. I use my nose to flip the bowl over and watch the brown nuggets scatter all over the kitchen floor. That ought to teach my buddy that next time to cover the nuggets with a paper towel before laying the slice of cheese in the bowl.

I squeeze through the doggy door and walk down the back steps into the yard. I look around and don't see any of the other guys waiting to worship the ground I walk on. I really wasn't expecting to, but I was still hoping Empty might be around. I'm kind of antsy to get down to Plaza Pizza before all the pepperoni slices are given away.

The sound of a rattling of the gate causes me to spin around and see what's going on. I'm surprised to see Truck walking into the backyard.

"Hey, Mixer, what's up?" he asks.

"The ceiling," I reply.

Truck looks around the backyard and then peers through the chain-link fence to Butch's buddy's backyard. I don't have a clue as to why that should capture his attention. Butch, Jim and Dandy are still inside the house, and I don't see anything interesting about watching grass grow.

Finally, Truck looks at me and says, "I was hoping to catch you out and about. I know you always wake up before your pals."

I briefly wonder if I should invite Truck in for a bowl of Frosted Mini Wheats then I decide against it. I don't feel like washing dishes. I could offer him the bowl my buddy left sitting on the coffee table, but I'm not sure if Truck likes leftovers.

"Is there anything special that you wanted to see me about?" I ask.

"Yeah," Truck replies while rolling his neck like he's trying to work a kink out of it. "I've put all my boys out on the street, and they still haven't heard anything. All the word is that something big is going down, and it involves you Ruffians. Other than that, nobody is saying anything. My boys are even getting nervous, and they don't rattle easily."

"I think it's the Russians," I say. "Empty wants to hunt them down and confront them, but Butch thinks we need to keep a low profile and find out what is going to happen before we make any kind of move. I'm torn as I can see both of their points."

"Well," Truck replies as he keeps intently studying Butch's buddy's backyard. "I wouldn't make any rash decisions. You want to make sure your decision is the right one."

"If I agreed further, I still couldn't agree additionally," I reply, and I'm enjoying the look on Truck's face while he tries to make sense out of that answer.

"So, are you the only Ruffian that ever gets up this early?" he casually asks.

I don't answer right away as I watch Goldie sashaying down the street. Wow. The motion to the ocean she puts into swinging her hips would even make a St. Bernard think about losing his religion. That Ed is one lucky dog.

I finally force myself to quit staring at Goldie and look at Truck while I answer, "Empty always has to grab some serious mirror time after he wakes up. Butch likes to sleep late, and Dandy never comes outside until he sees what's shaking and baking on The Cooking Channel. Jim will be out shortly. He always likes his time alone in the morning to ponder on the world's events and get his thoughts in order. Then he'll go back inside to watch The History Channel while Butch and Dandy take care of their personal needs. If you see how the possum is hanging."

Truck grimaces as he replies, "So, Jim goes back inside when Butch and Dandy come outside, so Butch and Dandy can use the bathroom in peace."

"You got it, potato chip."

Truck arches his right eyebrow as he looks at me and asks, "If you're outside when Jim wants his time alone, doesn't that defeat the purpose of Jim being outside?"

I think I know what Truck is saying even though I don't know what a purpose is. If nothing else I'm going back to obedience school and get my CED, Canine Educational Diploma. I see where I really need to buckle up my vocabulary.

"I go back inside when Jim comes out," I answer. "You have to give a fellow his time alone when he needs it. I'll go back inside and grab a snack, tear up something and take a catnap, though the catnaps were a lot more fun when Sally was around. Come to think of it, we never napped when we were taking our catnaps if you know what I'm talking about? Whoop whoop."

"I don't need to hear about that part of your life," Truck dryly replies.

"Sorry," I say. "It's a shame Goldie is taken. I wouldn't mind doing the whoop whoop with her during a catnap."

"Get your mind out of the gutter," Truck snaps. "So, you're telling me that every morning Jim is alone in the backyard, and no one else is around to disturb him."

"That's what I'm saying," I reply. "Jim needs the time alone to recharge his mental batteries. After all, he is the intellectual of our little group."

"That's interesting," Truck says while rubbing his chin with his right paw. "I guess when you're a genius you would need time alone to recharge your brain."

I don't know why Truck is suddenly wearing a little smile on his face, but I don't ask him. I'm not that type of dog.

"How long is Jim in the backyard by himself," he asks and before I can answer he starts a chorus of yaps at the loud garbage truck rumbling down the street.

When he's finally barked out, I answer his question by saying, "He usually only spends ten to fifteen minutes alone, and then he's good to go."

Truck suddenly spins around and says, "I've got to go, Mixer. I forgot to do something."

"Okay," I reply. "Take care, Truck."

"See ya, Mixer. I wouldn't want to flea ya."

CHAPTER 49

While I'm watching Truck leave through the open gate, I notice Empty walking toward the chain-link fence out of the corner of my eye. Empty silently glides along on his buddy's carpet of grass and effortlessly bounds over the top of the fence.

As he trots toward me, I tell him, "Show off. You could have used the gate like a normal dog. I hope that you're not trying to show off for me because I'm not that kind of dog."

"Never thought you were," he replies, "but normal is so boring."

I can't argue that point, so I say, "Truck had some interesting things to say. It appears none of his contacts on the street have heard anything about what's supposed to be going down."

Empty cocks his head as he says, "That's very strange. Truck usually knows what's going down on the street before the street does. This big thing that's supposed to happen must really be a deep secret for somebody. I wonder what's supposed to happen to us."

"We'll find out soon enough," I reply, and I even impress myself with that answer.

Empty isn't impressed and he counters, "I could have figured that one out myself, fur breath. Well, whatever happens, I know that we'll be ready for it."

Before I can reply, we hear the sound of a backdoor banging and watch Jim run into his buddy's backyard. He makes a couple of laps around the yard and then heads behind the hybrid tea rose bush to take care of his morning business.

"You have to love outdoor plumbing," Empty says, "but don't watch.

You know how sensitive Jim is about people watching him use the bathroom."

"We're not people, we're dogs," I point out.

"Whatever," Empty snorts.

"I wonder if Jim sleeps with his glasses on?" I inquire without really expecting an answer. Empty probably knows that's a rhetorical question. Great I know what a rhetorical is, but not a purpose. I wonder what the purpose of that is?

"Hey, fleas for brains, do you have any plans for this morning?" Empty asks snapping at a housefly buzzing around his head.

"Yep," I say. "I'm going to go down to Plaza Pizza. I'm in the mood for some pepperoni slices. I was going to see if you wanted to tag along. If any of us got caught walking the streets alone, it might not exactly turn out to be a birthday party for us with cake and ice cream."

Empty glances at me with a serious look on his face and says, "You got that right. If anything happened to you, who would I have to insult?"

How sweet. He really does care. We paw bump.

He glances over at Jim and says, "We probably need to get out of here. If he doesn't get his alone time, you know how grumpy Jim becomes."

"It's a shame that dogs can't eat chocolate," I reply. "When he starts getting grumpy we could always give him a Snickers candy bar."

Empty shakes his head back and forth and says, "That still wouldn't work. Jim doesn't like caramel."

"Then let's be bananas and split," I suggest.

"Maybe those two terrier twins will be down at Plaza Pizza," Empty says with a note of hope in his voice. "The last time I saw those two girls they were looking smoking hot with their skin-tight fur. Perhaps I can invite them over to share some serious mirror time."

"You're a dog," I say. "I know who you're talking about, but what are those babes names anyway? I've never found out."

"Scot and Tish," Empty replies. "I think they have a thing for me."

I ignore that and say, "I wish Goldie wasn't going steady with a hotdog. I wouldn't mind sharing pepperoni slices with her."

"Great Lassie in Heaven," Empty mutters while shaking his head back and forth. "You need to get over her. There are plenty of other fishes in the sea."

"I don't want a fish," I argue. "I want a dog."

"You can't be picky when you're swimming alone in the sea of love," he smirks.

"That's a whale of a thing to throw in my face," I shoot back.

"When it comes to love, your ship has sailed."

"Maybe I need to hook up with a Portuguese water dog."

"Why would you want to do that?"

"Because she would always be happy when her sailor was in port."

"Okay," Empty snaps. "I get the picture and there are some pictures that I don't want to visualize. I'm losing my taste for pepperoni."

"Well, let's head on then," I say, "or Jim's going to get paranoid thinking that we're spying on him. There's no sense in stressing him out."

We walk through the gate side by side, and neither one of us are saying anything. I know we're both thinking that we hope we get lucky when we get to Plaza Pizza, and I'm not talking about pepperoni slices. If the two terrier girls are there, this day could turn out to be wild. I've never dated a dog with an accent before.

Empty stops dead in his track and a low growl starts rumbling in his chest. I see the reason he abruptly stopped and why he has his war growl on. Standing in the middle of the street and staring at my buddy's house is the Russian wolfhound called Ivan.

"This is interesting," I say without turning my head to look at Empty.

"It's more than interesting, it's opportunistic," he replies.

I think about the morning the Russians chased me and had me cornered in Ms. Kolinsky's backyard, and I know what Empty is talking about.

"What time is it when two Ruffians chase one Russian?" I ask.

"I don't know," Empty replies.

"Two after one," I scream as I take off running toward the terrorist.

Ivan spots us and takes off running down the center of the street, then darts across to the opposite sidewalk.

"When we get close to him, Bark at him in English," I yell at Empty.

"I don't know any other language," Empty pants.

I'll give Ivan credit for one thing. He can really run when he has to. Empty and I are running all out and while we're gaining on him, it's a slow process.

I see something a few houses down that gives me a glimmer of hope. K.D. Mitchell is standing in her front yard holding her green water hose. Once again, it's not hooked up to the water faucet. She's just standing there, holding her water hose, and watching Ivan streak toward her.

"He's going to have to run by K.D. Mitchell," I gasp. "Maybe she'll take Ivan down for us. Ivan doesn't realize the trouble he's in."

"He's safe," Empty gasps back. "It's not after eleven o'clock yet."

Empty and I dart across the street to the opposite sidewalk, so we'll be on the same side of the street as Ivan.

The Russian streaks by K.D. Mitchell and she smiles sweetly at him. Empty and I rush by a few seconds later, and she glares at me. I stick my tongue out at her.

The terrorist tears around the corner as Empty gleefully yells, "Keep up the pace. We're gaining on him."

Empty and I round the corner and almost stumble over each other as we come to a stop and observe the deserted street. There's no sign of life on the street at all. There's not even any traffic from passing cars. It's like the world has swallowed Ivan alive.

"He's got to be hiding in a side yard or a backyard," I tell Empty.

Empty nods his head and says, "That's what I'm thinking as well. We're going to search all the yards one by one until we find him, and then we're finally going to have some answers."

"It's about time," I reply. "This cat and mouse game has gone on long enough."

Empty and I are both startled as two white, nylon nets drop over our heads, and strong hands grab our collars and start dragging us toward a blue Ford Cargo van.

I can't believe we just got nabbed by the dognappers on what was going to be one of the most important mornings of our lives. Empty is struggling to get away and almost makes his bid for freedom when another set of human hands grab his collar.

"Quit struggling," I tell Empty. "My buddy's phone number is on my dog tags. He'll come bail us out. We don't need to be charged with resisting arrest."

"It's entrapment," Empty snarls. "We weren't bothering any humans."

"Either way, the Russian is gone," I declare. "Let's make the best of it and wait for my buddy."

Empty and I allow ourselves to be placed in a cage inside the van. The dognappers van had two large custom windows installed on both sides of the van. I'm assuming they were there so the dog catchers could keep an eye on their charges when they were outside the van. Or, maybe they were there so the dogs could be tormented and see their loss of freedom.

The cargo van slowly drives by K.D. Mitchell's house. K.D. Mitchell holds the water hose in her left hand, and smiles and waves at us with her right hand.

Empty starts whimpering.

CHAPTER 50

After Empty and I are dognapped by the city workers, we're driven down to the shelter. Empty settles down enough to realize resisting would only make things worse. We're led down a short concrete hallway to a holding cage sufficient for the both of us.

The walk down the hallway is heart breaking as we pass cages filled with dogs barking and yelping at us. Some of the barks sound like the other dogs were happy to finally see a new face in the shelter. The other barks and yelps sound like desperate pleas for help.

Some dogs stare at us with no expression on their faces; it was if they had completely given up on their hopes and dreams. Sometimes life just doesn't turn out the way a dog hopes it will.

"I can't believe they locked us up in a cage like animals," Empty grumbles.

"They're human. They don't know any better," I reply.

"They give us water," Empty says as he stares disdainfully at a silver aluminum water bowl filled halfway with clear water, "but they don't offer to feed us."

"What is it that you think they should give us," I ask. I'm handling being locked up a lot better than Empty. I'm glad now that I watched all those yoga classes on television. It's helping me channel my inner canine and find my happy place.

"Some pizza, Netflix, and a mirror would be nice," Empty grouches.

I don't bother responding to that reply as I cock my head and listen to the barking of the other dogs. "How many of those dogs do you think will be lucky enough to get out of here and adopt a human?" I ask.

Empty looks at me and says, "Not nearly enough."

"Maybe my buddy will be here soon," I say hoping that will cheer up Empty. "He'll probably stop by McDonalds on the way home and buy us some ice cream."

Even the part about the ice cream doesn't cheer up Empty as he snaps, "It had to be K.D. Mitchell that ratted us out. What I can't figure out is why. It wasn't after eleven yet, so she was still supposed to be the nice K.D. Mitchell instead of the mean K.D. Mitchell."

"Well, I might have accidentally stuck my tongue out at her when we ran by."

Empty rolls his eyes and says, "Way to go, fur breath. You should have blown her a kiss instead. What I can't figure out is how she could call the city dognappers, and get them on the scene so quick. She couldn't possibly have had time."

"She probably saw them driving down the street and flagged them down," I suggest.

"Probably," Empty agrees, "but I'm still going to do some seriously revolting stuff to her morning newspaper. I'll wake up early just to do that."

The holding cage is large enough to walk around in, and I walk over to the west side of the cage as I spy an old black Labrador retriever with a muzzle full of gray hair watching us from the holding cage right next door to us.

"Hay said the cow," I say as I walk up to the bars. "What's your name?"

"Larjo," the Labrador replies and he has the saddest eyes I've ever seen on a dog.

"Nice to meet you, Larjo" I respond. "What did you do to get busted and sent here? We were framed. We're waiting on my buddy to find us and take us home."

Larjo drops his head and stares at the floor and whispers in a solemn voice, "I got advanced in years. I got too old to run and play, and when I started having hip problems, a new puppy adopted my buddy and I was brought here. My buddy lied to me and said we were going for a ride in the country, so I could ride with my head hanging out the window and breathe in some fresh country air. Instead, he brought me straight to the canine jail."

"That's awful," Empty says as he walks up. "Maybe you'll have a new buddy soon. It sounds like you're better off without your old buddy, the jerk."

Larjo shakes his head back and forth and says, "Nobody wants to be buddies with an old dog. I'll never get out of here. My buddy brought me here to die."

I look at Empty with an alarmed look on my face. There had to be a way to help Larjo, but I can't think of one.

As if reading my mind, Empty slowly shakes his head back and forth. He can't think of a way to help either.

"It's okay, though," Larjo says. "For the most part, I lived a good life."

My heart's breaking. There has to be some way to help this old dog.

My thoughts are interrupted by the yelling of a familiar voice, "Mixer, where are you, boy? Mixer, where are you?"

I look at Empty who grumbles, "It took him long enough to find us. Yell at him and tell him where we are. No, wait a second. That would freak him out. Bark a couple of times."

I let loose with a couple of loud barks, and the sound reverberates off the walls with a resounding echo.

"Great Lassie in Heaven," Empty gripes, "I think you busted my eardrums."

"There you are, boy," my buddy gasps with a sigh of relief. "I was so worried about you."

The city dognapper unlocks the door of the holding cage and my buddy steps in and throws his arms around my neck. "I was so worried about you," he cries again as he starts rubbing me behind the ears.

Okay, this is getting a little kinky here.

"He's glad to see you," Empty whispers. "It's not foreplay. Wag your tail and act happy and that kind of stuff."

I give my tail a couple of wags.

My buddy picks up the two brown leather leashes he dropped to the floor when he gave me my hug and snaps one each on mine and Empty's collars.

"I've already paid the fines," he says, "so we're free to go. We'll stop by McDonalds on the way, home, and I will buy you two some ice cream."

I give Empty my best I told you so look.

I look over at Larjo, and he's lying on the floor with his eyes closed. I see his sides shuddering, so I know he's sobbing where no one can hear him.

I make a snap decision. I sit down and lean back on the bars while whimpering.

"What is it, Mixer?" my buddy asks. "Is there something wrong?"

I whimper again.

My buddy gives the leash a gentle tug, and I resist it as I lean backward.

Empty lays down on the cold concrete floor and crosses his paws.

"What's going on with you two?" my buddy asks in confusion. "I thought you two would be ready to get out of here and go home."

I look through the bars at Larjo lying in his prone position.

"Oh I think I see," my buddy says as the light bulb in his mind clicks on. "You made a friend in here. Mixer, there's only room at the house for the two of us. We don't have the space for anybody else. That's why I don't have a girlfriend. There's not enough room."

My buddy doesn't have a girlfriend because there's not enough room? All those years of drinking chocolate milk have made him delusional. He wants a girlfriend as badly as I want some movie producer to finally wake up and make a modern Rin Tin Tin movie.

"You understand don't you, Mixer?" my buddy asks in a gentle voice while rubbing my chest. If his hands get any lower somebody is going to get bit, and I'm not talking about me.

I look over at Empty for help, and he mouths the words, "Start howling."

We both start howling.

"Stop it, please stop that," my buddy wails.

We howl louder.

"Okay, okay," my buddy cries. "My mother has been lonely ever since she retired from work. It might be good for her to have a companion. Let me go do the paperwork, and I'll see about taking your friend to my mother's house."

We watch the retreating back of my buddy and Empty says, "I can't believe that crap worked. I'd never bet on it in a million years."

I look over at Larjo, and he's sitting up and staring at us with a glimmer of hope in his eyes. I'm hoping my buddy can pull it off.

An hour later, all three of us are piled in my buddy's car as we drive off from the shelter. My buddy is telling Larjo everything about his mother and the big backyard he can play in. Larjo doesn't want to freak him out and blow this opportunity, so he doesn't say anything back.

I think the best part of the whole day turned out when Larjo had his head hanging out the car's window with ice cream all over his lips, and grinning like a puppy.

CHAPTER 51

After my buddy drops Empty and me off at our homes, he takes off to deliver Larjo to his new home. Larjo has his head hanging out the window and is barking like he's the happiest dog in the world. That's because he is probably the happiest dog in the world. He got busted out of the joint and now is headed to a home where he'll be cherished and loved.

"It kind of leaves a lump in your throat, doesn't it?" Empty says as he watches my buddy's car get smaller in the distance.

"It's funny how things work out," I reply. "If I hadn't stuck my tongue out at K.D. Mitchell, we wouldn't have gotten busted by the goon squad, and Larjo would still be in lockup."

"Yeah," he agreed, "you finally put your tongue to some good use."

"I always put my tongue to good use," I brag.

"That's not what Sally used to say," he shoots back at me.

I don't know what to say to that, so I ignore it. I'll think of a snappy comeback after I have a nice long nap. For some reason, I'm as tired as a dog.

"I'm going to go grab some mirror time," Empty says. "Are you going to be at the meeting tonight?"

"Of course I'm going to be at the meeting," I answer. "We have a lot to talk about."

We paw bump.

I watch Empty walk toward his house and yell, "Hey, Empty?"

"Yeah, what now," he asks without turning around to look at me.

"How can you tell when a sink is exhausted?" I yell.

"I don't know," he hollers backs.

"It's drained," I scream.

Empty still doesn't turn around to look at me, but I see him shaking his head back and forth and muttering to himself as he walks away.

I grin and walk through the open gate, so I can use the doggy door in the back and enter the house. I walk into the kitchen and check my food and water bowls. The water bowl is filled with my daily expectations of clean, fresh water. The food bowl is filled with Dyson's dog food and much to my surprise, there's an additional treat lying on top of the Dyson dog food. There is an Oscar Mayer Cheese Dog wiener neatly sliced into five pieces and laid out in a straight row.

My buddy must have filled the bowls before he embarked on his 'Freedom Journey' to spring me, Empty, and Larjo from the big house. I wolf down the five delicious pieces of cheese wiener, and take a long drink out of my water bowl. I'm surprised again. The water bowl isn't filled with regular tap water. It's filled with bottled Ozarka natural spring water bottled from springs in Texas. My buddy must have really been worried about me to have broken out the imported stuff. I guess he wanted me to come home to a nice surprise.

I walk into the bedroom to take advantage of the time alone and snag a much-needed power nap. I leap on top of the bed and walk around in a couple of small circles on top of the mattress until I find a spot I think will be the most comfortable. It's really a waste of time since I sleep in the exact same spot every time.

I look at my buddy's pillow lying on the side of the bed I allow him to sleep on. After all the heroic actions he performed today, and after having such a wonderful surprise waiting for me when I got home, it would be wrong to mess with his pillow today.

Okay, I can live with being wrong. I use my nose to flip his pillow off the bed and onto the bedroom's olive-green shag carpet floor. He's going to freak.

I must have been more tired than I realized. With all the noises that occur in the neighborhood daily, none of the daily noises wake me up. What brings me out of my sweet slumber, and it was sweetened because I dreamt that Goldie and I were romping together in a flower-filled cow pasture, is my nose.

I wake up with my nose twitching and eagerly sniffing the air. I know why I'm sniffing. I smell bacon. That can only mean one thing. My buddy is cooking us breakfast for supper. We're going to have bacon, biscuits, scrambled eggs, grits, gravy, coffee and milk. Actually, my buddy is going to have all that. All I want is the bacon.

I leap off the bed and notice that my buddy's pillow is not lying on the floor. He must have spotted where I accidentally knocked it off the bed and moved it to a safe place.

I rush into the kitchen without even bothering to check and see which weather girl is on The Weather Channel. I wouldn't mind seeing some nice cumulus clouds, but we're talking bacon. Honest to goodness, thank you Mr. Pig, bacon swimming in a lake of delicious grease.

I rush into the kitchen and skid to a stop when I see my buddy. He's walking around in a long white sleeping gown decorated with a big picture of a blue Huckleberry Hound smiling from the front of the gown. I look down and see he's wearing two pink fluffy house shoes with a gold bell on the toes of each of the shoes.

Okay, Butch would be jealous of the house shoes, but I back up a couple of steps. This is way more than I bargained for. I only came into the kitchen for slaughtered pig.

My buddy sees me, waves a black, plastic spatula in my direction, and says, "There's my sleepyhead. I was wondering when you were going to wake up."

I'm tempted to ask him about his clothing fashion statement, but I know he'll tell me in time, so I don't say anything.

"Mother loved Larjo," he squeals. "The two of them really hit it off. I think they're going to be very happy together."

I'm thrilled for Larjo, but not so much with my buddy for his squealing. If this keeps up, I may have to have him committed. He needs help.

"Mixer, don't you love my outfit," he gasps with a huge smile on his face as he twirls around and the edge of the night gown hanging below his knees flitters in the kitchen air.

I look around the kitchen to see if I can spot any empty bottles of chocolate milk. That would explain everything, but nope, I don't see any sitting around.

"I can explain this outfit," my buddy says.

I wait.

"I read," he continues, "that women love men who are comfortable in their own skin."

Well, duh, I start to tell him. I've never seen a human wearing anybody else's skin.

"Anyway," he carries on as he waves the black spatula around in the air, "the article said that women like men who aren't afraid to experiment in their clothes. So I had this gown and house shoe's custom made, so when I get a girlfriend, I can prove that I'm a modern type of guy."

For my buddy, that line of thinking actually makes sense, so I'm not going to argue with him. I lick my lips and stare at the mound of bacon lying on a nine-inch paper plate on the kitchen counter. A paper towel is underneath the bacon to absorb the grease.

"I've come up with a new idea for a rap song," he tells me in his happy voice.

I close my eyes and groan.

"I'm going to come up with a supper rap song. I don't think anybody has ever done one before. It will be wonderful," he squeals again.

Okay, my buddy has now squealed more times than that fried pig lying on the kitchen counter ever thought about doing.

My buddy starts spinning around the kitchen while rapping into the black plastic spatula he's holding in his right hand.

"I put butter, salt, and pepper on my grits.
Some people use sugar, just a little bit."
I like my eggs scrambled, fluffy and yellow.
Nothing's too good for this hungry fellow.
I like my gravy like I like my girls.
A little spicy, you ought to give it a twirl.
Throw in a red tomato because they don't have a pit.
Then you have a wonderful meal any way you slice it.
I like breakfast for breakfast and breakfast for supper.
I put my leftovers in a bowl made by Tupper.
I like my biscuits flaky and light.
I gotta keep my figure so my jeans don't get tight.
And don't forget about sausage and bacon.
I'm not from Georgia, but I've heard of Macon."

My buddy twirls around and starts twerking in the doorway for the girls on The Weather Channel.

I can't take anymore. It's time to act while his back is turned.

I rush over to the kitchen counter, lean up on it, and grab the mound of bacon in my mouth. My buddy will thank me. He needs to watch his cholesterol.

I'm almost through the doggy door when I hear my buddy wail in despair, "Mixer."

CHAPTER 52

"Thanks for bringing snacks," Empty mumbles around a couple of slices of bacon. "This hickory smoked thick sliced bacon sure hits the spot."

"I saw Rachael cooking with some peppered bacon," Dandy says. "I wouldn't mind trying some of that one day."

"Darling," Butch croons as he brushes some bacon crumbs off the side of his mouth with his right paw, "peppered bacon would absolutely wreak havoc on your sinuses."

"The next time you bring snacks do you think that you could bring some biscuits as well?" Jim asks. "I haven't had a bacon biscuit sandwich in years."

"I'll do my best," I promise."

"I'll bring the snacks tomorrow night," Empty says. "My buddy is planning on having pizza, so I'm sure that I can snag some pieces of pizza crust."

"Pizza was originally flat bread," Jim says as he breaks into one of his famous lectures. "The term pizza was actually used in 997 AD in a place called Gaeta, Italy. The Romans used bread called focaccia, but the Romans referred to it as panis focacius. Focaccia is Italian flat bread baked in the oven which is similar in style and texture to pizza dough. The Romans would add toppings to their bread. In 1889, a pizza was made for Margherita of Savoy, the Queen consort of Italy, garnished with tomatoes, mozzarella, and basil to represent the national colors of the Italian flag. By the late 18th century, the poor people around Naples were adding tomato to their yeast-based flat bread, and the modern pizza began."

Empty looks over at Dandy and says, "Wow."

"I've only scratched the service," Jim says. "The subject is so fascinating that I could go on about it all night. Did you know that tomatoes were brought to Europe in the 16th century from the Americas, and many Europeans originally refused to eat them because they thought the tomato was a poisonous plant?"

"Darling, that's so interesting," Butch yawns, "but let's continue this conversation tomorrow night when we're actually munching on pizza crust."

"Okay," Jim says as he pushes his glasses back up his nose and starts energetically scratching at a flea roaming behind his left ear.

I look over at Butch and say, "My buddy has a pair of pink fuzzy house slippers with a gold bell attached to the toes."

A dreamy look crosses Butch's face as he gushes, "That is so positively to die for. I simply must see them one day. Can you imagine climbing in between the sheets while wearing those at a Holiday Inn Express with a giant French poodle? It would absolutely drive Alphonse crazy. That yummy making session would probably straighten out the curls in his fur."

Empty starts making gagging sounds.

"Oh please grow up," Butch tells Empty. "Besides, what's this rumor I heard about you and Mixer getting busted and then rescuing a senior citizen from the shelter?"

"It's no rumor," Empty replies. "We got nabbed this afternoon, and Mixer's buddy came and got us. While we were being wrongly incarcerated, we met a senior black Labrador retriever named Larjo. Mixer's buddy bailed him out of the joint as well, and then the buddy dropped us off at the house and carried Larjo away."

Butch looks over at me and says, "Please explain, sweets."

I shrug my shoulders and say, "My buddy decided to let Larjo adopt his mother. He'll have a nice house to live in and a large backyard to roam around and warm himself in the sun."

"That is so lovely," Butch smiles. "I'm glad when we adopt senior citizen humans. The poor things don't often realize how much they depend on us. However, I'm curious as to what circumstances warranted you two being nailed. Y'all are usually much more careful than that."

"We were chasing one of the terrorists," Empty says as if that should explain everything.

The smile immediately leaves Butch's face as he stares at Empty. "That's not something I was aware of. Why were you two dear boys chasing the terrorist all by yourselves?"

"We caught him in front of my buddy's house," I speak up. "It's like he was trying to make plans of some sort. We hoped to catch him and finally get some answers."

"This changes everything," Butch says as he narrows his eyes. "If they're bold enough to come where we live, then I feel our passive approach to this situation must be addressed in a more aggressive manner."

"Are we finally going to take off the kid gloves and get serious about this thing?" Empty asks with an eager gleam in his eyes and hope in his voice.

"Darling," Butch replies in a monotone voice. "We're going to take off the gloves, boots, and dog tags. "I'm afraid that they have positively made it personal now."

"So, you think this big thing that is supposed to come down is because of the Russian wolfhounds and not the Fang Mafia?" I ask.

"Oh, we're going to inquire about the activities of the Fang Mafia as well," Butch says while casting a worried look over in Jim and Dandy's direction. "We might have to enlist the aid of our friend, Truck, and utilize some of his resources."

Jim and Dandy catch the worried gaze Butch gives then and Dandy says, "You don't have to worry about us. We know how to fight."

"And," Jim says, "I've been watching some mixed martial arts matches on cable. I think I've watched enough of them on television to pull out a few surprise moves."

Butch's eyes soften as he says, "I know you two darlings know how to fight and aren't afraid to, but I'm hoping we can head this off so you don't have to fight."

Empty looks over at me and says, "Do you want me to look Truck up tomorrow and see what kind of help he can give us?"

"No," Butch says while clearing his throat, "The two of you need to look Truck up tomorrow. I think it would be best if we always stay in at least pairs for the time being. We need to utilize that old motto of: There is safety in numbers."

"Good point," I say.

Empty looks over at me and asks, "Is noonish a good time for you? I want to catch some mirror time in the morning, and then we can head out. Truck's usually somewhere close to the park around noon."

"That works for me," I say. "It'll give me an excuse to sleep in."

"When have you ever needed an excuse?" he counters.

"I'm always up before you," I counter his counter.

"I'll see what I can find on Google," Jim says.

"I won't spend all day watching Rachael," Dandy volunteers.

"Good, we have a plan," Butch says. "Now let's not patrol and call it a night, so we can all catch a good night's sleep."

"Let's do it," Dandy yelps.

We gather around, do a group high five and yell, "We are The Ruffians."

CHAPTER 53

Vicktor, Boris, and Ivan sat beside the large green trash dumpster sitting behind Crashaw's Crab Castle, while munching on tossed crab cakes from the noon's daily buffet.

"I always love it when I find a decent seafood restaurant," Ivan said around of a mouthful of broiled crabmeat.

"This place doesn't spare any expense," Vicktor observed, as he started in on his third crab cake. "They definitely use Alaskan king crab meat in their cakes. If I had a touch of Worcestershire sauce to put on top of them, I would rate these as the best crab cakes I have ever eaten, and I've eaten my fill of crab cakes."

"They are good," Boris agreed, "but I was hoping we might be able to score some salmon tonight. They say you should eat fish twice a week."

"I'm not sure if that applies to dogs," Ivan argued.

"Can't we just enjoy a nice meal out without arguing?" Vicktor asked.

"You're right," Ivan said.

"Hey, Ivan," Boris asked. "Could you please pass me one of those French fries lying beside that water puddle behind your hind feet?"

"No problem," Ivan replied while taking another bite of his crab cake without making any movement toward passing Boris any of the French fries.

"Jerk," Boris muttered under his breath.

"Well, Ivan, do you have any news to share with us?" Vicktor asked.

Ivan looked around to make sure any unfriendly ears weren't listening and then whispered in a low conspiratorial voice, "I'll take out the beagle tomorrow. By this time tomorrow, The Ruffians will be minus one dog."

"Excellent," Vicktor proclaimed. "There are those who will be pleased to hear the good news. This should be the beginning of the end for The Ruffians."

"What are the odds for a successful execution?" Boris asked in a matter of fact tone.

Ivan smiled and said, "The beagle will never know what happened."

CHAPTER 54

The Godfather was a happy dog. He was laid back with his head in Sally's lap while Sally was dipping into a can of Honey Boy Pink Salmon and feeding The Godfather tiny bites of the delicious and moist, but unfortunate fish. Tiny rivers of juice ran down the sides of The Godfather's mouth as he smacked and licked his lips in total contentment.

The Fang Mafia was scattered around the yard in prone positions, and all were wearing the satisfied smiles of a job well done.

"Everything is set, boss," Blackjack stated. "We're taking the beagle down tomorrow. Twenty-four hours henceforth we can officially quit worrying about The Ruffians sticking their noses in places they don't belong."

"I still want to take out Mixer," Carjack drawled. "After what he did to my danglers, he deserves everything that he has coming to him."

"I've been thinking about that," The Godfather slowly spoke in the tone of someone who doesn't have a care in the world. "After we finish our job, you can take out Mixer as a bonus."

"Thanks, boss," Carjack gratefully acknowledged.

"You're such a bad boy," Sally purred into The Godfather's ear. "I love it. What are you going to do with the beagle's body?"

"Well," The Godfather asked through half-closed eyes to no one in particular. "Where are you going to hide the body?"

"There's that patch of woods east of the city's landfill," Slapjack spoke up. "It's overrun with bushes, vines, and snakes. Nobody, neither canine nor human, ever goes in there, so we think that will be the perfect spot. Jim will disappear to never be seen again."

"This is so exciting," Sally purred. "I simply must be allowed to see this. Even though I wish it was Mixer, it's going to be a dream come true to see The Ruffians suffer. I love it. I simply do. I think the thug life is what I was born to do."

"You're such an evil, twisted creature," The Godfather replied. "It makes me wonder where you've been all my life."

Sally bent down and kissed The Godfather on the forehead as she fed him another morsel of the delicious salmon who would have much rather been swimming upriver instead of in The Godfather's happy little stomach.

"I can't believe all this is finally coming true," Hijack spoke up. "All those months of planning are finally starting to pay off. This town is going to be ours."

"And I'm going to be the first lady of the most notorious gang in animal history," Sally cooed. "I almost get weepy with joy just thinking about it."

"If Carjack gets to take out Mixer, I should be allowed to take out Empty," Blackjack complained. "He's been a thorn in my side for years."

"We've come too far to let personal feelings get in the way," The Godfather admonished. "When all is said and done The Ruffians and every other dog in town will be permanently out of our way. You're going to have to be happy with that."

"Yeah, you're right," Blackjack agreed while licking his lips, and staring at the can of Honey Boy Pink Salmon.

Sally caught him staring at the can and coughed up a hair ball in his direction. "This salmon is for The Godfather," she hissed. "If you want fish, go find your own."

"Well, what about those wolfhounds we've been hearing about?" Slapjack inquired. "Has anybody heard why they're here?"

"Maybe they're tourists," Hijack volunteered.

"Please explain yourself," The Godfather mumbled around a mouthful of the now definitely not happy about the situation fish.

"Remember that old movie theater, *The Myric*, which shut down a couple of summers ago?" Hijack asked looking around at the faces of his partners in crime.

"What does a movie theater have to do with the wolfhounds?" Blackjack snapped.

"If you'll quit interrupting, I'll tell you," Hijack growled.

"I love watching furry testosterone levels at play," Sally purred. "You boys are making me weak in my knees."

Hijack ignored the feline barb and said, "They've reopened last year. Now they show old movies in it on the weekends."

"I think I see where you're going with this," Slapjack joined in. "I hadn't thought about it, but you might have a point worth considering."

"Would you two start making some type of sense before you give me a headache?" Carjack pleaded. "What does a movie theater have to do with anything?"

"They're having a James Bond marathon every weekend this month," Hijack replied.

"So, it could be the wolfhounds are in town so they can watch *From Russia with Love* as many times as they want for the price of one ticket."

"How have you boys made it this far without someone doing the thinking for you?" Sally hissed as she dropped another tidbit of salmon in The Godfather's open mouth.

"What are you talking about, Sally?" Hijack asked as he looked around in confusion at the other three members of the Fang Mafia.

Blackjack, Carjack, and Slapjack all shrugged their shoulders as they looked back at Hijack. They were as confused as anyone else by Sally's statement.

"Think about it," Sally spat out in an impatient voice. "The only candy they sell at the Myric's concession counter is Milk Duds, and you know that dogs can't eat chocolate."

"You have a point," Hijack reluctantly agreed.

"They don't sell popcorn?" Carjack asked in mild confusion.

"Popcorn isn't candy," Slapjack admitted.

"It is if it's candy corn," Hijack argued.

"You don't pop candy corn," Blackjack all knowingly pointed out.

"Does it matter?" Sally asked. "Those Russians aren't in town to go to the movies, and I can't believe you four didn't spend more time trying to figure out who they really are."

"We've been too busy making plans to take Jim out of the picture," Blackjack argued in protest. "That's what the boss wants. The beagle will never know what hit him."

"It really doesn't matter," The Godfather mumbled through half-closed eyelids in total contentment. "They haven't interfered with our plans. If they stick their noses in our business, we'll take care of them. If they haven't pulled any funny business yet, I don't think they're going to. We probably worried over nothing."

"Yes, boss," the Fang Mafia replied in unison.

"Open wide, honey blossom," Sally purred.

The Godfather opened his mouth, and Sally dropped the last bite of juicy salmon into The Godfather's mouth.

CHAPTER 55

As much as Jim loved his fellow Ruffians, he enjoyed his few minutes of time alone in the morning. It gave him time to plan out his day and ruminate about the various events happening to the world. He liked to keep abreast of the things that were happening in the human's world even if the other guys didn't pay much attention to it.

He wasn't worried about having his time alone disturbed. Dandy would head straight for the television as soon as his paws hit the floor. Butch liked to sleep in, though Butch had an inner psychic alarm clock, so if he didn't sense Jim back in the house at a certain time he would come looking for him. Jim was on the receiving end of more than one gentle scolding about the dangers of staying outside too long by himself in the backyard.

Dandy liked to sleep in as much as Butch, and after waking, Empty would grab a few serious hours of mirror time so he could admire his own body.

The only Ruffian that might disturb Jim was Mixer since Mixer was an early riser. Mixer generally allowed Jim his few minutes of time alone without disturbing him, but no one at any time knew what Mixer was going to do, Jim contemplated. Jim amended that to no one had a clue what Mixer was going to do or say.

Jim was thinking about the special he watched about outlaws and gunfighters on The Western Channel the night before. He was surprised to learn that some of the more famous people truthfully weren't good shots, and their reputations were over inflated and in some cases completely made up. He wondered if a Hollywood producer was ever going to make a western about how the Old West honestly was.

His main concern this morning was that his buddy didn't leave his laptop computer turned on when he left for work. Jim wanted to see what news he could find on Google, and he wasn't a big fan of using the desktop computer. It was hard to keep his balance in the black leather office swivel chair. Plus, Dandy liked to run by and spin the chair around in circles at the most unsuspecting moments.

His thoughts were interrupted by the sound of someone saying, "Good Morning, Jim, what's up? And please don't say the ceiling like Mixer always does."

Jim spun around, and his eyes lit up with happiness at the sight of Truck walking toward him. Truck had always been one of his non-Ruffian favorite dogs.

"Hi, Truck," he said. "I'm enjoying a few minutes of solitude before the rest of the guys wake up. Once they're awake time alone is over with."

"Oh, I'm sorry," Truck apologized. "If you want me to, I'll leave. I know how well it is to have time alone. It's important to take advantage of it when you get the opportunity."

"No, you're fine," Jim said as he pushed his glasses back up his nose. "We really don't get a chance to talk very often on a one to one basis. Besides, what brings you over to this side of town so early in the day?"

"I wanted to take a stroll and see how the other half lived," Truck lied while snapping at a horsefly buzzing about his head.

"Well, we have a few minutes to talk before Butch comes looking for me," Jim admitted.

"Does Butch come looking for you very often?" Truck casually asked while licking his lips, and casting a nervous glance toward the backdoor of the house.

"I don't know how he does it," Jim said, "but if he senses I've been in the backyard too long by myself, he'll come get me and then go back to bed."

"Yeah, you and Dandy are really lucky to have Butch watching over the two of you," Truck stated. "Most dogs don't have that kind of protection."

"It's not protection," Jim laughed. "He does it because we're family."

"I'm surprised Mixer isn't out and about," Truck casually mentioned. "He seems like he's never been one to let the bone get buried too deep."

"He's probably awake," Jim admitted, "but he's good about not disturbing my time alone. He and Empty were up this time yesterday, but they left me alone. I think they had something they wanted to do."

"Empty was up as well?" Truck asked with more than a hint of nervousness in his voice.

"Yeah, but that's the exception and not the rule," Jim replied.

"What's this about Empty and Mixer got busted by the city dognappers yesterday? Is there any truth to that story, or is it just another street rumor?"

"No, it's true," Jim said while glancing toward the backdoor of the house. It had almost reached the point where Butch would be coming out to look for him, and he was really enjoying the opportunity to chat with Truck one on one.

"I'm surprised, they got busted," Truck admitted. "They are both too street savvy to allow something like that to happen to them."

"Normally, I would agree, but they caught one of the Russian terrorists in front of Mixer's house, and they got distracted while trying to catch him."

Truck's eyes widen a little as he asked, "One of the wolfhounds was here in the neighborhood?"

"Yeah," Jim said, "but I don't think we'll see any of them around here again."

Truck glanced toward the backdoor of the house again, and this time he detected some shadowy movement alongside the corner of the house. It was time. The hit was going down, and he needed to be gone before Butch or any of the other Ruffians showed up. He needed some way to distract Jim.

"Is that honeysuckle growing on the top of the back fence?" Truck asked while hoping Jim's natural love of science would provide the distraction.

"It is," Jim proudly stated. "That particular vine is a *Lonicera canadensis* also known as the American fly honeysuckle."

"That's amazing," Truck said. "I didn't realize there was more than one type of honeysuckle. I thought a honeysuckle was a honeysuckle."

"There have been one-hundred and eighty species of honeysuckle identified around the world, "Jim bragged while once again pushing his glasses back up his nose. "It's a fascinating subject. The name Lonicera is actually derived from a Renaissance botanist Adam Lonicer."

Truck caught the rush of movement out of the corner of his eye and turned his head, so he wouldn't see the hit go down. It was too late to stop it now.

"Honeysuckle is widely valued as a garden plant," Jim continued without being aware of anything unusual happening.

Truck was wishing now he had never made the deal. Jim didn't deserve this.

Truck closed his eyes and shuddered at Jim's surprised yelp.

Then the only sound was the sound of Jim's body making a soft thud as it slumped to the grassy carpet. The silence was deafening.

CHAPTER 56

I've been lying awake in bed for a couple of hours because sometime during the night, I found that comfortable spot where you don't move. If I wasn't thirsty, I'd stay in a bed a couple more hours. I stand up on the mattress and look at the room. I don't see anything I can knock off onto the floor. Even my buddy's pillow is missing from the bed. So he thinks that he has Mixer proofed the room. Two can play that game. I hope he realizes that he's gotten himself into a war that he has no hopes of winning.

I give my hips a couple of shakes and leap from the bed onto the olive-green shag carpet. Instead of heading for the living room, I walk down the short hallway and enter the bathroom on the right side of the hall. I look around the small bathroom, and I spot my treasure in the human waste recycling center.

My buddy's Oral-B battery toothbrush with disposable bristles is lying on top of the sink beside the ceramic Donald Duck soap holder. I glance over at the toilet and see that my luck is even better than I can hope for. The toilet lid is open. I do some quick mental calculations, make some adjustments for the angle of the drop, place my nose at a ninety-degree angle on the left side of the toothbrush, take a deep breath, slowly exhale for three seconds, hold my breath, and flick my nose sideways.

The toothbrush looks like the spinning rotors of a Westland Lynx helicopter as it spins through the air and lands inside the toilet bowl with a loud plop as drops of water splash up out of the bowl and onto the beige linoleum covered floor. My work here is done. I can't help but feel a sense of pride in a job well done. My buddy is gonna freak.

I leave the bathroom and head down the hallway toward the living room. I stop dead in my tracks in the living room. My buddy left the television turned on, and I stare at the girl on The Weather Channel. Wow. She's talking about a warm front passing through the Midwest and I can see why. I wouldn't mind having her warm front pass over me.

I reluctantly tear myself away from the television to go inspect my food and water bowls in the kitchen. The water bowl, as usual, is filled with clean, fresh water. I check my food bowl. I'm hoping for barbeque or some Kentucky Fried Chicken. I feel like a baseball player because when I look in my food bowl, I know that I've struck out. The bowl is filled to the brim with brown chicken flavored soybean nuggets. The dry dog food isn't even Dyson's dog food. I use my nose to flip the bowl and watch as the nuggets scatter all across the kitchen floor. While my buddy is sweeping up the mess, he might as well get on his knees and use his toothbrush to scrub the cracks on the floor. I doubt that he's going to use it to brush his teeth anymore.

I'm thinking about what else I can get into when my thoughts are interrupted by the terrible sounds of someone screaming in pain. I cock my head as the screams begin again, and then I realize the sounds of anguish are coming from Butch's buddy's backyard.

I rush through the doggy door and out of the corner of my eye, I see Empty leaping over the chain-link fence into my buddy's backyard. He must have heard the screams at the same time I did. I rush down the back steps and, side by side, Empty and me race across my buddy's backyard and leap over the fence and into Butch's backyard.

Butch's face is contorted into a mask of rage as he holds a screaming Dandy against his body. It's heartbreaking to see the look of grief on Dandy's face, and his awful screams feel like they're tearing my soul apart. I glance at Empty and I notice the tears in his eyes so I know Empty feels the same way I do.

"What's this about?" Empty finally chokes out in a muffled voice.

"Look on the ground," Butch sobs as he pulls Dandy tighter to him while Dandy screams in anguish again.

Empty and I look down on the lawn and notice Jim's broken glasses lying beside a note scrawled in barely legible handwriting. Empty and I lean down to read the note.

Dear Ruffians,

We got the beagle. That's why we left his glasses. If you don't want the same thing happening to you, quit trying to find out why the squirrels in the park have no nuts. Their nuts are none of your business. We have our eyes on you. If we think, you're still trying to stick your nose in business that doesn't concern you, the other beagle will get it next. Then we will take care of the rest of you one by one. You don't know the powers you are messing with. The beagle never stood a chance. Just remember, Jim is a good dog, but if you don't listen to us, he'll be doggone.

Have a nice day,

The bad dogs.

Empty looks at me with wide eyes as we straighten up and whispers in a hoarse voice, "Great Lassie in Heaven, I never thought that it would happen to one of us."

"I didn't either," I reply while trying to hold back a sob.

"We're never going to be able to yell we are The Ruffians again," Dandy wails. "Why would they do this to Jim? Why would they do that to my best friend?"

Empty looks at Butch and says, "We're going to find out who did this, and then we're going to have our revenge."

"You can positively count on it," Butch sobs.

Empty and I gather around and try to console Dandy the best we can.

Empty looks at me and says, "Don't even think about making a joke."

"There's no way that's going to happen," I answer.

"I know," he says while nodding his head. "I don't know what I'm saying. I'm confused about who would want to do this to Jim, and my heart feels like it's breaking into a million pieces."

"I feel the same way," I respond. "I can't believe any of this."

"I'm going to take Dandy into the house and put him to bed," Butch mumbles in a soft voice while rubbing his nose with his paw. "I need to see if I can get him to rest for a while."

"That's a good idea," Empty says. "Mixer and I are going to hit the streets and start asking questions. We're going to find whoever did this."

"We'll check on you two when we get back," I add. "If we find someone who had anything to do with this and Empty goes berserk, I'm not going to try to stop him."

"Please don't," Butch says in a stronger tone of voice, "but remember when we find out who the ringleader is behind all this, he's mine. I don't see a very bright future in store for him."

"You got it," Empty and I reply in unison.

We watch Butch lead a sobbing Dandy back into the house, and the back door closes slowly behind them.

"I'm not sure that's a promise I can keep to Butch," Empty softly says.

"You better," I reply in a sad voice. "Jim was like his son."

Empty looks at me and growls, "Are you ready to go kick some butt?"

"Yep, I'm a lean, mean butt kicking machine!"

CHAPTER 57

Empty and I are standing by the bleachers of the west soccer field and watching a speeding hotdog hurtling toward us across the field at breakneck speed.

"I'm not in a mood to put up with a talking hotdog this morning," Empty says.

"Well, you never have kicked his buns," I say. "This might be a good time to start."

"Gosh, I never expected to see you two here this morning," Ed from Puerto Rico gasps as he slides to a stop in front of Empty and me.

"We really weren't planning on being here this morning," Empty says without volunteering any more information.

"I don't guess that you've seen any Russian wolfhounds walking in the park this morning," I ask Ed and hope that the answer is yes.

"No," Ed says while shaking his head back and forth. "You two are the first dogs that I've seen at the park all morning."

I look at Empty and say, "If no dogs are in the park this morning, there must be a lock down happening all over town. They're afraid to come outside."

"Is it really true?" Ed asks.

"Is what true?" Empty inquires. "True is often determined on who is saying what."

"That's too complicated for me to gnaw on," Ed admits, "but is it true that something happened to one of The Ruffians?"

Empty looks at me and says, "The word's already out on the street. That's going to make our job harder. Most dogs are staying behind locked doors, and the ones we're after are just going to go deeper into hiding."

"They're not going to hide deep enough," I brag. "We'll catch them."

"Possibly Truck knows something," Empty replies. "When we find him, perhaps he'll be able to feed us some new information."

"I'm so sorry," Ed says. "I never thought anything would happen to a Ruffian."

"It's okay," Empty gruffly answers. "I guess it was bound to happen one day."

"You and Truck have become pals," I tell Ed. "Have you seen him this morning?"

Ed looks at me with serious eyes and says, "No, and that is strange. Usually, we have a little chat in the morning. I hope nothing happened to him."

"That's great," Empty grumbles. "Our best source of getting any information isn't around either. We're going to have to track him down."

"Our tracker is out of commission," I point out.

"You goofball," Empty says. "We're dogs. We ought to be able to sniff him out."

"Yeah, if we knew a good starting point of where to begin," I reply.

Empty shrugs his shoulders and replies, "You might have a point, fur breath."

"Where's Goldie?" I casually ask Ed while hopefully looking around. She's one of the few dogs that look just as good either coming or going.

"She says that she's not coming outside until this mystery is solved," Ed tells me. "I'll stop by her buddy's house later this morning for some pizza and Kibbles' n Bits."

"You're a lucky dog," I say.

"Don't I know it," Ed replies.

"Ed, why are you out at the park?" Empty impulsively asks.

"Oh, I had to take my buddy for a walk this morning," Ed answers. "He was getting restless being cooped up in the house, so I thought a walk would do him good."

"Yeah," I agree. "You have to walk them daily, or they get bent out of shape."

"You never walk your buddy," Empty says.

"I can never get him away from The Weather Channel long enough to walk him," I protest. "Besides, until he gets his chocolate milk problem under control, it might be best not to bring him out in public."

"I forgot about that," Empty admits. "For once in your life, you might be right."

"I've got to go," Ed yells as he whirls around and takes off running across the soccer field in the opposite direction.

"He can run," I say. "I wish I had his energy."

About that time, Ed looks over his right shoulder and yells, "Good luck, guys. I hope you find the lowlife who took Jim out of the picture."

"That's very interesting," I say while looking at Empty.

"There's nothing interesting about a speeding hotdog," Empty grouses.

"For once, think with your head and not your muscles," I scold.

"What's that supposed to mean," Empty snaps. "Who died and made you Albert Einstein?"

"He said, 'Good luck on finding who took Jim out of the picture'. We never mentioned any names. How did he know that it was Jim? It could have just as easily been Dandy."

"You have a point," Empty muses out loud while rubbing his chin with his paw.

"Well, he's gone now," I say. "We'll ask him about it the next time we see him. Besides, we probably need to head back and check on Butch and Dandy. I feel like a Whirlpool washing machine standing out here."

"What's that supposed to mean?" Empty asks.

"It means the park was a total washout," I reply.

"Yeah," Empty grunts. "Let's head back and check on those two, and then I think we need to make a visit to Little Italy and see The Godfather."

"Cool," I say. "I'm in the mood for some Italian."

Empty and I are walking back home in silence when I ask him, "Empty?"

"Yeah?"

"Why did the hotdog get the hamburger pregnant?"

"I don't know," Empty admits.

"Because it forgot to use a condiment," I holler.

"That is so lame," he grumbles.

"It wasn't that bad," I protest. "I've told worse."

We keep walking in silence, and then I hear Empty snickering under his breath.

"What are you snickering about?" I ask.

"I was thinking about your hamburger joke," he admits.

"Well, I hope it got your mind off of our miseries for a couple of minutes," I say.

"That it did," he admits.

"Then it worked."

"Thanks, Mixer."

"You're welcome, Empty."

We paw bump.

Then we walk the rest of the way home in silence.

CHAPTER 58

Empty and I got back to Butch's buddy's house and found Butch sitting all alone and staring at the note still lying upon the ground.

He looks up at us with sad eyes and softly asks, "How did it go at the park?"

"It didn't go at the park," Empty replies. "The only dog we saw was Ed from Puerto Rico. It looks like the word is out on the street about what happened to Jim, so all the dogs in town are staying inside. It looks like a complete and total canine lock down."

"How's Dandy doing?" I ask.

Butch slowly shakes his head back forth as he says, "The little darling isn't doing well at all. I put him to bed and finally got him to fall asleep. I'm going to keep him inside for a couple of days. I think he needs a lot of bedrest."

"That's a good idea," I agree. "It's going to take us all a long time to get over what happened. I'm not sure Dandy will ever get over losing Jim."

Empty and I involuntarily take a step backward when Butch glares at us with the coldest set of eyes I've ever seen in a dog. "I know of some others who will never get over what happened," he harshly whispers. "When we find the ones responsible for poor Jim's demise, I'm going to make sure they are never capable of getting over anything again."

"That's already a given," Empty replies. "Since we didn't discover anything at the park, Mixer and I are going to snoop around The Godfather's place and see what we can find out in Little Italy. There has to be a clue somewhere. We just have to find it."

A wary look enters Butch's eyes as he says, "Darling, I'm not sure that's a good idea. If there is any trouble, the Fang Mafia will have you badly outnumbered. I can't leave Dandy, so it's going to be a couple of days before I can help in the investigation."

"You don't have to worry," I say. "We're only going to snoop around. If it looks like there is going to be a confrontation, we'll back off and leave."

"I'm still not sure about this," Butch admits. "Empty can be a hothead at the most inopportune time, and you have a tendency to instigate trouble."

Once again, I'm reminded why my decision to drop out of obedience school was a poor choice. I have no idea what a tendency is.

"We'll be careful," Empty promises. "We'll be in and out without anybody ever knowing we're there."

"I'm still not certain about this," Butch replies while looking Empty and me in the eyes. "If anything should happen to either one of you, I'm positively not confident that I would be able to handle it. I've already lost one dear friend who I love deeply. I'm not sure I could take losing another loved one so soon."

Empty and I start looking everywhere but at Butch when he starts using the 'L' word.

"Wow, look at that one cloud floating over the Malone's house," I say, "It kind of looks like Elvis. I've never seen that before."

"I see what you're talking about," Empty replies. "Thank you for pointing that out. Thank you very much. Well, that gust of wind took care of that cloud formation. It broke it up."

"Elvis has left the building," I answer.

"You two beat all I've ever seen," Butch scolds. "Somebody says love around either one of you, and you both get nervous and shaky."

"Don't worry, we're going to be careful snooping around The Godfather's house," Empty says to change the subject.

"Well, if you must do it, please be careful," Butch sighs in resignation.

"We will," I answer. "Just take care of Dandy."

"Oh you can count on that, darling. You can positively count on it," Butch answers as he looks me in the eyes. The cold set of eyes are back in his expression. I know what that means. Before all this is done and over with somebody is going to get seriously hurt.

"Let's go, fur breath," Empty tells me as we paw bump with Butch.

We take our time walking toward The Godfather's house. Neither one of us can think of any reason to rush the trip. The Godfather isn't going anywhere.

We're slowly strolling down the sidewalk when we spot K.D. Mitchell on the other side of the street. She's standing in her front yard holding her green water hose, which once again isn't hooked up to the faucet, and glaring at us.

Empty glares back at her and tells me, "I don't care if it is after eleven in the morning, and she's the mean K.D. Mitchell. If we didn't have business to attend to, I'd go take care of K.D. Mitchell right now for causing us to get busted."

"I hear ya," I agree, "but I guess she's the reason Larjo gained his freedom. If we hadn't got busted, he would still be locked up in the big house."

"There is that," Empty grudgingly admits.

Empty and I walk in silence the rest of the way to Little Italy. We don't have to talk. I know that we're both thinking of Jim, and how much we miss our buddy.

We're in for a rude awakening when we finally reach The Godfather's home. The place looks like it's been deserted. There's no sign of The Godfather or the Fang Mafia. There's an empty can of Honey Boy Pink Salmon lying beside the corner of The Godfather's doghouse, but other than that, it looks completely abandoned.

"This is weird," Empty mutters to himself. "It looks like they all packed up and left."

"Yeah, I'm glad we're not math teachers," I say.

Empty looks at me, cocks his head, and asks, "What's that supposed to mean?"

"It means something isn't adding up," I say.

Empty ignores that remark as a curious expression crosses his face and says, "Think about it. Somebody put a hit out on Jim. Now both the terrorists and The Godfather and his goons are nowhere to be found. Do you think they might have been working together, and we were wrong the whole time thinking that they were on opposite sides?"

"I'm going to check out the inside of the doghouse," I tell Empty. "Maybe they left something behind that will help us."

"Good idea," Empty says. "While you're checking the inside of the doghouse, I'll be seeing what I can find out here."

I wiggle inside the doghouse and one of the first things I notice is the scent of Sally's odor lingering in the air. So Sally and The Godfather must have really been doing the furry rub with each other after all. I feel a slight twinge of jealousy.

Then I spot something laying on the plywood floor in the far corner of the doghouse which makes my heart leap for joy. "I found something," I yell at Empty. "It's awesome."

"What did you find," he yells back.

I can barely contain the glee in my voice as I holler, "A cd of 'The Doobie Brothers Greatest Hits'. I'm keeping this."

"You're going to make me a copy of it," Empty says as I wiggle back out of The Godfather's former abode.

"Did you find anything?" I ask as I stand up and look around the deserted yard.

"I got nothing," he says. "I'm having a hard time believing The Godfather would skip town. All he ever wanted to do was be the biggest dogfish in the pond."

"And own a nice home with dogwood trees around," I add.

"We might as well call it a day," Empty says. "We need to be around in case Butch or Dandy needs us."

"Maybe we can find Truck tomorrow, and hopefully he'll have something that we can use to figure this whole mess out."

"I'm serious about you burning me a copy of that cd," Empty says. "I like classic rock as much as you do, and you know I love The Doobie Brothers."

"You got it," I say.

We walk home singing in loud voices for the world to hear.

"I'd like to hear some funky Dixieland.
Pretty mama come and take me by the hand.
By the hand, take me by the hand, pretty mama.
Come and dance with your daddy all night long.
I want to honky tonk, honky tonk, honky tonk.
With you all night long."

CHAPTER 59

I use the doggy door to enter the house. As I'm entering, I hear the sounds of The Weather Channel blaring from the television in the living room. That doesn't bother me. What bothers me is the empty drinking glass I see on the kitchen counter.

The inside of the glass has a dark stain on it. That can only mean one thing. My buddy has already been into the chocolate milk. And if he didn't eat lunch that means he's been drinking on an empty stomach. I'm tempted to turn around and leave. I don't know what I'm going to find in the living room. I have a feeling that it isn't going to be pretty.

I walk through the doorway into the living room and stop and stare at my buddy. He's wearing a pair of faded blue jeans, red, plastic flip-flops, and no shirt. I'm glad Empty and I didn't stop for a quick bite of lunch. After seeing my buddy sitting in his recliner shirtless, I'm not sure that I would be able to keep anything down that was in my stomach.

My buddy notices me staring at him out of the corner of his eye and says, as he turns to look at me, "Hi, Mixer, I haven't been into the chocolate milk."

I don't know what I'm going to do about his denial. Now he's outright lying to me. Even if he hadn't said a word, the chocolate mustache above his upper lip would have gotten him busted. He still hasn't learned to hide the evidence.

I decide to deal with all those issues at a later date. Right now, I'm curious why my buddy is holding a banjo across his lap. I mentally run a million scenarios through my mind, and none of them turn out well. I'm not sure what my buddy is up to, but I'm pretty sure that I'm not going to like it. Instead of asking, I decide to wait for an explanation.

"Mixer, I bought a banjo," he says.

Well, that's great. The useless fountain of information spouts again. I've already figured out that he bought a banjo. I want to know the reason why he bought a banjo.

He smiles and says, "I've been thinking."

I close my eyes and stifle a groan. Here we go again.

"There's a possibility that my Butterscotch Ivory rap career might not work out. I have to be realistic about making it big in the entertainment industry."

I open my eyes and stare at him. Okay, he's making sense so far. Maybe we're on the verge of putting his dreams of stardom behind us.

"That's why I bought a banjo," he proudly states. "If Butterscotch Ivory doesn't work out, I'm going to have another on stage persona as a substitute plan."

I roll my eyes and don't even try to hide the groan this time.

"I don't think there's anybody doing banjo rap," he says in a sincere voice. "So I'm going to be the pioneer of banjo rap. I'm going to call myself the Banjo Bangster. Instead of being a gangster, I'll be a Bangster because I have a banjo."

I bet if I check the half-gallon of chocolate milk inside the refrigerator, I'll find it completely empty. He's really deep in the sauce this time.

He runs his fingers over the strings of the banjo, and it makes a banjo sound.

"That's what you call plucking," he tells me in his all-knowing voice. "You pluck a banjo. That's why when I'm on stage, I'll have all the pretty women join me, and everybody can watch us pluck together. People are going to pay to watch me, and beautiful girls, pluck."

I sit down, hard. As far as I know my buddy has never plucked once in his life, and now he expects people to pay to watch him pluck on stage?

"All the ladies can rub their hands all over my chest hairs while we're plucking," he continues. "That ought to make the plucking a lot more enjoyable."

I stare at the one-half-inch gray hair growing in the center of his chest. I hope all those beautiful women bring a magnifying glass with them.

"That's why I'm not wearing a shirt," he confesses. "If I'm going to be plucking with pretty women on stage, I want to get used to plucking with my shirt off."

I lean forward and I fall into a prone position beside the coffee table. I can't handle any more of this while sitting down.

"Hey, I have a wonderful idea," he proclaims as a smile lights up his face. "We'll get you on stage as well at some point during the show, and people can watch us pluck together."

I growl.

"I don't have to go to work tomorrow, so if you want to, we can practice plucking all night. That way, we'll be used to plucking each other by the time we make it on stage. Did you think the day would ever come where people would pay to watch us pluck together?"

My buddy needs more help than even what I realized. He's definitely sleeping on the couch tonight. If he thinks he's going to pluck me, he's going to be sorely disappointed. Plus, if he tries to, he's going to have bite-marks all over his body. Wait a second. What if he likes being bitten while he's plucking? Maybe biting isn't such a good idea. After me, Butch, Dandy, and Empty take care of business, I'm going to run away from home.

"Mixer, don't you want to be pluck buddies?" he asks in a somber voice.

I growl again, and this time I show my teeth.

"Okay," he sighs in a resigned voice. "If it's going to make you that unhappy, I won't ever bring up the subject of us plucking together again."

Good. He's finally showing some common sense. Maybe the chocolate milk is wearing off. However, he's still sleeping on the couch tonight.

His face brightens as he says, "Do you want to hear the first banjo rap song I wrote?"

I close my eyes and pretend that I'm asleep. It doesn't work. I hear the banjo strings make an awful racket as he runs his fingers over them.

"They called me the Banjo Bangster.
I wear red flip-flops because I'm not a gangster.
I showed my banjo to a lady and said you must have good luck.
Because if you play your cards right, we may pluck.
My banjo has five strings.
I see on your fingers, you don't have any rings.
Let's go grab a soda and two straws we can suck.
Then I'll grab my banjo, and we can pluck.
Some banjos only have four strings.
Others have six, and those are fancy things.
Be careful where you walk, and don't step in that muck.
You don't want mud on your fingers when we start to pluck.
If you don't want to trip, just grab my arm.
Then I'll tell you about my life on the farm.
I've got a cow and a dog and a goat and a duck.
But, we'll chase them out of the room when we start to pluck.
I'm being a little forward; I don't know your name.
Why don't you let me take you to a hockey game?
We'll watch the players on the ice chase the puck.

And if we get bored, we can always pluck.
I know a pretty patch of woods that is very near.
We could go to it and watch the deer.
You could be my doe, I'd be your buck.
Then we could go to the meadow and finally pluck."

"Mixer, how did you like my first banjo rap song?" my buddy yells with entirely too much excitement in his voice.

I keep my eyes closed and growl.

"Mixer," he wails.

CHAPTER 60

I wake up listening to the sounds of The Weather Channel floating in from the living room. I remember that my buddy doesn't have to go to the place he calls work today. I stand on the mattress and look around the room. I don't see anything that I can knock off onto the floor. Okay, my buddy thinks he has pulled a slick one. I'll get even with him later.

I give my hip a couple of shakes and leap off the bed onto the olive-green shag carpet. I look around the room and underneath the bed. There's nothing I can find to use to freak out my buddy. Then I see his banjo leaning against the wall in the corner. That opens up a whole new can of worms, and I'm not even fishing. It's good news for me. It's bad news for my buddy.

My bladder feels like it's about to burst, and I really need to get to the crabapple tree in the backyard and take care of my personal business. If you look at a banjo long enough, you can vaguely visualize a tree. I walk over to the banjo and stare at it. If my buddy keeps the banjo, it's only going to get him into trouble. Besides that, my bladder isn't going to empty itself. I hike my leg up over the front of the banjo. The banjo's strings make plinking noises as they are soaked with my morning liquid river of relief. It sounds like music to my ears.

I walk into the living room and the banjo boy is sitting in his recliner wearing a new pair of Scooby Doo pajamas and eating a bowl of Kellogg's Apple Jacks.

"Good morning, Mixer," he says. "After I finish eating my cereal, I'm going to practice on my banjo. I've decided to practice one hour every day."

I start to tell him that probably isn't going to happen, but I decide he'll be able to figure that one out on his own. So instead of saying anything, I keep walking to check out the food and water bowls.

The water bowl is filled with clean, fresh water, and the food bowl is filled with Dyson dog food. It looks like my buddy is finally learning.

I enjoy a long refreshing drink of water and stroll over to the doggy door to go outside. I'm halfway through the doggy door when I hear my buddy yell in pain from the bedroom, "Mixer!"

I keep on going outside. My buddy is probably going to need some time alone to compose himself. And being a compassionate kind of dog, I'm going to let him have his time alone. I hope he knows how lucky he is that I own him.

I walk into the backyard and look around. None of the guys are up yet, but there's a furry body sitting patiently under the crabapple tree. I wonder what Sally is doing here.

I walk over to the tree and say, "What's red and black, squeaks, and goes around and around?"

"I don't know," she says.

"A mouse in a blender," I holler.

"Always the comedian," she hisses.

"I thought you would like a mouse joke," I protest.

"I like my mice rare and not pureed," she spits out at me.

"Is there a certain reason you're sitting in my buddy's backyard, or did you get to missing me so much you have to come gaze at my angelic face with awe?"

"Don't flatter yourself, Mixer."

"Why not? Are you going to do it for me? After all, I was the best lover you have ever had. It's only natural that you can't get over me."

Sally stands and arches her back as she hisses, "What makes you think that?"

"Because I could always make you purr like a cat," I brag.

"Whatever. I only stopped by to say how sorry I am about what happened to Jim."

That's the last thing I expect Sally to say. I make a snap decision that I'm going to enroll in obedience school again. I'm going to take a math and art class. I'm no canine artist, but there's something about this picture that isn't adding up. Sally is The Godfather's girl, we think The Godfather is partially behind about what happened to Jim, and here she is telling me that's she's sorry for what happened.

"Does The Godfather know you're here?" I warily ask.

Her eyes flash in anger as she replies, "The Godfather doesn't own me. No male owns me. However, I will say he's been better to me than you ever were. At least, he hasn't dumped me like a bad habit because of a fear of commitment."

I feel sorry for her. It's evident that she's using anger as a way to cover up her deep-rooted feelings of love she has for me. I don't blame her. If I ever dumped myself, I'd have a hard time getting over me as well. I'm unforgettable like that.

"If it had been me instead of Jim, who got taken out, what would you have done?" I inquire in an offhand canine type of voice.

"I'd still be celebrating," she says and her words have more acid in them than a Duracell AA battery.

Okay, maybe she isn't quite as fond of me as I think.

"But it wasn't you," she spits out at me, "it was Jim, and I always liked that boy. I like Dandy as well. It's you and Empty I can do without."

"I'm not surprised you already know about what happened since you're with The Godfather, but if we find out he's the one behind all this, we're going to take him out."

"You're not smart enough to catch The Godfather," she hisses. "Besides, you would never get past the Fang Mafia."

"We have Butch," I simply state.

Sally swallows a couple of times, and a panicked look crosses her face at the mention of Butch's name. I guess she was so in awe of me that she forgot about Butch. It's never a good thing to forget about Butch, especially, when he's in a bad mood.

"I'm not worried," she arrogantly replies. "Not even Butch would hurt a lady."

"You're not a lady, you're a cat," I point out.

"You know what I'm talking about. Butch would never hurt a female."

"Do you want me to tell the rest of the guys you stopped by to offer your condolences?" I ask. "It might make Dandy feel better."

"I quit caring what you did a long time ago," she growls while coughing up a hair ball and spitting it at me.

I duck as it flies harmlessly over my head.

"That's it, I'm done," she says. "I dropped by to say I'm sorry about what happened to Jim. I did it, and now I'm out of here."

I watch Sally walk away toward the gate. I think she's putting a little too many wiggles in her hips. She still wants me. But, who wouldn't?

CHAPTER 61

Sally and Truck strolled side by side on the gravel pathway by the duck pond in the park underneath the illumination of silvery moonlight. They were speaking in subdued tones as both knew the sounds carried farther in the cool night air. Without the normal daytime activities and noises of the park covering the din of conversation, they felt their hushed tones still sounded like shouts from a mountaintop.

"I saw Mixer today and offered my condolences," Sally spoke without looking at Truck.

"How did that conversation go?" Truck asked while checking the movements of an opossum running across the pathway in front them.

"Swimmingly," Sally sighed. "I can't talk to that dog without having the urge to claw his eyes out. And that wise-cracking mouth of his doesn't ever make matters easier."

"Yeah," Truck acknowledged, "when you two broke up you took the breakup hard. You were really traveling down a dark path for a while, and I wasn't sure there was any way to pull you back from it."

"We didn't have a breakup," Sally corrected Truck. "That jerk dumped me."

"True," Truck agreed. "I hate to say this, but it was probably the best for both of you. You have too much of an independent nature to allow yourself to be tied down, and Mixer is Mixer. The breakup was bound to happen sooner or later. It just happened sooner."

"I guess you're right," Sally purred. "I want to thank you for being there for me when I was going through such a rough stretch in my life. I'm not sure I'd have ever made it without your friendship. You were my constant source of strength."

"It's what friends do," Truck replied.

"What are you going to do?" Sally asked while finally looking at Truck with concern etched on her feline face. "You took both dog biscuits from The Godfather and the Russians. You made good on your promise to one group, but you betrayed the other."

"If given the chance, I'm sure that I'm going to be made an example of," Truck conceded. "That's why I turned the Shih Tzu's loose on the street. If they hear anything, they'll let me know. Plus, I'm hiding out at their buddy's house. I should be safe for a while."

"A while isn't going to last forever," Sally pointed out. "You need to make plans and, whatever they are, you better act on them pronto."

"I've already set the wheels in motions," Truck bragged. "That's what has always kept me ahead of the rest of the pack. Did Mixer mention anything about who they're going to go after? Knowing Butch, he'll go after everybody."

"He didn't bring up the Russians, so I think they are leaning toward going after The Godfather to start with."

Truck let out a low whistle as he replied, "That's going to put you in a tough spot. You might want to disappear for a few days until this thing blows over."

"No," Sally replied while shaking her head. "They'll still have the Fang Mafia to deal with, and with The Ruffians being one dog short, it should give the advantage to the mob."

"You know Empty doesn't care about the odds, as long as he gets to fight, and Butch is in a class all alone when it comes to mayhem and violence."

"They have Mixer," Sally snorted. "That shouldn't increase The Ruffians odds of winning. In fact, it may lessen them."

Truck chuckled as he looked at Sally and said, "Don't sell your former boyfriend short. Mixer doesn't like to fight, but when push comes to shove, he's no slouch."

"I don't think Dandy is going to be much use to them," Sally said as she stared at a sleeping duck. She briefly thought about having Peking duck for supper, but let the idea slip away from her mind. She didn't feel like going through all the trouble of a hunt, plus she wasn't thrilled about duck meat to start with. The lucky duck kept on sleeping.

"It's about to get interesting," Truck confirmed. "That's why I'm keeping a low profile. There are some dogs that aren't very happy with me right now."

"You'll come out smelling like a rose," Sally said. "You always do."

"That I'm not sure about," Truck admitted. "This is big. The biggest thing I've ever been involved in. However, at least it's not boring,"

"Nothing is boring around you," Sally laughed. "You always have something interesting going on in your life."

"Well, it's going to be over soon, and then we'll see what happens next in our very not mundane lives," Truck chuckled.

"I'll be glad when it is over," Sally admitted, "but was taking Jim out the only option available? I liked that boy."

Truck took the time to investigate a discarded French fry lying beside the gravel path before answering and finally said, "I thought and thought about it. The Ruffians had to be neutralized before they stuck their noses in the wrong business. Taking Jim out of the picture seemed to be the easiest way. It was either him or Dandy."

"I hope he didn't suffer," Sally softly replied.

"I was there when it happened," Truck answered in an equally soft tone of voice. "Jim didn't suffer. He never knew what hit him."

"But what are you going to do if Butch finds out you're the one who set his friend up?" Sally asked while laying a paw on Truck's shoulder.

A wave of cold fear washed over Truck's body as he thought of an angered Butch coming after him. "I prefer not to think about that," he said.

"Okay, I admit the hit on Jim had to happen," Sally confessed, "but it still hasn't neutralized The Ruffians. They're bound and determined to discover who put the contract out on Jim. I don't think they're going to back off."

"It doesn't matter," Truck said. "Everything is set in place now. I don't think The Ruffians have time to get their noses stuck in the wrong business."

"I guess I should head on back home," Sally said. "The Godfather is probably going to be missing me soon, plus he did promise to give me a back rub tonight."

"That's probably a good idea," Truck admitted. "I need to check in with the Shih Tzu's. They might not have had time to pick up on anything yet, but you never know. There are a lot of loose tongues in this town."

"The next time there's a contract put out on a dog in this town, please make sure it's Mixer." Sally pleaded.

"I hope there isn't a next time," Truck confessed.

"Well, crap," Sally pouted.

"I'll talk to you soon," Truck said as he gave Sally a light kiss on the cheek.

"See you later, Truck."

CHAPTER 62

Butch, Empty, and I are sitting in my buddy's backyard on a lazy Sunday morning. The neighborhood is unusually quiet as most of the dogs around town choose to remain hidden away in their buddy's homes or backyards. The news about Jim spread like wildfire to the neighboring communities. All the animals seem to be of the mind that whatever was happening was a long way from being over. We feel the same way.

"How's Dandy doing?" I ask Butch while munching on a vanilla cream-filled donut that my buddy carelessly left lying on the coffee table.

Butch yawns and says, "He's not doing well at all. All he wants to do is lay in bed. I can barely get him to eat or drink. He's not even watching Rachael on television, and that used to be one of his passions. I positively don't know what I'm going to do about him."

"Well, you can't blame him," Empty grumbles. "We haven't come close to finding out what's going on. The Fang Mafia and the Russian terrorists have all disappeared. Even Truck isn't anywhere to be seen. It's like everybody has vanished."

"Come to think of it, even Ed from Puerto Rico isn't at the park anymore," I say. "I don't care about seeing him, but when he dropped out of sight, so did Goldie, and I do want to see her. She's hiding her feelings, but I know she wants me."

"You need to get over that," Empty scolds. "She was never going to be your girl. You got beat out by a speeding hotdog."

"Well, she never gave you a second look either," I point out. "You had more than one chance to kick that hotdog's buns and didn't."

"Oh please," Butch says interrupting us. "Must I simply endure listening to another argument from you two? I'm not in the mood and you two would argue about something you both absolutely agreed on. It does get tiresome listening to the constant bickering."

"It's what we do," I say.

"And do it very well," Empty brags.

"Great Lassie in Heaven, I have an idea," Empty proclaims while clapping his front paws together.

I look over at Empty and say, "Be like a baby with a mouthful of cereal and spit it out."

Empty rolls his eyes and shakes his head as he continues, "Tomorrow morning is the free buffet at Mahoney's Meat Market. That should get some dogs out and about. We haven't exactly been highly visible on the streets ourselves. Butch, we all know you had to stay close to Dandy, but if we go to the buffet in the morning as a group maybe who's after us will be tempted to take us all down in one swoop."

"Plus, it would be a great way to get Dandy to eat," I point out.

"The plan does have some merit," Butch concedes, "but if Dandy doesn't feel like making the trip down to the meat market, I'm not sure I want to force him to attend the buffet."

"I understand," Empty counters, "but the longer we delay in going into some type of action, the leads are going to start getting cold."

"We have to have a lead first," I remind Empty.

"Shut up, fur breath."

Empty and I paw bump.

"Well, it positively would be a chance to get some fresh meat into the poor little darling's body," Butch muses out loud. "Right now, he's not eating enough to keep a bird alive."

"Then we have a plan," I agree.

"Besides," Butch adds, "there is a rumor that a new Bassett hound has moved into town. He's supposed to be really buffed. I wouldn't mind checking him out."

Empty starts making gagging sounds while shoving his paw in and out of his mouth.

"Oh grow up," Butch tells Empty. "If they aren't bothering you, there's nothing wrong with two consenting dogs making yummy."

Empty's gagging sounds gets louder.

I decide to change the subject. I don't want them to get started in on me that I used to date a cat. They never did really understand that relationship.

"Are we going to chase the mailman around the block a couple of times on the way to the meat market?" I ask. "Dandy always enjoyed playing that game."

"Oh dear me," Butch moans. "I think we should probably skip that event. Our postal carrier isn't as young as he used to be."

"But we never bit him," Empty argues. "All we did was chase him and listen to those funny little screams he makes while running."

"With all the problems we're currently dealing with, I don't think we should take a chance on having harassment charges being brought against us," Butch contends.

"Okay, you might have a valid point," Empty agrees.

Once again, my dropping out of obedience school is biting me where the flea used to. I don't have the foggiest idea what a valid is.

"I'll talk to Dandy and see if I can get the little darling excited about going to the buffet. I'd love to see him smile again."

Empty and I sagely nod our heads in agreement. That's what wise dogs do.

"Well, I'm going to go check on Dandy," Butch says as he stands and stretches. "You two try to play nice with each other, and I'll see you in the morning."

"See you, Butch," Empty and me say in unison.

We watch Butch jump over the chain-link fence and into his buddy's backyard and disappear into the house.

Empty looks at me and says, "What are you going to do today?"

"When my buddy gets home from church, I think that I'll have him take me for some ice cream. I can't think of anything more important he has to do."

A thoughtful look crosses Empty's face, and he surprises me by saying, "Sometimes I think it would be nice to be human."

"Why would you want to be a human?" I inquire.

"Think about it, Mixer," Empty says. "They don't have to deal with ticks or fleas. They don't have to deal with a burglar breaking into the house because that's our job. Basically, compared to the pressure of being a dog, humans don't have any pressure at all to deal with."

"I see your point," I answer.

"Well, I'm going to go grab some serious mirror time while I have the house all to myself," he says. "I never get near enough time alone."

"Yeah, I could always grab a power nap," I reply.

"Mixer, we're going to find those responsible for putting the contract out on Jim, and when we find them, we're going to get our revenge," Empty says in a steely, determined voice.

"I never thought otherwise," I honestly answer.

"To Jim," he says.

"To Jim," I agree.

We paw bump.

CHAPTER 63

I'm glad Butch could talk Dandy into going to the free buffet at Mahoney's Meat Market. I can tell he's lost a little weight, and instead of the happy beagle I've always known, his eyes, which are usually filled with happiness and good humor, are now the saddest looking eyes I've ever seen on a dog. When any of us ask him a question, he replies with a one-word answer in a barely audible voice.

I can see the worry in Empty's eyes as he whispers out of the corner of his mouth, "Dandy isn't doing well at all. We have to do something to help him."

"I know," I whisper back. "Maybe we can pick him up a ham bone at the meat market. He's always enjoyed chewing on those."

"Good thinking," Empty answers. "I'm hoping I can pick up a foxy chick as well."

"You're a dog," I respond.

"Well, guys, are you all ready to march down to the meat market and enjoy a delicious meal?" Butch asks in a way too cheerful voice. I know why he's talking that way. He's trying to pick up Dandy's spirit and make him feel better.

"Lead the way, oh fearless leader of the canine world," Empty barks out.

"I'll even show you all the best cuts of meat to select," I brag, "because nobody beats my meat."

"Yeah," Dandy glumly says.

"Let's journey forth and claim our banquet," Butch proclaims.

We walk through the gate leading to my buddy's backyard, and the first thing I notice is the postman's white Jeep parked at the corner of the street.

I lick my lips in anticipation of the chase. There's nothing like starting the week off with a little exercise.

Butch notices my actions and warns, "Mixer, we agreed to leave the mailman alone."

I start to whimper and then decide to put on my big dog britches. After all, I did agree with the plan to leave the mailman alone.

We finally realize that we aren't going draw Dandy into any animated conversations, and pretty much proceed on our canine cuisine crusade in silence. I'm hoping some five-star select choices of scraps will improve Dandy's mood.

Empty finally breaks the silence as we're walking in front of Lancaster's Laundromat and says, "I hope there are some hot babes at the buffet this morning."

"You have such a one-track mind," Butch responds. "There are so many wonderful things in the world to ponder on that continuing to dwell on one subject which leaves you missing out on the little things which in themselves are the larger things in life we take for granted."

Empty doesn't answer. We both know when Butch is pretending that he's a philosopher to let it go, and Butch will eventually come back to reality.

"If there are no babes, you could always take a donkey to Pizza Hut," I tell Empty.

Empty shakes his head back and forth and says, "I know better than to ask this, but why would I want to take a donkey to Pizza Hut?"

"So you can get a pizza ass," I proudly answer.

"I knew better than to ask," Empty grumbles. "I freaking knew better."

Then I hear the sound that makes my heart swell with pride. I hear Dandy let out a small giggle. That's one of the prettiest sounds I've heard in a long time.

"Nice job, fur breath," Empty mutters under his breath, and holds out a paw for a paw bump.

We turn the corner at Fourth Street and Myrtle Lane, which puts us only two blocks away from Mahoney's. I can't help, but think of Jim and how he loved to attend the buffet. He enjoyed telling us all about what he saw on The Discovery Channel while munching on scraps of top sirloin. I never met a dog who loved top sirloin as much as Jim did. I can almost hear him yelling, "Hey, Mixer. Hey, fellows."

"Hey, Mixer. Hey, fellows."

"I can actually hear Jim yelling at us in my thoughts," I tell Empty.

"That's weird," he says. "I was thinking the same thing."

"That's positively spooky," Butch drools. "I was hearing the little darling in my mind as well. I guess we all miss him so much."

"Hey, fellows."

"There goes the voice again," I say out loud to no one in particular.

Dandy breaks into a series of frantic barks and then he switches over to English. "Hey, guys, look across the street."

We look across the street and see Jim racing around the empty booths of the vacated farmer's market toward us. He's wearing a huge smile on his face, and his brown ears are streaming in the air like a banner behind an airplane.

"How is this positively possible?" Butch sobs. "My little darling is alive."

"It's Jim! It's Jim!" Dandy yells while twirling in circles.

"This isn't good," Empty yells in an alarmed voice. "He's not slowing down to look both ways before he crosses the street. He's not paying any attention to the traffic."

We start yelling for Jim to stop and look both ways before crossing the street.

Either he can't understand what we're saying, or for some reason he's ignoring us. I see the reason Jim is ignoring us. He's being chased by the Russian wolfhound called Ivan, and Ivan is quickly gaining ground on Jim.

I hear a loud growl rumble deep in Empty's chest, and I know he spots the terrorist as well. The growl is beginning to sound like a freight train passing through crosstown at noon.

Then everything seems to be moving in slow motion. A maroon Chrysler cargo delivery van rounds the corner of Myrtle Lane at a high rate of speed. Edison's Electronics is painted in bright yellow block lettering on the side of the van. I know there's no way the driver of the van can see Jim, and Jim is so intent on getting to us that he doesn't notice the van.

I look around and see my pals staring in horror at the scene before us. An elderly lady pushing a blue plastic shopping cart from the local drugstore is looking out toward the street with her right hand covering her mouth.

I yell at Jim to stop, but it feels like my words are lost in a vacuum.

"Stop, oh please stop, darling," I hear Butch yell.

I hear Dandy and Empty yelling for Jim to notice the van.

Jim tears off the curb and onto the street with his smile growing larger as each step brings him closer to us. He's so focused on us that he doesn't notice the van.

I close my eyes.

I hear Butch scream in horror.

I hear Dandy and Empty frantically yell, "Stop!"

I hear the sound, the sick, thudding sound of an object being struck by a vehicle.

I hear the screeching of the van's tires as the driver slams on the brakes.

I can't even begin to stop the tears.

CHAPTER 64

I hear a voice say, "Mixer, why are you crying?"

I open one of my eyes and see Jim looking up at me with a curious expression on his face. I open both eyes, clear my throat and say, "I'm not crying. My allergies are acting up, but I thought for sure that you had been run over by that delivery van."

"If that old lady hadn't saved my life, I would have," Jim explains. "I was so excited to see you guys, that I never noticed the van."

I look over Jim's head and see the maroon delivery van stopped in the middle of the street with a white powder scattered all across the windshield. The van's driver is trying to scrape the powder off the windshield with his hands and the only thing he's accomplishing is creating a bigger mess. I see his lips move as he is talking to himself and shaking his head back and forth.

"Now I'm really confused," I tell Jim. "What did that old lady do?"

"Well, when she saw I didn't notice the van, and the driver wasn't slowing down, she threw a small two pound bag of flour and it splattered all over the windshield. The driver didn't have any choice but to stop because he couldn't see a thing."

I turned to glance at the old lady pushing her blue buggy down the sidewalk while taking the time to glance over her left shoulder and glare daggers at the delivery van.

"Okay, that explains the squealing of the tires and the small thud I heard," I say, "but I heard Butch screaming in terror. What was that all about?"

"He stepped in a crack on the sidewalk and chipped a nail," Empty says as he and Butch walk up to stand by Jim and me.

"It isn't just any toenail polish," Butch snorts. "It's Essie Borrowed & Blue polish, and that stuff doesn't grow on trees. I was absolutely appalled when I noticed the chipped nail."

"Jim, are you okay?" The Russian terrorist asks as he walks up to stand behind Jim.

I catch a blur of movement out of the corner of my eye, and Ivan is knocked backward into the street, and he goes down under a fury of snarling fangs.

"Stop it, Butch, Ivan saved my life," Jim yells.

I hear Ivan's yelps of pain and howls of terror as he's defenseless under Butch's brutal assault. Ivan's howls of pain go quiet as I see the reason why. He can't scream anymore because Butch has his fangs in his throat.

"Stop him," a frantic looking Jim screams at Empty and me. "Ivan saved my life."

Empty looks at me, shrugs his shoulders, and breaks into a run toward Butch. At the last second, he lowers his shoulder and the force of the collision breaks Butch's stranglehold on Ivan as he's knocked head over heels toward the center of the street.

Butch is instantly on his feet, and I see the slobber dripping off his fangs as he advances toward Empty. Empty stands with his rear legs spread wide, and I see nothing good coming out of this situation. I know Empty isn't going to back down.

"Stop it, Butch," Jim yells as he tries to block Butch's raging advance. "Butch, Ivan saved my life."

Butch stops and stares at Jim and the madness in his eyes slowly fades and is replaced by recognition and confusion. "What did you say, darling?" he asks.

"I said Ivan saved my life," Jim repeats as Dandy comes to stand beside him, and they high five each other.

Butch looks over at Empty and says, "I'm so absolutely embarrassed about my behavior. I hope you can forgive me knowing the duress I've been under."

"No problem," Empty says. "Let's get to the meat market and snag some breakfast."

They paw bump.

"You might want to ask questions first before you go all crazy like that again," Ivan gasps as he walks toward us. "You could have at least read the dog tag on my collar."

I read Ivan's dog tag out loud, "D.B.I."

"That's right," Ivan says while rubbing his throat. "I work for the Dog Bureau of Investigation. Your friend assaulted an agent."

Empty looks at me and asks, "Have we ever beat up a fed before?"

"We've never seen one before," I reply.

"Would someone please explain to me what's going on," Butch pleads. "I'm so positively confused right now."

"Perhaps, I would be able to shed some light on the subject," a familiar voice interrupts.

I turn around and see Ed from Puerto Rico, and standing beside him is Goldie. That doesn't surprise me, but what does surprise me is the sight of Truck and Sally standing behind them. I'm wondering who's going to show up next.

"This is great," Empty grumbles. "If any more dogs show up, there will barely be enough scraps left at the buffet to feed a gopher in a bingo hall."

"Shush, darling," Butch scolds. "I simply can't wait for an explanation."

"I'm the Director of Intelligence for the Dog Bureau of Investigation," Ed says. "I'm based in Puerto Rico because that's where we have our satellite feed."

I look over at Goldie and ask, "And you are?"

"Special Agent Goldie," she replies. "That's why I could never go out with you. I'm forbidden from mixing business with pleasure."

"He'd just dump you," Sally hisses.

I ignore that.

"As I was saying," Ed continues, "we've had you Ruffians on our radar for a while now. We've even thought about approaching you for some freelance work. However, something always came up to prevent that. The reason we're here now is because of The Godfather. He's originated the grandiose scheme of gathering all the nuts in town and using them to poison Dyson dogfood."

"So that's why the squirrels are running around the park without any nuts," Empty grumbles. "And The Godfather claimed that he didn't know why the squirrels were behaving so squirrelly. We should have known not to believe him."

"That is correct," Ed says. "The Godfather originally let it be known that any squirrels that got caught storing nuts would be eliminated. When the squirrels started eating all the nuts, The Godfather amended that to any squirrels caught eating nuts would be eliminated as well."

Empty looks at me and says, "That's why the squirrels would spit the nuts out of their mouths when they saw us at the park."

"They thought we were hit dogs," I reply. "That's nuts."

"We know you Ruffians and The Godfather had issues in the past, so I couldn't recruit any of you to work with us. There might have been a temptation to make it personal," Ed continues. "Our original plan was to intimidate you, so you wouldn't stick your noses into the business about the squirrels. When that didn't work we decided to kidnap Jim. We figured that was our best option. With you thinking Jim had been taken out of the picture permanently, none of you would want to pursue the matter any further for fear of your own lives."

"Darling, where did they hide you at?" Butch inquires while looking at Jim.

"At first they were going to have me camp out in that little patch of woods by the city landfill," Dandy replies, "but Ivan decided there might be too many snakes crawling around, so he put me up at a Holiday Inn Express. I even got Netflix and all the free pizza I could eat."

"Why didn't you try to escape?" Empty asks.

"Would you give up Netflix and free pizza?" Jim counters.

"Good point," Empty agrees.

"But we had another complication rise up, which also made the kidnapping of Jim a necessity. The Godfather was going to actually have the Fang Mafia kill Jim and hide his body in that same patch of woods. We couldn't let that happen to a citizen while on our watch. Supposedly, The Godfather was going to have it done to ensure that you Ruffians didn't stick your noses into his nutty plan, but I think he wanted it done just because he's that mean."

"This is interesting," I say, "but how did you find out about The Godfather's plans?"

"I told Ed and Truck about the plan," Sally hisses.

"You double crossed The Godfather?" Dandy asks with a hint of awe in his voice.

"Not exactly," Ed says while answering Dandy's question. "We recruited Sally to come work for us as an undercover agent. She's the first foxy feline to ever be admitted to the D.B.I."

"Why did you agree to spy on The Godfather for the D.B.I?" I ask.

"What else was I to do?" she spits at me "It's not like I have a love life anymore to keep me busy, and it wasn't that great when I had one."

I hear Empty snickering behind me.

"Why would you positively tell Truck about it?" Butch inquires.

"Truck and I got adopted out of the shelter on the same day," Sally responds. "I tell him everything. We're family."

"That's how we could recruit Truck to set up Jim. We needed to make it look like the real thing, so we paid him off with dog biscuits. It's ironic The Godfather made the same offer to Truck."

"If all this is true, why were you chasing Jim?" Empty asks Ivan.

"I wasn't chasing him. I was bringing him home. We've located where The Godfather has all the nuts stored. We're making the bust this morning. He and the Fang Mafia are hiding in an old closed down furniture factory. Boris and Vicktor are already down there keeping an eye on things."

"We're going down there with you," Empty snarls in his stubborn voice.

"You can't," Ed emphatically states. "You're civilians. We can't allow you to accompany us on a precise military-style police action."

"Darling, I'm just absolutely, positively giggling with joy at the thought of you trying to stop us," Butch croons.

"I can't believe you did a double adverb abuse," Jim mutters with a scowl on his face.

"You may want to rethink that one, boss," Ivan says while pointing at Butch. "Swear them in as honorary D.B.I. agents just for this one bust. For a girl, he fights like a guy."

"Thanks," Butch beams.

"This goes against my better judgment," Ed says, "but you are all now official honorary D.B.I. agents. Your position with the agency will expire at noon."

I look over at Empty and say, "We're cops. We ought to post this on Facebook."

"Nobody would ever believe it," he says.

"Yeah, you're probably right."

"Could we please cut out all the chitchat and proceed to our location?" Butch pleads. "I'm positively dying to see The Godfather."

CHAPTER 65

Ed's talking as we leisurely stroll toward the closed down furniture factory where The Godfather and the Fang Mafia are hiding out. Ed wants us to take our time, so we can work out a feasible attack formation. He stresses over and over how important it is to have good tactics. Plus, he's also worried if we rush down to the abandoned factory, we'll stir up a racket and warn the Fang Mafia of our presence.

"I can't stress enough the importance of taking The Godfather alive," Ed says.

Butch snorts.

"I mean it," Ed emphatically states while glaring at Butch. "We have to make an example out of The Godfather. If there are any other career criminal canines out there that are dreaming of power and dominating the animal kingdom, they need to be aware of how foolish those dreams are because they will never escape the long paw of the law."

Butch starts whistling.

"I mean it," Ed vehemently states, "If I don't have your word that The Godfather will be taken alive, I'm going to revoke your honorary membership in the Dog Bureau of Investigation. I'm not going to allow personal feelings to jeopardize a law enforcement mission. Now do I have your word that you will help apprehend The Godfather and bring him to justice alive?"

"Sure," Butch replies.

I'm impressed by Ed. The little fellow has an aura of power surrounding him. It's no wonder that he rose to such a prominent position in the D.B.I. I also noticed that Butch said sure instead of positively. There's only one explanation for that. Butch is still planning on doing his own thing when we reach the furniture factory.

I look behind me at Sally and ask in my sexiest voice, "What are you doing coming along on a dog bust?"

That seductive voice is going to get to her. There's no way that she's not going to get weak in the knees when she realizes that beddable voice is directed toward her. She's going to be butter in my paws.

She stares at me and hisses, "Because I'm a member of the D.B.I., you idiot."

I turn my head and stare straight ahead. I feel sorry for Sally. It must be torture for her to be this close to me and have to mask her feelings that she still holds in her heart for me. She would have to be an actress of extraordinary talents. She must have taken acting lessons because so far she's making it look real.

We walk pass the Claassen's Corduroy Clothing Closet on the corner of Crossover and Cypress streets and hang a hard right on Industrial Drive as we head toward the former furniture factory in the abandoned industrial park. There used to be several warehouses and factories in the old industrial park, but one by one they slowly closed down. It makes sense that it would be a perfect hiding place for The Godfather and the Fang Mafia. They could come and go as they pleased and no one would be around to notice their movements.

I need to concentrate on the upcoming bust. I need to steady myself and become a lean, mean fighting machine. I decide upon a fail proof strategy. I'm going to hang back and let Empty and Butch take out the Fang Mafia. I'll be their backup in case they need me. I'm proud of myself when I realize that I'm the kind of dog that has my friend's backs.

"Remember," Ed whispers as we enter the parking lot of the old factory. "Boris and Vicktor are already hiding in the vicinity watching our every move. They have our backs covered. The Fang Mafia doesn't stand a chance."

We slowly and quietly walk across the gray asphalt parking lot toward the factory. We notice that Slapjack, Carjack, and Hijack are standing in front of the building and checking out their surroundings. Blackjack is standing off to one side.

"Remember," Ed urgently whispers in a low voice, "nobody is to make a move until I give the word."

"Word," Empty yells and he, Jim, and Dandy take off running across the debris covered parking lot toward the Fang Mafia.

Jim and Dandy are baying their war cries as they streak toward the mafia boys. I look back at Butch, who's showing no intention of joining in the charge. I know why. He's waiting until he spots The Godfather.

Butch looks at me and says, "Mixer, would you positively please join your friends in this much-anticipated melee?"

Well, crap. So much for my plan of letting Butch and Empty take down the Fang Mafia.

I streak across the parking lot and catch up to Empty, Jim, and Dandy. We're a canine skirmish line as the four of us race across the pot hole, weed covered parking lot. The four members of the Fang Mafia have spotted us and are standing ready with fangs bared to embrace the upcoming battle.

The epic battle that was always inevitable has finally arrived. The Fang Mafia versus The Ruffians. There hasn't been a battle of this worldly proportion since Coke versus Pepsi.

The mobsters are standing with their legs spread wide, and I notice the drool dripping off their fangs, and the hatred dancing in their eyes as they wait to tear us limb from limb.

Jim charges toward Slapjack. Dandy is making a beeline toward Hijack. I keep flying in a straight line toward Carjack, while Empty veers off and charges Blackjack.

Above all the growling and snarling filling the morning air, I wait until we are close enough to smell the foul, hot breath of the Fang Mafia in our faces before I yell, "Mixer-fu!"

As soon as I yell those magical words, I flip my back legs out from underneath me and slide underneath Carjack's body. Jim and Dandy follow suit as Jim slides up underneath Slapjack, and Dandy disappears from sight under Hijack's massive bulk.

Well, surprise surprise, what do you know? I have a set of danglers in front of my face. I reach up and clamped down with my teeth and squeeze with all of my might.

Bleah! I wish Carjack had been the kind of dog whose mother taught him to take a bath at least once every Saturday night. It really doesn't matter. I don't care if you washed them with four bottles of Pine Sol and three bottles of Mr. Clean, the bottom line is that danglers are never going to taste like chicken.

I feel Carjack's body tense up as he mutters between clenched teeth, "Oh, no. Not again."

Carjack tenses his body and falls over on his side without another sound. I scramble to my paws and quickly look around. Slapjack and Hijack are lying on their sides and moaning for their mommies. Jim is using his hind paws to kick rock and scattered debris over Slapjack's prone body while Dandy is standing over Hijack and making motions with his front paws like he's shoveling up the poop.

I glance over where Empty and Blackjack are engaged in a life-or-death struggle. Empty's on top of Blackjack and I hear the mob boy's howl of terror as he screams, "Get off me. I had my fur washed this morning, and you're messing it up. Get off me, I say."

Empty slowly backs away as Ed from Puerto Rico, Goldie, and Sally rush up to the scene.

I turn my attention to observe Butch, who's standing rock solid like a statue in the town's square as only his head is moving. I know if the battle turned against us, he would have been in the middle of the fray. I also know he's looking for The Godfather. I have a bad feeling things aren't going to turn out well for the little mafia chieftain.

I feel a pressure against my legs and look down to see Sally rubbing against me with her back arched. I'm wondering why my stomach is growling, but then I realize that it's not growling at all. It's Sally's purring.

"You know how I love violence," she moans, "and I got absolutely turned on by the way you handled yourself. I didn't think you had it in you. Jim still has one more free night on his voucher for a room at the Holiday Inn Express. How about a little Netflix, pizza, fun, and me?"

What can I say? A dog has to do what a dog has to do.

CHAPTER 66

I'm surprised to see Ivan walking out of the factory with Boris and Vicktor sheepishly following behind him with their heads drooping toward the ground.

"Where have you two been?" Ed barks at his subordinates as he rushes over to meet them.

Boris and Vicktor look at each other and then resume their intent staring at the ground without bothering to provide an answer to their boss.

"You two agents better look me in the eyes," Ed growls. "I want an explanation as why you two were absent from the tactical maneuver."

"I found them locked inside a broom closet," Ivan answers before Boris and Vicktor can respond. I can't help but notice the twinkle in Ivan's eyes, and the glee in his voice.

Ed rolls his eyes and asks in astonishment, "How did you two get locked inside a broom closet? This was supposed to have been a precise tactical operation and you two were supposed to have already been in a position to attack our criminal adversaries."

"It's not our fault, boss," Boris protests. "We were getting into our position to ambush the Fang Mafia when we caught the smell of Pedigree Beef and Country Stew dog food. There was an opened package of it lying on the floor of the broom closet."

"It was entrapment," Vicktor adds. "We went in to investigate and that's when a member of the Fang Mafia slammed the door behind us and locked us inside the closet."

"So you were thinking with your stomach and not with your brains," Ed snarls. "You could have jeopardized the entire operation. For two professionally trained agents, you showed a serious lack of judgment, and you will return with me to Puerto Rico for six weeks of remedial training."

This is great. Our backup got backed up.

"Yes, boss," Boris and Victor reply and neither looks very happy about their fate.

I look at Ivan and ask, "What about you?"

Ivan shrugs his shoulders and answers, "I go wherever I'm needed. The bureau will give me my next assignment on a need to know basis."

I hear a loud commotion at the far end of the parking lot, and I look over to see what the racket is all about. Great Lassie in Heaven, I see a mob of toy Pomeranians, French poodles, Chihuahuas, dachshunds, and pugs racing toward us. I can barely hear myself think over their barking and howling. There have to be at least two hundred of them.

I look over at Truck who says, "I wasn't sure what all we were walking into, so I called for some backup. There's no way The Godfather is going to escape."

I'm glad he says there's no way The Godfather is going to escape because about that time, The Godfather streaks out of the front door of the abandoned factory and around the corner of the building. He's escaping.

Butch spies the fleeing little felon and breaks into a run and starts chasing the mastermind of madness. The Godfather better not slow down or stop to catch his breath.

Just as Butch rounds the corner of the building, Empty yells at me, "Mixer, Butch is going to kill The Godfather. Go after him."

I break into a dead run and as I'm tearing around the side of the former furniture home I have two thoughts. One, I'm chasing Butch. Two, what do I do when I catch up to him?

Empty never actually told me to catch Butch. He said to go after him. I quit running and break into a slow walk. I'm still doing what Empty told me, I'm just not doing it very fast.

I'm glad I quit running because as I'm walking by an open door in the side of the building an Irish setter steps outside. I stop and stare at her. She's beautiful. If I play my cards right, maybe we can have a quick romp inside the cutting room.

First, I'm going to dazzle her with my charm and wit and sweep her off her paws. I've never met a redhead who was immune to the charms of the Mixer.

"You're name must be Needle, because I sure want a shot at you." I say.

She yawns. I love it when a female plays hard to get.

"You're name must be catheter because urine in my heart forever." There's no way that she's going to be able to resist that line.

She stares at me. She's probably looking for an excuse to stare into my romantic eyes.

"Do you have an ice pack, because I broke my leg falling in love with you?"

She pushes past me and walks away without giving me another glance. I shouldn't have used so much charm on her. She's intimidated.

I continue to walk after Butch.

About that time, The Godfather comes flying around the far corner of the tin building. I'm amazed. He's actually flying in mid-air. I see why he's flying in mid-air. Butch is holding The Godfather by his red collar.

"Put me down," The Godfather rasps. "You Ruffians are in so much trouble. When I get done with you, The Ruffians will wish they had never heard of The Godfather."

I look at Butch, who rolls his eyes.

We walk back toward the front of the factory in silence because I can't think of anything to say, and Butch can't talk while he's holding The Godfather in his mouth.

The Godfather is kicking his little legs in the air trying his best to escape. I decide to torture him a bit.

"Hey, Godfather, Sally and I are going to the Holiday Inn Express. Do you want me to film it and put it on YouTube, so you'll have something to watch in prison?"

The Godfather starts frantically kicking wilder, as he huffs, "I'm going to get you for this, Mixer. Nobody steals my girl."

Butch gives me a hard hip bump to get me to shut up.

We finally make it back to the milling canine mob in front of the factory and Butch drops The Godfather in front of Ed.

Empty walks up and says, "Good job."

We paw bump.

"I was sure that you were going to kill him," Empty tells Butch.

"Oh, darling, I positively thought about it. I'm famished and I dearly love Mexican food, but I thought why should I give this little tyrant an easy way out. I'd much rather see him locked up with a bulldog named Bubba. He's going to make somebody a great prison wife," Butch replies.

"We'll take it from here," Ed barks. "I want to thank you for your help in getting The Godfather and the Fang Mafia off the streets. From this point on, the local K-9 unit will be assisting us. You are no longer members of the D.B.I."

"For a hotdog, you're not bad," Empty tells Ed.

"You still have time to kick his buns," I add.

Butch looks over at Ivan and says, "Do you want to sneak away somewhere private? I touch your badge, and you touch mine. I've never made yummy with a federal agent before."

Empty sticks his paw in his mouth and starts making gagging sounds.

CHAPTER 67

I'm half crawling and partly dragging my body back to my buddy's house. There isn't a joint in my body that isn't aching. Sally and I raised the roof at the Holiday Inn Express. I forgot what an animal she is in bed.

I notice the mailman walking down the sidewalk on the other side of the street. I would bark at him, but my tongue is too sore. There's a reason that it's sore, but I'm going to keep that secret to myself. I'm not the type of dog that kisses and tells.

I also have more important matters to worry about. K.D. Mitchell is standing in her front yard and staring at me while holding her green water hose. I know it's after eleven a.m. because eleven was the checkout time for our room at the Holiday Inn Express. So, I'll be facing the mean K.D. Mitchell. I think about crossing over to the other side of the street, but in my weakened condition, I know deep in my heart that I'll never make it.

I keep stumbling down the sidewalk toward K.D. Mitchell. I'm going to wind up the main ingredient in a doggy pot pie and there's nothing I can do about it. I accept my fate and bravely advance down the sidewalk. K.D. Mitchell may take me out of the ball game permanently, but she'll never take my pride.

K.D. Mitchell smiles at me. Great Lassie in Heaven, what's going on? K.D. Mitchell isn't mean. It's after eleven a.m., and K.D. Mitchell is nice. The Godfather and the Fang Mafia are gone and so is the mean K.D. Mitchell. I try to smile back, but my lips hurt too much. There's a reason for that as well. Let's just say that I had Sally purring like a cat.

I finally make it back to my buddy's house and wearily crawl through the doggy door in the back of the house. Out of habit, I check my food and water bowls. The water bowl is filled with clean, fresh water. The food bowl is filled with Dyson dog food. I use my nose to flip over the food bowl and watch those delicious tidbits of Dyson dog food scatter across the kitchen floor. I guess there are some habits that I'm never going to be able to break.

I move my exhausted body into the living room and find my buddy watching The Weather Channel. I'm hoping that he doesn't notice me. All I want to do is make it to the bedroom and sleep for about the next three or four years. I'm so tired that I have a feeling that when I do crash I'm going to sleep like a dog.

My buddy notices me.

"Mixer, look what I have," my buddy laughs.

I look.

He holds aloft a clear plastic drinking glass that's filled with a white liquid. "I'm not drinking chocolate milk," he proudly proclaims with a smile on his face. "I'm drinking whole milk. I've given up drinking chocolate milk."

I'm stunned. I'm in such a state of shock that I don't say anything. My buddy has survived his journey down the treacherous river of chocolate milk and returned safely. I'm proud of him. I never thought I would see this day.

"And I'm drinking healthy," he says. "This whole milk is actually two percent reduced-fat milk."

I grimace. Leave it up to my buddy to ruin a perfectly good glass of milk.

"Mixer, you're going to be so proud of me," he says with a happy smile. "I've decided that I'm not going to be an author or a rapper."

I sagely nod because it seems the wise thing to do.

"I'm going to become a male model," he yells. "I'm going to model underwear."

I sit down, hard. I start to tell my buddy that his career will probably be brief, but I decide to let him figure that one out on his own, so I don't say anything.

"Think about it, Mixer," he cries in a jovial voice. "I'm going to be on television commercials and billboards all across the country. People everywhere will see me wearing only my underwear. I'm in all likelihood going to become so famous that I'll almost certainly be offered a contract to star in a movie. Women all across the nation will see how I look in my underwear. I'm probably going to wind up with a girlfriend."

It's the milk I decide. It's not just the chocolate milk. It's all milk. My buddy is very milk intolerant. That has to be the answer. My buddy can't handle milk. I may be wrong, but I'm pretty sure that his momma didn't breast feed.

"I went to Walmart and picked up a six-pack of Fruit of the Loom boxer briefs, so I can practice modeling in the bathroom tonight. That full-length mirror hanging on the door is going to be perfect to practice in front of."

That's it. I'm getting my buddy a blow up doll. He needs something to occupy his time. I think about getting him a male blow up doll just to see his reaction, but then I realize that he would only wind up getting Butch to blow it up for him.

"If you want to, I'll let you watch me model my new underwear," he solemnly says while nodding his head up and down.

That's it. This conversation has definitely taken a kinky twist to it. I'm out of here.

I start walking toward the bedroom when my buddy says, "Come on over here, old friend of mine, and let me rub your belly and scratch you behind the ears."

I ignore that and slowly advance toward the bedroom. I pretend that I don't see his outstretched hand. I know it's tough love, but someone has to practice it.

"Mixer," he wails.

EPILOGUE

We're sitting in my buddy's backyard for our nightly meeting. Butch is walking around with a dreamy look upon his face, and Jim and Dandy giggle every time he walks into the crabapple tree.

Empty looks at me and asks, "So are you and Sally once again an official couple?"

"No, I just gave her memories to last a lifetime," I brag. "Sally has to go to the Dog Bureau of Identification's basic training. After she finishes her advanced training, who knows where she will be stationed? I'll probably never see her again. However, we blew off the roof at the Holiday Inn Express."

"You're a dog," Empty says.

We paw bump.

"Ivan and I wound up at the Motel Six," Butch croons. "And we positively left the light on. In fact, we turned on everything if you know what I mean."

Empty immediately doubles over and starts making gagging sounds.

"It was fun to finally be able to watch Rachael again without having to worry," Dandy gushes. "She looked especially delish this afternoon."

"We have to be diligent," Jim warns while pushing his glasses back up his nose. "The Godfather and the Fang Mafia might finally be locked up where they belong, but who knows what other hardened canines might move into town with foul intentions preying in the back of their minds. We can't rest on our laurels. If our services are once again needed to combat the evils in this world, we must be ready to spring into action at a moment's notice."

Empty looks at me and asks, "What did he say?"

"Don't forget where you hid the bone," I reply.

"Gotcha."

"I positively love the way Russians make yummy," Butch says to no one in particular.

Empty looks at me and says, "It's going to be a while before we're going to be able to pull him out of la la land. If he's this way after going to a Motel Six, I guess it's a good thing that he didn't wind up at a Ramada Inn. We'd never get him back to the real world."

"Don't think I didn't catch that adverb abuse," Jim fusses at Butch. "Sometimes I honestly don't know what I'm going to do with you."

"Are we going to patrol tonight?" I ask Empty.

Empty nods his head toward Butch and says, "Do you really want to take him out in public acting and looking like that."

"Good point," I say.

"I'm glad the squirrels in the park have their nuts back," Dandy pipes in. "Not having any nuts is not a way for a squirrel to live."

"It's not a way for any animal to live," Empty concedes.

"I'm glad Sally didn't have nuts," I say.

"I'm glad Ivan did," Butch drools.

"Let's do it," Jim yells.

We know what he's talking about.

We gather around, do a group high five, and yell, "We are The Ruffians!"

The End

ABOUT THE AUTHOR

Rick Johnson currently lives in Tupelo, MS. He's an avid animal enthusiast and his favorite hobbies are taking long walks, traveling with, and telling jokes to The Dog.

Rickjohnson1789@gmail.com
TWITTER
FACEBOOK
GOODREADS

LOOK FOR THESE OTHER GREAT STORIES
FROM
RICK JOHNSON

TRAILER TRASH

LOVE IN THE BOX

DOG'S BEST GOOBER

HEIRLOOM PLANTATION

www.ingramcontent.com/pod-product-compliance
Lightning Source LLC
Chambersburg PA
CBHW072205170626
46813CB00003B/805